The Caine Prize for African Writing 2014

The Gonjon Pin
and other stories

The Caine Prize for African Writing 2014

The Gonjon Pin
and other stories

New Internationalist

The Caine Prize for African Writing 2014
The Gonjon Pin and other stories

First published in 2014 in Europe, North America and Australasia by
New Internationalist Publications Ltd
The Old Music Hall
106-108 Cowley Road
Oxford
OX4 1JE, UK
newint.org

First published in 2014 in Southern Africa by
Jacana Media (Pty) Ltd
10 Orange Street
Sunnyside
Auckland Park 2092
South Africa
+2711 628 3200
jacana.co.za

Design by New Internationalist.

Printed by Bell and Bain Ltd, UK.
who hold environmental accreditation ISO 14001.

British Library Cataloguing-in-Publication Data.
A catalogue record for this book is available from the British Library.

Library of Congress Cataloging-in-Publication Data.
A catalog record for this book is available from the Library of Congress.

New Internationalist ISBN 978-1-78026-174-4
Jacana ISBN 978-1-4314-2026-1

Contents

Introduction

Selected from a record number of eligible entries, 140 stories from 17 African countries, this anthology contains the five stories from the 15th annual Caine Prize shortlist, which was announced by Nobel Prize winner and Patron of the Caine Prize Professor Wole Soyinka, as part of the opening ceremonies for the UNESCO World Book Capital 2014 celebration in Port Harcourt, Nigeria. After last year's domination by Nigerian writers, there are no Nigerians on the 2014 shortlist, and Billy Kahora has been shortlisted for the second time in three years.

The Chair of Judges, award-winning author Jackie Kay MBE, described the shortlist as: 'Compelling, lyrical, thought-provoking and engaging. From a daughter's unusual way of grieving for her father, to a memorable swim with a grandmother, a young boy's fascination with a gorilla's conversation, a dramatic faux family meeting, and a woman who is forced to sell her eggs, the subjects are as diverse as they are entertaining.' She added: 'The standard of entries was exceptionally high – so much so that it was actually very difficult for the judges to whittle it down to a shortlist of only five stories. We were heartened by how many entrants were drawn to explorations of a gay narrative. What a golden age for the African short story, and how exciting to see real originality – with so many writers bringing something different to the form.'

The 2014 shortlist comprises:

- Diane Awerbuck (South Africa) 'Phosphorescence' from *Cabin Fever* (Umuzi, South Africa)
- Efemia Chela (Ghana/Zambia) 'Chicken' from *Feast, Famine and Potluck* (Short Story Day Africa, Cape Town, 2013)

- Tendai Huchu (Zimbabwe) 'The Intervention' from *Open Road Review* (New Delhi, 2013)
- Billy Kahora (Kenya) 'The Gorilla's Apprentice' in *Granta* (London 2010)
- Okwiri Oduor (Kenya) 'My Father's Head' in *Feast, Famine and Potluck* (Short Story Day Africa, Cape Town, 2013)

Joining Jackie Kay on the panel of judges are distinguished novelist and playwright Gillian Slovo; Zimbabwean journalist Percy Zvomuya; Assistant Professor at Georgetown University, Nicole Rizzuto; and the winner of the Caine Prize in 2001, Helon Habila. To commemorate 15 years of the Caine Prize this year, £500 will be awarded to each shortlisted writer. Once again, the winner of the £10,000 Caine Prize will be given the opportunity to take up a month's residence at Georgetown University, as a Writer-in-Residence at the Lannan Center for Poetics and Social Practice. The award will cover all travel and living expenses. The winner will also be invited to take part in the Open Book Festival in Cape Town in September 2014, the StoryMoja Hay Festival in Nairobi and the Ake Festival in Abeokuta, Nigeria.

This book also contains the stories that emerged from this year's Caine Prize workshop, which was held in Zimbabwe for the first time. In the Vumba, near Mutare, we assembled 12 talented writers at the Leopard Rock Hotel, where we were bordered to the east by the mountains of Mozambique. We are immensely grateful to Angeline Kamba, Irene Staunton and Edzo Wisman for their useful advice and to the Beit Trust and Exotix for providing the majority of the funding. Three of the writers who took part were Nigerians shortlisted in 2013 and six were local Zimbabwean writers; the others hailed from Kenya, Somalia and Ghana. During 12 days of peace and quiet the workshop participants were guided by Nii Ayikwei Parkes (Ghana) and Henrietta Rose-Innes (South Africa), who won the Caine Prize in 2008.

Halfway through the workshop the writers visited four schools near Mutare in groups of three or four to speak to and read to the students. Accounts of some of these highly successful events at Hillcrest, St Werburgh, Hartzell High and St Augustine's are detailed on the Caine Prize blog (http://caineprize.blogspot.co.uk/).

After the workshop the group returned to Harare for an event (on 1 April) at the newly refurbished Harare City Library in partnership with the Library and the British Council. Nii Parkes hosted a conversation about new trends in African literature with Clifton Gachagua from Kenya, Barbara Mhangami from Zimbabwe and Elnathan John from Nigeria. Farayi Mungoshi also spoke briefly about the newly published novel *Branching Streams Flow in the Dark*, by his father, Charles Mungoshi, that begins with a short story written at a Caine Prize workshop in Kenya back in 2005. A stimulating evening was enjoyed by all.

The following day (2 April), the writers were invited to read excerpts of their work at the Tambira Hub in the new Meikles MegaMarket in Harare. The event was hosted by Tinashe Mushakavanhu. Shoppers were in for a treat, as they heard stories and poems from Lawrence Hoba, Philani Nyoni, Elnathan John, Abubakar Adam Ibrahim, Barbara Mhangami, Bryony Rheam, Gertrude Zhuwao and Clifton Gachagua. The writers were then themselves in for a treat with a lunch at Meikles Hotel in the kitchen of La Fontaine restaurant.

We hoped by bringing the Caine Prize workshop and the writers involved to Zimbabwe that the literature and publishing sector in the country would be enlivened and encouraged. AmaBooks co-publishes the Caine Prize anthology in Zimbabwe and Weaver Press publishes a number of Caine Prize winners such as Brian Chikwava and NoViolet Bulawayo. We hope the opportunity to meet Caine Prize authors and to talk about books and writing will have encouraged locals to join the library and buy a few books as well as to keep up to date with all the Caine Prize does each year. The anthology is also available in Ghana, Uganda, South Africa, Zambia, Nigeria and Kenya through our co-publishers. It can be read as an e-book supported by Kindle, iBooks and Kobo and we are continuing to develop our partnership with the literacy NGO Worldreader to make award-winning stories available free to African readers via an app on their mobile phones.

The principal sponsors of the 2014 Prize were the Oppenheimer Memorial Trust, the Booker Prize Foundation, the Miles Morland Foundation, Sigrid Rausing and Eric Abraham, Weatherly International plc, China Africa Resources plc and CSL Stockbrokers. The Beit Trust primarily supported the workshop in Zimbabwe, with Exotix, and support was also received from the British Council, the Culture Fund, the EU delegation, Cambria and Kenya Airways, which provided travel grants for workshop participants. There were other generous private donations, and vital help in kind was given by: the Royal Over-Seas League; Bodley's Librarian; the Rector of Exeter College, Oxford; the Royal African Society; Marion Wallace of the British Library; Tricia Wombell, Co-ordinator of the Black Reading Group and Black Book News; the Southbank Centre; Asma Shah and Abenilde Sousa from Ladies Who L-Earn; Vicky Unwin and Clare Cooper at Art First; and Brixton Library. We are immensely grateful for all this help, most of which has been given regularly over the past years and without which the Caine Prize would not be Africa's leading literary award.

Lizzy Attree
Director of the Caine Prize for African Writing

Caine Prize 2014
Shortlisted Stories

Phosphorescence

Diane Awerbuck

'IT GETS THE BLOOD GOING, MY DEAR.'
Her granddaughter stared disbelievingly at Alice's answer, straight on, in a way that Alice herself would never have dared to regard her elders, especially her own grandmother. Brittany shook her dyed fringe down and replaced the earphone of her iPod, signalling the end of interaction. Alice could hear the notes' angry reverberation in her granddaughter's skull, like bees. She assumed that Brittany's throat was still too raw for much speech.

Alice tucked her own wispy hair into her rubber cap and draped the old striped towel over the rocks, her flesh goosebumped in anticipation. She began her simple, resolute walk towards the whitewashed pathway to Graaf's Pool, as she had every evening for more than 50 years, feeling the lightness as she always did, feeling like a showgirl, feeling like a bride.

It didn't show on the outside, Alice knew. Brittany was watching her progress, her face in the dusk unlined, her eyes sleepy and blank, idly counting Alice's sun spots like the pips on dice. Being 16 meant not having to care about damage, not even the kind you did to yourself on a Saturday night with a bottle of Panado. 'It takes eight pills to cause permanent liver damage,' the reproving nurse in the Medi-Clinic had said as she removed the pan with its swirls of charcoal and vomit. 'Eight. You are a very lucky girl.' The pan had slopped dangerously.

Brittany didn't feel lucky. She sat on the sand and waited

for moonrise because her grandmother had thought it was a good idea to get her off the couch and out of the flat, but when she looked at the water now she saw only her sharp edges refracted: she was immune to the smell and sound of the sea, and everything in it.

Under Brittany's dumb gaze Alice straightened her back in her black costume as much as she could, grateful for the coming dark. Still, her bones curved like forceps and there was only so much good posture could do. Her son Sidney, the plastic surgeon, always said that it was the skeleton you couldn't change. Boob jobs, tummy tucks, facelifts were easy to execute, but when your patients hauled themselves up from their towels on the sand to hobble to the water, they hunched over like the old ladies they were. Plastic surgery was as much a mystery to Alice as the idea that in another century Sidney himself had emerged, smeared and screaming, from her body. She couldn't imagine wilfully visiting radical change upon herself.

Her granddaughter evidently could. It was, lately, all that Brittany thought about. Last weekend's attempt to cut herself loose from them altogether had ended in her sullen flight to Cape Town. She would stay with Alice in the beachfront flat until the new school term started in Jo'burg. She needed a change of scene, Sidney had said, from behind the phone on his mahogany desk. Get her away from those people she hangs out with. Alice had a sudden vision of Brittany as a red-striped dishcloth on a washing line. No-one had said 'suicide', but the word had stung like a thrown stone.

Alice lifted the construction tape that was meant to bar her from the walkway and ducked under it. She was careful in the way that people who know the cost of falling are. She was familiar with the water arriving from the other side of the planet, with it leaving as it did, rapidly. The rocks on either side were slippery, but the path this evening was more than usually treacherous, splattered with periodic candle wax melting weakly. Small groups of people had taken to coming to the pool in a kind of nightly vigil. They sat on the rocks. From her flat Alice could see the tiny flames flickering in the dark.

Now she shaded her eyes and squinted back at the play area above the strip of sand where Brittany sat motionless. There was no-one else at this time of day except for the workers. The municipality couldn't leave the place alone. Men still mowed relentlessly, sending the shorn blades of grass into the air over their heads; they raked and trimmed. Others, with SOLID WASTE emblazoned on their backs, scooped up the stinking kelp in sacks and tipped them into the waiting lorries. One woman raked the sand. Alice wondered if she also rearranged the shells. They were always obstructing the promenade, four or five men working on the sewage plant located right next to Mouille Point Lighthouse, the smell of decay wafting onshore with the wind to all the travellers who sat sipping lattes, a reminder of the contents of their expensive insides.

Since the municipality had first tacked the demolition notices to the lampposts, swimmers had stopped coming to Graaf's Pool, spooked by the tape. There had been one or two nostalgic articles in the free suburban papers and a small, largely ignored, outcry, mainly from the gay men who used the pool as their own. Alice was glad that there was someone else who felt the same clench of heart at the destruction of this half-secret place.

The bulldozers appeared a few weeks later and were left on the lawns overnight, expectant. That first night Alice woke up every few hours from her light old-woman's doze and thought that she could hear their metal ticking as it contracted, their hinged claws creaking in the wind that also rattled the notices on the lampposts, that pulled at the strings of coloured light bulbs swinging between them, regardless.

But the lights would go too. It would all go. The ellipsis made her afraid of the changes that could be forced on a body overnight, without consent. Still, the carnage and the flattening hadn't happened yet. The old Jews sat on their benches and the rentboys washed their used parts in the showers; children in transparent underpants paddled in the shallows and seagulls perched on the poured concrete pillars of the promenade, the red dots on their beaks like blood.

Maybe the men from the municipality had forgotten about bulldozing Graaf's Pool. The machines had been squatting for nearly 28 days now, leaving stretches of dead yellow grass under their bellies. Alice marked each reprieve on her tidal calendar, the way she had when she was first married and had to diarize her cycle: safe-unsafe-safe. Everything we know is pulled towards the moon; the earth can hold onto most of its subjects, except water. That recedes and swells as we turn by degrees, so slowly that we feel it only as a change in the pressure between the ears.

Alice saw that the levels were low when she reached the pool, below even the cement line left by the workers who whitewashed the walls twice every season. High tide this morning had lapped against the retaining wall of the promenade, the waves splashing passers-by with their dirty brown foam. Brittany, hugging herself at the window, had almost smiled at their squeals and jumps. Low tide tonight, under the rabbit's moon, would abandon the sand for the far shore.

Alice didn't hesitate; she never did. The water froze your marrow solid. It was always better to immerse yourself. The shock ended sooner; you adjusted. She pushed off from the wall, keeping her eyes open though the salt stung, watching the bottom. Sometimes things washed in with the tide and couldn't wash out again: a transparent octopus had once flailed at her in terror.

With every length she swam, Alice wondered if this one would be her last, if a man with roses of sweat on his T-shirt and a paunch over his belt would order her out of the water; she would have to lift herself out to lie panting on the rocks before him, an ancient mermaid, scaly and songless.

No-one came. Alice gave up her lengths and clung to the side. Lately she tired more easily. She leaned back on her elbows and regarded the sky. It was almost purple now, the first stars out, the volume of the traffic turning up a notch as other people sat down to dinner, peered into cocktails, listened to music in bars. Alice studied the lights on the shore. She could barely make Brittany's figure out but she could imagine her pose: hugging her knees, legs crossed at the ankles, impenetrable.

Alice kicked her feet in the water, feeling its resistance. What if this really was the last time she swam in Graaf's Pool? The misery of the subtraction astounded her. She wanted some tribute, a final act. Alice glanced around and saw she was still alone. She took off her cap, a few tiny hairs at the nape yanked out in her hurry. She slipped the straps of her costume off her speckled shoulders, and the sand trapped in the folds of her body sank to the bottom of the pool. The rest of the black nylon was easily pulled over her belly and thighs. It floated away from her grasp, the shed thing in the water like a sealskin. Alice wondered why she had ever bothered with it. She dived experimentally; the currents swirled between her legs, the temperature changing as the cold met the warm, as if she had cast off decades with the material. It really did get the blood going.

When Alice broke the surface she already knew what was waiting. Brittany stood at the edge of the pool, fully clothed in the darkness.

'You were gone so long,' she said. Alice regarded her steadily. Somewhere behind her the costume was bobbing like seaweed. I wonder if she can see my pubic hair, she thought.

'You never know,' she told Brittany. 'The next time we come here, the pool might be gone.'

Her granddaughter shrugged in the night air. Her hands were jammed into the pockets of her hooded top. They said, very clearly, *That's not an excuse.*

'How cold is it, anyway?'

'Colder than an ice-cream headache,' said Alice. Colder than a near-death experience in the Emergency Room, she said in her head. 'Don't slip on the wax.'

Brittany bent and unlaced her sneakers. She divested herself of her ankle socks and her black jeans, her haunches thin as a deer's. Her top went next, then the shirts – three of them, layered archaeologically – until she was standing in her girlish underwear, a mystifying combination of cotton and wire scaffolding. She doesn't need a bra, thought Alice, looking at her unpromising chest. Why is she even wearing one? Her granddaughter's body was a collection of straws, white in the moonlight.

Brittany stored her iPod carefully in her top and then stood for a moment longer. She bent down and tumbled her panties over her knees and bony feet, fumbled at the clasp of her triple A. It left lines on her body that Alice saw briefly, and then Brittany fell forward into the water. Alice had to stroke backwards in a flurry to avoid being bombed.

Brittany came up for air and the two of them grinned at each other, treading water. With their hair wet they didn't look very different.

'It's really cold!' she gasped. It wasn't an accusation. Alice splashed a little seawater at her and swam out of reach.

'Don't be a baby.'

Brittany was waving her arms like tentacles and craning her neck from side to side.

'Look!'

Alice obeyed. The water around them had a greenish cast to it. When Brittany moved her limbs the little lights moved with her: she was trailing phosphorescence from every fingertip.

'What is it?'

'Plankton,' said Alice. 'Like fireflies.' She didn't add that dinoflagellates occurred in concentration when raw sewage was present in the water. Let Brittany have something that wasn't spoiled. The two of them fell quiet. Above them the moon was swollen orange and fully risen, the rabbit scrabbling his paws to prevent his fall into mortality as the earth and sun lined up.

At first Alice thought that the massive flood of light was natural. She was about to remark on the moon's brightness when they heard the engines start. Then the men's voices carried to them in bass notes over the walkway. Brittany made sense of it first.

'Gran! It's the bulldozers!'

The men from the municipality hadn't forgotten. They were just waiting for spring tide: the highest high tide that had washed over the promenade this morning – and the lowest low tide at 9pm that would leave Graaf's Pool dry enough to demolish. They would have the full moon to see by even without the enormous generators and the blinding stadium-strength lights. Their artificial beams lit up the pool and the two women in it in a parody of daylight. She hasn't called me Gran since she was little, Alice thought obscurely.

The men's shouts took on a different timbre, and she began to be afraid.

'Gran! What are we going to do?'

Alice considered the options. Brittany at least could get dressed here, but her own costume was long gone, a gift given back to the sea. She would have to walk back naked and then stumble around, trying to find her towel on the rocks.

'We'll have to go back.' She could feel herself shrinking, osteoporotic with shame.

'Gran, no.' The idea horrified Brittany, but Alice had no others.

The voices were coming closer. Alice thought she could hear the sound of the men's shoes on the walkway, but that was impossible. It was solid concrete. It must be the bulldozers, starting up. The vibrations made her teeth click lightly together with the same insectile hum transmitted by the men with the edge-trimmers. Suddenly she was exasperated.

'Well, what do you want me to do?'

She instantly regretted snapping at Brittany. Her granddaughter's eyes were enormous, her hair plastered to her head like one of those Japanese cartoon girls Alice saw everywhere. What were they called?

The two of them were silent.

'What if we did it in stretches?'

'What do you mean?'

'If you got out now, quickly, and then I did too, and if we were both very quiet...'

It made a certain sense, Alice supposed. Especially for someone who was used to being under the radar.

'Gran, we have to go now. The longer we wait...'

Alice nodded, considering. They might as well. 'But how do we cross the road?' It sounded like a joke.

'There's another way.'

'What other way?'

'Come. I'll show you.'

By degrees they hauled themselves out of the pool, the phosphorescence slipping off them like scales. While Brittany dressed as fast as she could, Alice crept and hid, crept and hid in the shadows of the rocks, keeping parallel with the walkway as much as she could. She slipped once on the candle wax, lacerating her palms. She wondered if her bloody handprints would still be there in the morning.

The men had reached the pool and were setting up more lights, angling the first bulldozer. Were they just going to push the rubble into the sea? The two women didn't stay to watch. In increments they got to the beach without using the walkway, terrified and exhilarated.

On the flat sand of the beach, Brittany tried to take her grandmother's hand, but the slashes hurt too much. Oh God, thought Alice, I'm smearing blood all over her. By the time they reached the flat they would look like the last demented refugees from *Lord of the Flies*. She gritted her teeth, shivering, and surrendered to Brittany's guidance.

The door was small, built flush with the retaining wall of the promenade, invisible at high tide. Even now it receded into the shadow thrown by the overhanging lip of the boardwalk above it.

'What's this, Brit?'

'A door. A tunnel, I think. Maybe it goes over the road. Under, I mean. We can cross.'

'Brittany,' Alice enunciated, 'we don't know for certain where it goes.'

'Gran, we don't really have a choice.'

If Alice was honest with herself she would recognize her pride surfacing, flailing like a small transparent octopus. How was it possible that she had been coming to this place for half a century, and never noticed the door? Or had she seen it and cast it off as a storeroom, a boat shed, somewhere the municipality kept its spades? And how had her granddaughter – her stick-thin, dyed-fringe, suicidal granddaughter – seen it at once for what it was?

'How did you know about the tunnel?'

'While you were swimming, I went for a walk. It was just here.'

It was just here.

Alice sighed. 'All right. Let's try. But if there's anything funny in there – anything at all – I'll walk naked across Beach Road like Lady Godiva!'

'Okay.'

'Okay.'

The boards of the door were weathered grey and splintering. When Brittany tugged at the rusted padlock, the chain came off and lay in her hands like a medal. They peered into the dark mustiness. At the far end, over the road, was a dimly illuminated rectangle. Alice thought sharply of the Cango Caves and how she was stuck there once in the Chimney, 30 years ago, when they were on a caravan tour of the country. ('How do you remember which ones are stalactites and which ones are stalagmites?' Sidney had sung out. 'Tits hang down!') The lights were going off in the Caves too, now, because algae was growing in response to the false warmth, the determined renewal of cells carpeting the stalactites like plaque.

Alice coughed. She could feel the spores settling in her lungs.

'Let's go, then.'

The two women – one naked, one fully clothed – ducked under the lintel and made their way into the darkness, aiming for the light. Behind them the earth shook as the bulldozers ate away at the dry boundaries of Graaf's Pool. The cement walls crumbled and then turned to powder, and the candle wax was washed out with them. The phosphorescence was gone, sucked back out to sea, clinging to a black costume that caught on the kelp and washed up at Three Anchor Bay in the morning.

Inside the tunnel the two women were dumb with the smell of crypts and limestone. Their feet were wet with the puddles they splashed through, numb at the extremities. For some of the way, they held hands.

Diane Awerbuck is the author of *Gardening at Night* (2003), which was awarded the Commonwealth Best First Book Award (Africa and the Caribbean) and was shortlisted for the International Dublin IMPAC Award.

Her work has been published internationally and translated into a number of languages. Awerbuck develops educational materials, reviews fiction for the South African *Sunday Times*, and writes for *Mail&Guardian*'s Thoughtleader. Awerbuck's collection of short stories, *Cabin Fever*, which included 'Phosphorescence', was published by Umuzi. Her most recent full-length work, *Home Remedies*, was published in 2012. Her doctoral work and non-fiction deal with trauma, narrative and the public sphere.

Chicken

Efemia Chela

I

It was a departure of sorts, last time I saw them. Or maybe not at all. I had left sigh by sigh, breath by breath over the years. By the time my leaving party came, I was somewhere else entirely. From this place, I watched fairy lights being looped low over long tables and rose bushes being pruned. The matching china came out with the crystal glasses. The guards in our gated community were paid off to pre-empt noise complaints, as were the local police. Our racist neighbours were invited in time for them to book a night away. A credit card and a note on the fridge told me to go and buy a new dress ('At least knee-length, Kaba!!').

The entire dusty front yard was swept. Forthright, our maid, swept it once from the middle to the left and once from the middle to the right, ensuring even distribution. She minced around the edges of the yard until she reached the right spot. Then she lovingly gave the earth a centre parting, like she was doing the hair of the daughter she seldom saw. Deftly, she made concentric circles with the rake, making certain not to be backed into a corner as she was in life. Paving would have been more in line with the style of the double-storey house, the stiff mahogany headboard in my parents' bedroom and the greedy water feature in the atrium. 'From the dust we came and to it we return,' my father said cryptically whenever anyone asked why. Our relatives whispered in covens that BaBasil should have gotten 'crazy paving'. They were adept at spending money that wasn't theirs and would never be, due to equal measures of indolence and bad luck.

The same relatives called me down to some new-found duty. I slouched my way to them and despaired again that these women would never know me as an equal. Instead, I was a comedic interlude breaking up days of haggling in markets, turning smelly offal into scrumptious delicacies, hand-washing thin and dim-coloured children's clothes, and serving dinner to their husbands on knees that could grate cheese. I pitied them too much to be truly angry.

Celebrations transformed them into long-lost gods and goddesses. We enticed them with Baker's Assorted biscuits, school shoes and endless pots of tea. They descended from the village and came to town. Sacrifices were made; I kissed most of my haircare products and magazines goodbye. But it was worth it even though they were near strangers tied to us by nothing more than genetics, a sense of duty and vague sentimentality. Who else could pound *fufu* for hours without complaint until it reached the correct unctuous and delightfully gloopy texture that Sister Constance demanded? Uncle Samu, my mother's brother, had driven away his third wife with a steady rain of vomit and beatings. As the family's best drunk, he could play palm-wine sommelier. His bathtub brew was mockingly clear. Getting drunk on it felt like being mugged. And by midnight he and Mma Virginia, who according to family legend were kissing cousins in the literal and sordid sense, could always be counted on to break out 'The Electric Slide' to the entertainment of everyone watching.

My aunties' voices rang out from a corner of the garden that had escaped my mother's plot to turn it into a suburban Tuscan nightmare. I weaved between the tacky replicas of Greek statues I had studied at university. The statues bulged like marble tumours from the lawn. A brown sea snail slid round The Boxer's temple. A rogue feather blew past Venus in the wind. Sister Constance smacked her lips against her remaining teeth in disgust: 'You took so long. They spoil you-o!'

I didn't reply and just contorted my features into what I thought was penance and respect. 'Let them have this,' I thought. 'They'll let me go soon.' After all, my mother, if she heard I had been too insolent, was far worse than all of them combined.

They told me to kill them – three plain white chickens. Expressionless and unsuspecting, they pecked the air while I shuddered above them, a wavering shadow. I searched myself for strength and violence while rolling up the sleeves of my blue Paul Smith shirt. 'I guess I'll have to kiss this goodbye too,' I thought glumly. I was about to look like an extra who found themselves in the wrong place at the wrong time in a Quentin Tarantino film. I curled my sweaty fingers around a knife that someone had pressed into my right hand. I remember thinking how blunt it seemed; inappropriate for the task ahead. But then I grabbed a chicken and felt its frailty.

'Wring and cut, Kaba. Wring and cut!' someone shouted.

I was too queasy an executioner. My shaking exacerbated the death-flapping of the fowls and their blood spurts. I kept going. One. Two. Three. Gone in a couple of minutes. I barely heard the meat hitting the silver-bottomed tub. I was roused from my trance by the glee-creased face of Aunt Lovemore. As I tried to make my way to a shower, one shirt-sleeve dripping, my mind emptied and all that remained was something someone once said to me or maybe... I couldn't tell where it was from. I still can't tell. It was:

'so much depends
upon

a red wheel
barrow

glazed with rain
water

beside the white
chickens.'

The feast was that night. I looked at myself in the back of a serving spoon that had some stray grains of white rice smeared on it. No-one would need it. Who could be bothered with Basmati when there was *kenke* to be unwrapped from wilted banana leaves like a present? When *nshima* so soft and personable was at the serving table in a large white quivering pile just waiting for some *kapenta* and an eager palate to come by? No, the Basmati would be given to the beggars who came by in the morning and expected nothing less from one of the town's richest families. Our generosity fostered expensive tastes.

My parents' cross-cultural marriage made for an exciting culinary event. From my father's side came slow-cooked beef shin in a giant, dented tin pot. Simply done, relying only on the innate flavour of the marbled red cubes of flesh and thinly sliced onion getting to know each other for hours. It was smoked by open charcoal fire and lightly seasoned with nothing but the flecks of salty sweat from nervy Auntie Nchimunya constantly leaning over the steaming pot. Mushrooms were cooked as simply as Sister Chanda's existence. Fungi were hoped for in the night and foraged for at dawn. My favourites were curly-edged, red on top with a yellow underskirt and fried in butter. My lip curled as someone passed me a bowl of *uisashi*, wild greens and peanuts mashed into a bitty green mess. Little cousins cheekily defied their rank and begged for the prized parsons' noses from the grilled chickens. My chickens. Their shiny mouths indicated they'd already had more than enough chicken for the night and their age. Tauntingly, I popped one of the tails into my mouth and refused to pass them the crammed tray.

My mother, desperate not to be upstaged by her husband, reminded us all of her issue. The Fante chief's daughter, swathed in *kente*, brought *kontombire*. It was a swamp-like spinach stew flooded with palm oil, thickened with *egusi*, specked with smoked mackerel and quartered hard-boiled eggs. It was carried to the table by three people, in a boat-shaped wood tureen from our mezzanine kitchen and the ancient forests of Ghana. Even her mother-in-law was impressed. She unwrinkled her forehead and loosened her fists a little, revealing her fingers stained so yellow by the sauce. From behind my thick pane of one-way glass, I saw my uncle had a bit of red garden egg stuck in his beard, but munched along cheerily, stopping briefly only to push round glasses up the bridge of his Ampapata nose. He was ignoring his side of *waakye*. I was tempted to take it and scoff it myself but then I looked down, remembering the chunk of succulent grasscutter that I'd pinched from Ma Virginia's bowl of light soup, still slightly hairy with a bit of gristle dangling from it. She was busy scanning the party for Uncle Samu's characteristic beaten-in black fedora. Grasscutter, fried okra and plantain. Now that would be tasty.

The chair to my left was empty but I preferred it to the barrage of information about my 30-year-old cousin's upcoming wedding, courtesy of our great-grandmother on my right.

'Bridget is off the shelf! Ow-oh!

'Praise God! The glory is all yours, Jesus!

'She's so fat and in all the wrong places. Oh! And she insists on this mumbling. Gah! And the boys just weren't coming, you know. So many weddings she had to see and cry at but no-one was crying for her.

'Ei! You know you guys, you're just like your parents. You go abroad to these cold places where money is supposed to grow on trees. Even though there is no sun. You marry these white girls and boys who would die during our dry season, they are so thin. All bones. You get kept over there and we just hear news. Small-small news. And that you're making it big out there, with our name. But never come back. Oh God!

'But luckily this one never left. Just did what he was told to. A job, at least. Nothing much. But in the government, filing papers and not even important ones. So he will never get on the party's bad side like my brother did in the Sixties.

Eh-eh! No, we can't have all that trouble again. Even though, God willing, we would recover.

'Now I can say all my girls are settled. Uh-huh! I can die now. Someone else is responsible for them now. They will do as I did. They will live as I lived. I have made them so. I have taught them well. They will never lose themselves. That is enough. Yes. That is enough. What other claim does a wife have?'

A *chitenge*-covered desk beside the second buffet table was for the DJ. There was a stack of records and the glow of a MacBook illuminated my older brother's face. He played eclectically, switched from computer to record player. Computer to Supermalt. Supermalt to record player. Mostly high life, with Earth, Wind and Fire, Glen Miller and Elton John. The musical liturgy of the family. Everything he knew would please. Near the bottom of the pile of records I saw a tiny snail that had escaped being stewed, creeping slowly upside down on the underside of a WITCH LP.

The fairy lights doused everyone in a soft glow. I think I was happy dancing with my little niece in the dust to the music; my heels forgotten by the hedge. Our yard was crowded and noisy until the sun came up. When I woke up in the afternoon, the noise echoed and resonated within me. It had embossed my inner ear. I'd captured it all. My brother had mentioned once that the earth was a conductor of acoustical resonance. If it's true, maybe the same goes for people. The night played over and over again. I was there shrouded by night. I looked around the garden with moistened eyes, a bulb of white wine condensing in my hand. I saw growing piles of soiled dishes whisked away by staff. Cutlery gleaming like silver bones under the moonlight. The people, the scale, the grandeur. It wasn't really anything to do with me at all.

II

I never wanted to admit it to anyone, but times were tough. I'd just left university with a distinction no-one asked about. I barely managed to convince someone to hire me.

Employers thought eight years of tertiary studies had left a gaping hole where experience should have been. In the year that the markets crashed, I was assured that the crisis would have sorted itself out by the time I entered the job market. It was nothing like that. I probably should have studied something more practical, but stubbornly I believed in my research. That there was really a place in the world for what I believed in.

I rented a room in the bum end of town and there I plotted my future. I played clairvoyant, gazing over my neighbours' corrugated iron roofs into the cavernous eyes of the mountain. Those were abrasive mornings. I tried to ignore the strangers in the abandoned lot opposite my window. Girls returned there the morning after the fact, looking for their dignity in the dirt or lost plastic chandelier earrings. Boys sprayed their scent on the crumbling wall, eyes on the lookout for scrap metal. The train rattled by, creaking as if each stop would be its last. Sometimes it was. I was late to work often. Gaudy prostitutes swooped indoors like vampires at first glimpse of the rising sun and the garbage men, part-time fathers of their children.

My relationship with my parents festered. I could expect disapproving text messages and automatic EFTs into my account. They sent me a pittance for rent and over the years had made sure to cultivate the kind of unspoken relationship that meant I wouldn't dare to ask for more money. Every ping in my inbox signalled another accusation. They told me that I was still young and there was still time to start a law degree. I baulked; their alms lessened.

I tried not to let their unpleasantness taint my days, curdle the sea I swam in or sharpen the wind. That coastal wind, a blustering soundtrack to my days in that seaside city. It pranked me in public, lifting my skirt. I, and undoubtedly others, got used to a flash of my thigh and untrimmed hedge creeping just past the edge of my briefs. I wasn't having enough sex to be greatly concerned with my appearance down there. Nothing in my top drawer could be rightly termed lingerie. In a town where everyone, through lies or privilege, was cooler and richer than you, I felt like I didn't even have to try. It was liberating. I went where my heart led me. Took tables for one. That's not to say I was starved for sex though. Every so often things would happen.

Like at this party one weekend. The party went down at a formerly whites-only pub that had been reclaimed, much like the word 'slut' had been some years before. 'Oh my god! Eb! You little slut! I love you!' shrieked my friend, Alice, all arms and legs.

And at this moment, her arms were wrapped around the neck of her polyamorous boything, Eb. His real name was Ebenezer, I think. I was embarrassed by black parents who still handed out Dickensian names to their children as if it would advance them up the hegemony. Though kudos to those kids too dark to blush called Aloysius and Enid for rebranding themselves as Loyo and Nida. The colonial pub, all flaky gilt frames and lined beige wallpaper tempered by dark woods, was full of them. Of us, I mean. Another generation tasked with saving Africa, yet ignoring the brief. Overwhelmed, we sought to please ourselves as best we could, whether that meant siphoning profits off family businesses, accepting scholarships overseas and never looking back, or being assimilated into the incompetent state. Laughing, talking, smoking and dancing, we could have been young people on any continent.

A girl and a boy sat down beside me and, after a perfunctory hello, asked me to join their threesome. Rather a forward approach, I thought, but then the boy backed out after I feigned some interest. He ran off.

'I think he's spooked. Sorry. I–' she said, trying to salvage the situation.

I raised my eyebrows in response and she leant towards me in a way that could only mean one thing. She led the intrepid exploration of my mouth with a gentle suction that left me gasping at once for air and more of her. I gripped her side. We ended up in my single bed. I wasn't dogmatic enough in my desire to be a lesbian but I liked the symmetry of being with a woman. Breast to breast. Gender didn't matter really anyway. I talked to Alice over coffee about it. I remember saying:

'Boys.

Girls.

Whatever.

We're always just two people searching... fumbling towards something.'

Before she awoke, I surveyed her half-covered body. I was in awe, as I always was when someone wanted to have sex with me. And then I saw it. Holding down her bottom lip with a finger, I tried not to wake her while getting a better look. It was an inner lip tattoo. God, it must have hurt – an egg. A single egg. I didn't have time to ponder what it meant. She woke and instantly seemed embarrassed. Not by her fevered cries that split the night or the way she had gushed a little between her legs when her body was racked with pleasure. She was embarrassed by the window edges taped shut to keep out the cold. The suitcase instead of a dresser. My crusty two-plate stove that I made *nshima* and beans on every day trying not to shock myself or short circuit the whole floor. She dressed in silence, turned away. When she did turn back, she looked at me, her eyes softened by pity. A bite of the lip said she hadn't realized what happened last night was a charity event. She scuffed her Converse on the rough floor as if trapped and bored.

'It... it was lovely,' she said haltingly, trying not to meet my eyes again.

It was quiet for so long after that I nearly missed her squeak. 'You might need this more than I do,' she said, leaving R100, like a bird dropping, crumpled on the blue crate I called a nightstand. I didn't leave my room for two days after. The sheets trembled. But after my grief, I smoothed out what she thought I was worth and went and bought myself some fancy gin.

After that I worked harder at work than ever. I was one of 100 unpaid interns at the bottom of a global firm. Our only hope of getting hired was archiving gossip and evidence of affairs or theft amongst our superiors and using them as leverage once we became brave enough. I regret not being braver. My days went down the drain as I alphabetized contact lists and took coffee orders. I filed things. Then retrieved them for executives a couple of days later. Then was told to redo the filing system.

One night I was given orders by one of the art directors. She was having a crisis, she said. Meaning, she was on a deadline and her coke-addled brain had no vision for the client's product. It was two days to the big pitch and she needed to 'cleanse to create' so I had to rub all her erasers until I reached a clean surface on every inch of all 30 of them. Grumpily, I walked to her desk. First, I checked the pockets of the fawn-coloured jacket draped over her chair. I rustled for snacks, change or something to pep me up. Rustle. Rustle. But nothing. Except a business card. Rectangular and rounded at the edges, it read: Karama Adjaye Benin, Chief Recruiter, FutureChild Inc. The ovum bank you can trust.

III

I envied people who talked in certainties and absolutes. In plans and futures. I felt like I had nothing. Whether doubt, anger or hunger gnawed at my stomach became irrelevant. I set aside time at home to cry. I used the internet at work to find more jobs, but I was already stretched thin on that front. Sleep was for the in-between moments, wherever they fell. I lied my way into focus groups and market surveys for products I couldn't afford. My heels wore down. My gait changed. I saw myself in the blacked-out windows of a skyscraper en route to somewhere. At first I didn't realize who the hurried girl with the hunched back was. I looked again. She looked hunted.

I had to stay home trying to keep warm or risk having to party sober. I could coast through end-of-the-month weekend when everyone was generous at the bar or people threw parties at houses with cellars and drinks cabinets. Sometimes, at clubs like The Pound, I let old men call me a doll and dribble nonsense in my ear over synth beats and the squeak of pleather. I listened, smiled and was intermittently witty, but generally I only spoke to say, 'Double Jack, please.' They were men who lived on promises. I starved on hope. This was fourth-wave feminism.

I considered prostitution quite seriously after that one-night stand with Ananda. The concept didn't seem so far-fetched any more. In a way, the business card was my chance. Their offices were in an innocuous-looking building not far from the CBD. It was difficult to know what to wear, but I wanted to look like someone who deserved to be reproduced. I looked nervously out the window at the wet mist blurring anyone who had the temerity to leave the house. I picked my most ironed dress and a smart jacket and took a hardback book to read. This choice too was the source of some anguish as it needed to be big enough to hide my face in case I saw someone I knew, but also had to double as a tool to intrigue and impress the recruiter. My father had always said *Ulysses* would come in handy some day. I was angry that he was right.

The chrome chair felt sterile and sharp against my body. I looked around at the waiting room, gooey with pink branding about ethnically diverse angels, mama birds and dreams. All the framed stock photos were rosy assumptions of family life. I tried to concentrate on filling out the form handed to me. It was the only truth I had dealt with in a long time. I found it refreshing. I couldn't fail here. I was qualified to do this, to be a donor. I would get a bonus for every year of post-graduate study I had achieved.

Checking all the details, I was glad my natural mediocrity had its uses – healthy, black, 65 kg, brown-eyed woman. A non-smoking 24-year-old, with regular periods and taking no contraceptives. A little girl with pigtails and a pinafore smiled up at me from my lap. These photos would complete my personal zine, to be handed over to the agency for consideration. The girl was blissfully unaware of what was happening, just smiling shyly like she always would. I turned her over.

Why were the blank lines so easy when life was so hard? I looked so different on paper. Broken down into sections, I barely recognized myself. I felt that I had only ever heard of this woman, had never met her. I fake-read my book, which gave me time to really mull over what I was doing. I was sure it didn't matter. The eggs were just lying around inside of me going to waste on the twelfth of every month. From what I remembered from school, I had thousands of them in reserve. I was a veritable mine of genetic material. This was nothing to cry over.

I signed my contract while lying on my back, during one of several ultrasounds. Injection by injection I began to think that it was meant to be. Maybe it was the hormones. The red-headed woman doing the extraction sacrificed congeniality for professionalism. I gathered that she wore all white, even outside work. The only thing that differentiated her from a robot was her revelation that she had also been a donor, albeit in her thirties.

'I was just young enough. I had a lot of bills. I wanted to give the gift of parenthood to someone less fortunate,' she said, as if from a script.

To convey emotion, she punctuated her speech with weird bobs of the head. To make awkward conversation while doing my scans, she asked about my degree. I sensed misunderstanding. Sometime after third year, I had learnt to let the confusion pass without comment or justification. They'd see.

'Your ovaries are doing well.'

A few months later I was forced to look up at her like I had several times before. Her whole face was like clingfilm, wrapped fast across sinew and bone. I squinted up, then dropped my head down, away from the scrutiny of the powerful lights. My neck slackened as I breathed in the gas. I lost consciousness counting backwards.

'You're a hero now,' said Karama as I stumbled out, still a little woozy and anaesthetized. Trying to be kind, she crushed me into her body. I didn't feel like anyone's saviour, even though there were two red stigmata in my knickers. My phone beeped somewhere at the bottom of my bag letting me know that I had been paid. I ignored it.

After the extraction, I felt less lost. I knew exactly where I was and where I was going. I went home and climbed up the rickety fire escape to the roof, holding on fearfully to the rail afflicted with rust, making it wart-like to the touch. The cold mist cloaked me in damp as I stepped onto the crunchy pigeon-shit roof. I stood motionless looking down at the swaddled city. I knew what was hidden below the mist. Shacks slanted with uncertainty. Six-lane highways and car ads clinging to billboards beside them. Wide boulevards bordered by alien trees and thin housewives in cafés. Narrow byways lined with needles. Underfunded primary schools with middle-aged men parked outside trying not to eat the sweets they used as bait. Cold modern apartment blocks; all light, expense and lack of privacy. Secret leisure houses cowering behind high walls. Leaning road signs waiting to be stolen by students.

All of these places. I would never know where my child would be. No, I would. I would always be beating paths for it to follow. It would wind its way around my brain. I'd stage shadow-puppet shows on the walls of my skull, playing out its careers, hobbies and loves. One director, one spectator. I didn't want the child to be sheared between two lives, two minds, two imaginations. My own and its own. I pleaded to no-one that they would spare it, not rip it apart. I hoped my ghost would not smother it. That my wishes would not hamper it. I prayed it wouldn't be pained. Or nagged by the phantom limb – the gnawing mystery of my existence. I wanted its parents to take all the credit. I hoped they would never tell it.

That my donation would just be fiction.

Efemia Chela is a 21-year-old writer with her body in Cape Town and her heart in Japan. She had a bumpy childhood in Zambia, England, Ghana, Botswana and South Africa. She is married to a film camera. They go everywhere together and have many square children. She gets her thrills from remotely attending international fashion weeks, artistic intertextuality, old movies and tasting new cuisines. The short story 'Chicken' is her first published work, which originally appeared in *Feast, Famine and Potluck* `(Short Story Day Africa, Cape Town, 2013).

The Intervention

Tendai Huchu

The first thing I did when we got to Leicester was ask Precious to use the bathroom. I did my business super quick, because I wanted them to think I'd only gone in for a long piss, and her loo had one of those inexplicable doors with frosted glass. I flushed, washed my hands, gave the room a blast of the good ol' Glade, checked the bowl for skid marks and got out of there.

Z and I had come down from Newcastle where we'd been slugging and whoring for a couple of days until the natives ran us out with pitchforks. He was a little off with me, because all the way down the M1 I'd stopped him every half mile or so for a pee – not my fault, I have a condition. The problem, as he put it, wasn't so much my non-stop pit-stop requests, rather the fact that I refused to use the verges like a 'real man'. I admit, I was stoned and paranoid, but I'd heard this story from a mate about a bloke who had a mate who was answering nature on the verges when the ngonjos pulled up from nowhere, and get this, coz he was shaking it when they showed up, they did him for jerkin' the gherkin, and had the poor sod put on the register.

'This is my gororo, Simba. Simba, meet Precious,' Z said, using the exact same line he'd hit me with when introducing Sharon in Newcastle. Not that this knowledge was new to me, or that I didn't know of other girlfriends, but in that moment a wave of righteous indignation washed over me. But this never lasts long:

'Tafara nekukuzivai,' I said the mystic words and clapped my hands, old school.

'Pleased to meet you too,' Precious replied in English.

We repeated the ritual for Tamu and his girlfriend Sarah, Sylvia (Precious's mate), and some random Zimbo – a blazo in shorts whose name I can't quite remember. There was a lot of clapping and repeating of the mystical words, until Precious's two daughters came in. I don't remember their names, but one was older and the other was younger than the older one, yes, I'm sure that's correct. The kids didn't speak Shona, so we were introduced in English, and check this out: I was 'Uncle Simba'. The little one said something stupid like; 'Oh, Simba from the Lion King.' I wanted to twist her ear nice and proper like my teachers did back in the day, but ended up explaining that Simba meant strength and my full name, Simbarashe, meant God's strength, because names had to have meanings where we're from. Then again the 'rashe' could be God or the king, so a more apt translation that keeps the ambiguity is 'the Lord's strength'. The kid just looked at me blankly like I was talking effing Zulu.

'Would you like something to drink?' Precious asked.

'Tea,' Z said, and I gave him my wtf face.

'What about you, Simba?' she turned to me.

'I'll have a beer,' I said.

'Are you sure you wouldn't like some tea first?'

'Beer is my tea.' My little joke fell flat. The blazo looked at me with contempt. I reckon he must have been one of those Pentecostal types.

Precious got me a Bud. I couldn't believe I'd gone through that mini aggro for a Bud. Give me a wife-beater or a Sam Adams if you wanna get into it like that. My dad was hitting Black Labels at eight in the morning when I was growing up, and he never missed a day at work in 25 years. But I like to think that I drink for religious reasons, Biblical ones that is. And I'm not just talking about Jesus's first miracle, no man, Proverbs 31's the daddy, and I've got it all memorized, well, the important bits anyway:

Let beer be for those who are perishing,
wine for those who are in anguish!
Let them drink and forget their poverty
and remember their misery no more.

It's pretty plain to anyone with a rudimentary theological background that Liz, Phil, Charlie, Wills and my boy Harry, oh, and Kate and the baby too, are, by divine decree, advised to stay away from Noah's brew, and save it for us poor Third World immigrants.

Z asked for the channel to be flicked to the news. Precious stuck us on the BBC, but Z requested Al Jazeera instead. 'Maresults are coming and it's the only channel I trust,' he said. 'The winds of change are coming to our nation, just you wait and see.' We were hit with the Egyptian situation. I waited for it, Z was pro-Morsi and I was pro-coup, or was it the other way round? We'd spent so much time arguing about it until we became confused, but what I do know is that our positions on the issue were diametrically opposed and irreconcilable. He looked at me, gauging to see if I was going to say something. I held my peace and drank my crappy Bud.

'I used to think Egypt was such a nice country before all this madness happened,' the blazo said.

'Nice? They ain't done nothing since the Pyramids,' I replied.

'Do you always have to be so antagonistic?' Z said to me. 'That's such a racist thing to say. I mean, how would you feel if someone said that our people hadn't done anything since Great Zimbabwe?'

'I wouldn't feel nothing, because it's the truth. We were the greatest empire in the world, but look at us now, we're a nation of bums innit,' I replied, knowing this would goad him on.

'You're a prick. Ah, sorry, mune vana.' Z threw the kids an apologetic glance. 'Very sorry about the language.'

I fought to contain a snigger, tried to look injured even, and Z went on: 'Wait until the election results, everything's going to change, just you wait and see.'

The Egyptian thing just kept dragging on as they covered all the angles, the Islamic Brotherhood opinion, the Opposition opinion, the American opinion, the British opinion, the Arab League opinion, the UN opinion. Everyone had something to say about it. I zoned out, my eyes fixed on some indefinite point on the DVD collection next to the TV. There were photos on the wall of Precious and her kids, a social-work degree certificate from some third-tier university, and an empty rectangular shadow which I think must have been occupied by her ex-husband's picture. I wondered where he was and why he'd left. Maybe Z would leave her for the same reason.

Syria came on next and I felt a tinge of disappointment. In the last decade we'd shared the stage with Iraq and Afghanistan; now it seemed Zimbabwe couldn't make the headlines if it tried. Perhaps the world had gotten tired of us with our crazy politicians and starving billionaires, topped off with an ultra-crap cricket team, the same worn-out antics year in, year out; we'd gone the way of Big Brother 10.

I can't quite remember what else we spoke about, zoned out as I was, but I can guarantee it would have been among several topics Zimbos always regurgitate when congregating – how much better things were back home than in the UK (insert canned laughter), white people (racist bastards), Indians/ in some versions labelled Pakistanis (racist bastards), Nigerians/West Africans (racist bastards), when was the last time you went home? (answers vary), get rich quick schemes (that go nowhere), work (mostly care work and other such menial occupations), food (yes, the food was so much better back home... that is, when we had it). All I had to do was wear a slight smile on my face and nod along. Z looked like he was monitoring my behaviour and would chuck me out at the slightest provocation.

'Let's not forget why we're here, the young ones would like to present their story,' Precious announced, pointing at Tamu and Sarah.

'We are ready to listen,' the blazo said.

Israeli jets had encroached Syrian airspace.

'You're right, that's why we came,' said Cynthia.

This was outside the script. I was drinking too fast, as you do in boring company, my Bud was two-thirds done. The blazo leaned forward and wore a grave face, the kind old biddies wore padare back in the day when we went kumakaya.

'Sarah, perhaps you'd like to begin and then we can hear from Tamu,' Z said, like he was in on the whole thing. I sat up, or sank back in my chair.

'We'll help you in any way we can,' Precious said.

'Auntie, we've come to you "grown ups" because our relationship is in trouble,' Sarah said with great dignity. The blazo nodded to signal they'd done the right thing. 'You see, this "boy" and I have been going out for eight years. We met in high school in Mazowe, and we have been together ever since. I came here first and worked hard, with my own hands, until I raised enough money to buy him a ticket so that we could be together. I love him, but now I have doubts as to whether he sees a future for us.

'He promised to marry me three years ago and I'm still waiting. Every time I ask about it, he gets angry and defensive. He starts shouting things about money and work. But three years! Three whole years? He can afford to buy himself iPhones and video games, but he says he can't afford a wedding. I am tired. I can't wait forever, eight years we've been together...'

She went on, and on, and on, and on, and on, reciting a litany of accusations against Tamu, who sat stone faced with his arms folded across his chest. A couple of times he sighed, blowing out long breaths of exasperation.

'...because I can't really see why if he is interested, he can't at least begin to make an effort–'

'Will you *please* shut up,' Tamu finally said.

'See Auntie, see the way this "boy" talks to me,' Sarah pointed at him, jabbing her finger in the air.

'You've been talking for so long, iPads, computer games, I can't even remember what you started off saying. How can I respond when you keep talking? I need to say my side–'

'Iwe, don't interrupt me, it's still my turn to speak.'

'You can't expect me to keep quiet when you're talking nonsense. For one hour, everyone has had to sit and listen to your rubbish.'

'I haven't been speaking for an hour.'

'Okay, okay, please, let's try to be amicable,' Z said, holding up his hands. 'You both love each other. I know that because you wouldn't be here if you didn't, so we have to find a way of talking nicely to each other and see how we can help you solve this problem.'

'I think we should hear Tamu's side of the story, so we can better understand what is happening,' said Cynthia.

'That's right,' said the blazo.

Tamu opened his mouth to speak, but that's when we came on the news. Precious increased the volume on the TV. Tamu started saying something, or maybe he didn't speak, rather he turned his attention to Al Jazeera like the rest of us had done. The reporter was black, with a Shona accent, holding a clipboard, and she stood in front of a large green tent with the words 'POLLING STETION' written outside it. She spewed some chat about how the election had largely been peaceful and the results were coming soon. A crowd formed behind her, their necks craned, as they looked into the camera. We all held our breaths. The ticker on the bottom scrawled stuff about Egypt. The news reports which we'd followed in the previous weeks as they popped up sporadically on SKY, BBC, CNN, ITV and Channel 4, all spoke about how Zimbabweans were going to vote for change in this election. This of course meant that the Opposition would win, a fact we were asked to take for granted. That was the only acceptable outcome for which the media had groomed us. I took a sip and checked out the expectant faces around me. A nervous twitch made the left side of Z's mouth dance Gangnam Style.

The reporter's lips were moving. I thought she was a very comely woman, like an early Renée Cox portrait, and then quickly corrected my sexist impulse. My beer was at critical.

Was Precious going to offer a refill? I languished in my uncertainty, the future became a boot stamping on my face.

'Change is coming to Zimbabwe,' Z said.

'It's been a long time coming,' said the blazo.

'As soon as our victory is confirmed, I'm packing my bags, leaving this goddamn country and going home,' Z went on.

Which side was I on again?

'Ndizvozvo, change is coming, I can feel it.' The blazo was swept along by Z's optimism.

The reporter was saying something about the ZEC, and the SADC, and the AU, and the EU, and the UK, and the US, and the RSA, but she may not have mentioned some of these acronyms. The results were out. The Party had won. The Party had won. The Party had won. The Party had. The Party? I saw a joyful smile mixed in with relief on Z's face, because the Party's win was a victory for him too. He had an asylum claim pending with the Home Office and if the Opposition had won, he'd have been screwed. He quickly mastered himself and frowned, now wearing a new look, a cross between sorrow and anger.

'Those cheating bastards,' he shouted at the TV screen.

'I can't believe it,' said the blazo. 'It's all lies. Why did they even contest the election when the playing field had not been mowed?'

'Levelled,' I said.

'What?' the blazo asked.

'The playing field had not been *levelled*,' I replied.

'By mowing,' he said.

I closed my eyes and felt it pushing in from the void as it

so often did. It was a pressure from an unknown dimension, a place before thought where only feeling and emotion matter. It came to me often during moments of crisis. Sometimes it hit me while I slept, forcing me from my bed to my desk. It was the act of being taken over by something so deep within oneself that it could have been from outside oneself, a seismic force of such magnitude that I was thrust from my seat. My hands were thrown outwards as though I was on the cross, and then my voice cried out:

The children of Africa cry
Waa-waa-waa
When they should be laughing
Ki-ki-ki
Can you hear them, can you hear them.
Will you help them, will you help them.
The land of the fat hippopotamus
The home of the mighty Zambezi
The mystical ancestors
The wide African skies
The children of Africa cry
Waa-waa-waa
...

Out of me flowed a poetic response, a thermonuclear blast that left everyone stunned. Cynthia's mouth was wide open. Z blinked a couple of times. As it lifted, I felt naked and tired, so tired. I fell back onto my seat and tried to control my breathing. I reached into my pocket, took out a notebook and began to write the verse as I'd received it. My t-shirt felt clammy on my skin. Everyone was staring. Precious told the kids to go to bed.

'I'm sorry I didn't tell you,' Z apologized, 'Simba is a poet.'

'A poet?' someone said.

'I'm a member of the Zimbabwe Poets for Human Rights,' I said.

'What does that mean?' Precious asked. 'Like, forgive my ignorance, but how can one be a poet for Human Rights. Does this mean that as a poet for Human Rights you're not interested in love, landscapes, the stars, ordinary life?'

I was so exhausted from my poetic attack that I couldn't formulate a full response for her. The problem with our school system is that it never imparted the appreciation of higher art to any but a handful. The best I could do to educate her was to say that Poetry for Human Rights was the highest form of art. I'm not sure she understood, but she nodded and quickly brought me another beer. I drank in silence, pondering the awesome meaning of my new verse.

I caught Sarah looking at me, and in that moment understood that she was a kindred spirit. There's a sixth sense by which poetic souls become aware of one another. By poetic souls, I mean not only poets or readers of poetry, but those for whom poetry induces profound emotion and a heightened understanding of the world. Sarah had this soul, and the wide-eyed look she gave me from across the room gave me strength and a renewed conviction in my mission here on earth.

'We've been cheated again, but we will never accept this result. The people will mobilize across the country,' Z said.

'Rise up, ye, mighty race!' I cried.

'The people will take to the streets. We refuse to live under this dictatorship any longer. If the Arabs can do it, so can we,' he said.

'Behold, the African Spring flowers,' I said, waving my Bud, spilling libation for the ancestors on Precious's carpet.

'When we stand united like this, brothers, there's no force in this world that can hold us,' the blazo said. 'We will not accept this result.'

It was easy enough to say all these things 10,000 miles away from the epicentre. Nothing we said or did meant a fart, and that was the truth of it. I checked Twitter and

Facebook on my phone to see what everyone else was saying about it all.

'How can we in the diaspora know what people back home are thinking, or who they voted for?' Tamu said in a quiet voice, as though asking himself.

Not one of us had an answer for him.

The net was abuzz and everyone had an opinion on the result. A lot of people were celebrating. Some of these were Zimbabwean, and a great many of those were just Africans who didn't live in Zimbabwe. When I was a kid at the UZ (it was a different country then), I had an erection for Castro and Saddam, though I'd never have wanted to live in their countries.

'Would anyone else like something to drink?' Precious asked.

'I'll have a beer,' Z said, in a world-weary voice.

'Me too,' said the blazo. 'I quit last year, but what's the point?'

Cynthia asked for wine but got Lambrini instead. We nursed our drinks, staring at the TV, eager for more information. I got to thinking that Precious needed the wallpaper changed or maybe the walls needed a lick of paint. The carpet needed washing. A cellphone rang, it might have been mine. No-one answered it.

'I just need to know if he is going to do as he promised and marry me, or else I'll move on. I can't wait forever, I'm 25. This is not child's play. Some of my friends, people who were junior to us in school, are already married and starting families of their own,' Sarah started up again. 'Auntie, everyone here can see I am committed to this "boy". If money is a problem he should just say so.'

'Ndezvekumanikidzana here?' Tamu replied, gruffly like.

'You see, you see the way he talks to me like I'm a rag. I'm tired, that's it, it's over, Auntie.'

Sarah got up, picked up her handbag which was on the dodgy carpet and made for the door. I almost forgot myself and made to rise, but Precious was up before me and blocked Sarah's path using her considerable weight in a manner my skinny frame could only hope to approximate. She pleaded with her for a couple of minutes, saying certain things, the kind of things that calm people down when they're seeing red. I don't quite recall the exact words, but Precious said stuff about how one needs to be patient with men because deep down they are all spoilt little boys.

Tamu sort of sneered and stewed in his seat, making no attempt to keep Sarah from leaving. He looked like he was tired of the whole affair and had better things he'd rather have been doing with his time.

'I went through his phone, Auntie,' said Sarah, and Tamu sat up, attentive all of a sudden. 'You can't believe the things I saw in there.'

'You went through my phone?' Tamu shouted.

'Yes, I did.'

'It's my *personal* phone. Why would you do that? You see, this is why I don't want to be with you. How can I be with someone who doesn't trust me? My phone is private. That's an infringement of my sovereignty. Arrgh.'

'Let's calm down for a minute,' Z said. 'I can see everyone is getting angry, so how about we all calm down and try to figure this thing out.'

'Uncle, how can I be calm after what this "boy" has done?' said Sarah.

'You went through my bloody phone.'

'Let's all just calm down like Uncle Z said,' said Cynthia. She looked maternal and concerned.

Sarah glared at Tamu, who stared back defiantly.

In that moment, our complete and utter inadequacy to help this young couple became apparent to me. This thing, this intervention, that we were trying to do, was a sort of attempt to bring Shona, old school, ways of doing things to the UK, like we were Tetes and Sekurus, but we were found wanting. Z was a manwhore of the lowest kind, and the young couple would see this when one day, in the not so distant future, Precious would be crying with a mincemeat heart over how he dumped her suddenly, with no explanation. The blazo in the shorts and Cynthia were both sufficiently middle aged so they should have been married but they weren't. I didn't know what they were, divorced, widowed, single, whatever, but what I did know, looking at them, was that if neither of them could hold down a stable relationship, then they sure as hell shouldn't have been playing marriage counsellors. And Precious, poor Precious was compromised, if only because of the poor judgement she demonstrated by going out with my gororo, Z.

For my own part, I never cast a single stone in this entire charade. I was consumed with overwhelming fury, seeing what Tamu was doing to this little princess. How could he sit there, chatting nonsense about his privacy, as she trailed the list of names from his phone:

'Tracy, Laura, Chloe, Sekai, Cynthia, Jade, Lucy, Susan, Miranda, Irene, Chido…' Sarah spilled out this litany, like she'd memorized the whole thing.

'You shouldn't have gone through my bloody phone. You were looking for something, yeah, well, now you found it. I hope you're happy,' Tamu said.

'Am I not a beautiful woman, am I not beautiful?' She turned to me, but before I could answer Tamu blurted out:

'That's right, you forgot Sally and Michelle.'

'Come on, Tamu, you're not helping here,' Z said.

I wanted to get up and sock the 'boy' on the speaker proper. Sarah was crying. The two other ladies embraced her, Precious in front and Cynthia behind her, so she was sandwiched, like they were protecting her from another blow. I could feel a tremor in my hands. I clenched and unclenched my fists, felt a dullness, the mist descending. I got up with my fists clenched and the next thing I felt was Z grab my arm.

'Let's go for a smoke,' he said, as he led me out of the flat.

He hovered by me while I pinched out the seeds and rolled one. I searched in my pockets for a lighter, but couldn't find one. Z offered me his. I lit up, took a drag, and began to cry. Man, I wept like a pussy.

Tendai Huchu is the author of *The Hairdresser of Harare*. His short fiction and nonfiction has appeared in *Warscapes*, *Wasafiri*, *The Africa Report*, *The Zimbabwean*, *The Open Road Review*, *Kwani?05*, *A View from Here* and numerous other publications. In 2013 he received a Hawthornden Fellowship and a Sacatar Fellowship. His next novel will be *The Maestro, The Magistrate & The Mathematician*. 'The Intervention' originally appeared in *Open Road Review* (New Delhi, 2013).

The Gorilla's Apprentice

Billy Kahora

That last Sunday of 2007, just a few days before Jimmy Gikonyo's 18th birthday – when he would become ineligible to use his Nairobi Orphanage family pass – he went to see his old friend, Sebastian the gorilla. Jimmy sat silently on the bench next to the primate's pit waiting for Sebastian to recognize him. After a few minutes, Sebastian turned his gaze on Jimmy and walked towards the fence. The gorilla's eyes were rheumy, his movements slow and careful. Their interaction was now defined by that strange sense of inevitable nostalgia that death brings, even when the present has not yet slipped into the past. Jimmy removed the tattered pass from his pocket and read the fine print on the back: '*This lifetime family pass is only for couples and children under 18 years of age.*' There was a sign on the side of Sebastian's cage: 'Oldest Gorilla in the World. Captured and Saved from the Near Extinction of His Species After the Genocide in Rwanda. Sebastian, 56. Genus: Gorilla.'

The *Sunday Standard* beside him said: Nairobi, Kisumu, Kakamega and Coast Province in Post-Election Violence After Presidential Results Announced. That Sunday morning was strangely cold for late December. When Jimmy looked around, every one of the animals seemed to agree, each exhibiting a unique brand of irritation. 11am was the best time to visit the Orphanage. The church-going crowd that came in droves in the afternoon was still worshipping, so the place was empty.

He had come here first as a toddler. They acquired their family pass in the days when his father was a trustee of the

Friends of Nairobi National Park but his father soon found the trips boring and, for some years, Jimmy had come here alone with his mother.

When Jimmy was 12 his father left them, and Jimmy began to come on his own, except for the year he had been in and out of hospital. That year, he had borrowed a book called *Gorilla Adventure* by Willard Price from a school friend. He had read it from cover to cover, in the night, using a torch under the blanket and eventually falling asleep. He had woken up to find the book tangled and ruined in urine-stained sheets. He had received a beating from the owner that had only increased his love for the mountain gorilla. For the rest of his primary-school years he would take the lonely side in arguments about whether a gorilla could rumble a tiger, or whether a polar bear could kill a mountain gorilla.

Feeding time was Jimmy's favourite moment of the day at the park – sacks of cauliflower plopping into the hippo pool, the dainty-toed river horses huffing. Until Sebastian had fallen sick, Jimmy had helped the handlers in the feeding tasks: crashing meaty hunks against the carnivores' cages and forking in bales of grass and leaves for the others. These times became the fulcrum of his weeks, defining his priorities and spirit more than his mother's war with the doors of the small Kileleshwa flat they now lived in; her daily conflicts with the cheap dishes which she had to wash herself as they could no longer afford a maid; their strange and sometimes psychotic neighbours; her boyfriends. Week after week, year after year, he listened to the screeching conversations of vervets devouring tangerines, peel and all; the responding calls of parrot, ibis, egret: the magenta, indigo and turquoise noises fluttering in their throats like angry telephones going off at the same time.

It took him away from real life. Real life was Evelyn's College for Air Stewards and Stewardesses, which he had attended for a year. Real life was the thin couch he slept on at home. Real life was his mother screaming that he needed to face Real Life. Waking up on Sunday morning and staring at the thin torn curtains of the sitting room, the stained ceiling that sagged and fell a few inches every week and smelt of rat urine, Jimmy often felt he needed to leave the house before his mother asked him to join her and her latest boyfriend for breakfast. Real life was the honey in her voice, the gospel singing in the kitchen as she played Happy Family for her new man.

Jimmy was more sensitive to light than most. When he was 16, a blood clot had blacked out his sight for months and he had spent most of that year in hospital. 'Picture an ink stain under his scalp,' the doctors had told his mother. 'That's what's happening in your son's head.' The stain had eventually been sucked out, and the doctors triumphantly gave him large black X-ray sheets for his 17th birthday. After 15 months of seeing the world in partial eclipse, light came alive again for Jimmy in the Animal Orphanage – glinting off slithering green mambas and iridescent pythons, burning in the she-leopard's eyes high up in her tree.

Every July he had watched the two kudu shrug off the cold with dismissive, bristling acceptance, standing like sentinels blowing smoky breaths in a far corner of the enclosure. When the sun travelled back north from the Tropic of Capricorn over November, the two hyenas' hind legs unlocked and straightened, and they acquired a sort of grace. In August the thick-jawed zebras and black-bearded wildebeest, heeding the old migratory call, would tear from one side of their pen to the other and, finally exhausted, grind their bodies into the ground, raising dust.

Over the last year, as Sebastian became more subdued, Jimmy spent more of his Sunday keeping him company. He could sit for hours like Sebastian, rendering the world irrelevant. In the Animal Orphanage, everything outside became the watched. And Jimmy knew all about being watched. What his mum called love.

That last Sunday of the year there were still visitors at the Orphanage. They carried their apprehension like a badge a day after the election results were announced. All who passed the gorilla pit noticed the slightly built, light-skinned young man with brown hair, a zigzag bolt of lightning on the left side of his scalp, above one ear. He would have been thought good looking, but there was something wrong with the face – a tightness, a lack of mobility. Soon the crowds would arrive, some from church, others rural primary-school children in cheap, ugly browns and purples, wearing leather shoes with no socks, smelling of river-washed bodies, road dust, the corn-cob life, meals on a three-stoned hearth. Jimmy knew all about these children – had lived among them, and become one of them after his father had left and his mother had taken them to her parents' in Kerugoya for six months.

On holidays like today, foreign tourists would crawl out of minibuses and crowd the fence as they flipped through the pages of *Lonely Planet Kenya*, carrying water bottles, cameras, distended stomachs and buttocks, with their wiggling underarms like astronauts on the moon. They watched with strained smiles as their children actualized Mufasa and other television illusions, as they chatted about cutting their trip short, with all that was going on. The children made everyone jump, clanging the metal bars of the cage, trying to get Sebastian's attention, sticking out their tongues at the immovable hairy figure and having their photos taken. When the warders were not looking, they would throw paper cups and other odds and ends at Sebastian, who threw them back. When the sun crossed its highest point in the sky, faraway screams rent the air. The gazelles and impalas stopped grazing and looked up in their wary way, tensed to accelerate from zero to a hundred as they had always done. The old lions seemed to grin, yawning at a sound they understood only too well, and licked their chops. Smoke billowed in the air from a distance, and loud popping sounds could be heard. In half an hour, as if in response, the crowd had thinned, and Jimmy was left practically alone beside Sebastian's cage. In the beautiful, quiet afternoon they started their dance, small mimicking movements they shared. Scratches and hand flutters, heads bowed forward and swaying from side to side.

Jimmy listened to the faraway sounds once more and said: 'That must be Kibera. Maybe time I also left, old man.'

Over the last six months Sebastian had started to avoid making eye contact with Jimmy. At first Jimmy had taken offence, then he realized that Sebastian's eyesight was failing. He had cataracts, and his eyes and cheeks were stained with cakes and trails of mucus. Sometimes Sebastian would join their weekly ritual of movements for only a few sluggish moments, then turn away and slowly walk to the shade. Now they could hear screams coming from Kibera and Jimmy looked up to see a large mushroom cloud as a petrol station was set ablaze in Kenya's largest slum. Sebastian raised his head ever so slightly to catch the breeze, and he began to pace, nostrils flaring and mucus streaming. He lifted his palm and beat it on the ground along with the faraway popping of gunshots. Jimmy had read all the books there were on gorillas, and he knew about their sense of community, their empathy – their embracing of death.

Jimmy had been born not far from State House where the President lived. The house he remembered smelled like the Animal Orphanage. It smelled of the giant pet tortoise that had disappeared when he was eight. After he had cried for a week his mother brought him Coxy, and the house came to smell of rotting cabbage and rabbit urine. Later, when he was older, Mum allowed him to keep pigeons, and they added to the damp animal smell of the house. It smelled of the bottom of the garden where he eventually strangled Coxy and the second rabbit, Baby, and drowned their children, overwhelmed by three squirming litters of rabbits; the piles of shit to clear. His mother found him crying at the foot of the garden and said in consolation: 'What are rabbits anyway? Your father is a rabbit. Always up in some hole.'

He didn't keep pets after his father left. They moved into a small flat with skewed stairs and smirking girls in tight jeans who chewed minty gum all day and received visitors all night. Mum said it would still be all right because they were still in Kileleshwa and not far from State House. 'James,' she would call out, from the chemical haze of her dressing table, 'pass me the toe holder, pass me the nail-polish remover. Come on James, don't be spastic. Wait till you become a steward, you'll fly all over the world. With your mum's looks you'll be the best,' she would laugh in the early afternoon, a glass of Johnny Walker Black next to her. 'Then you can stop spending time with that old gorilla. You know, when your father left I thought that we would just die, but look at us now.' She would smear on her lipstick and flounce out of the apartment to meet a new man friend. (I've no time for boys. I need a man. James, will you be my man? Protect me.)

Sebastian rose, slowly coming to rest on knuckled palms. Jimmy watched the gorilla stand on his hind feet and move in the other direction, slowly, towards the other side of the cage. He was listening to something. Jimmy strained, and for a while he heard nothing – and then he felt against his skin rather than his ears, slow whirring sounds, followed by sharp, rapid clicks. A dark tall man walked into view. He walked with his head tilted. And with his dark glasses and sure firm steps, he could have been mistaken for a blind man. He went right to the edge of the gorilla pit, squatted, and, looking down, spoke to Sebastian in a series of tongue clicks, deep throat warbles and low humming. Sebastian bounded to the bottom of the wall standing fully upright, running in short bursts to the left and the right, beating his chest as if he were welcoming an old friend.

Then Jimmy distinctly heard the man say something in what he recognized as French. He could not understand any of the words, except *mon frère, mon vieux*. The gorilla-talking man walked away briskly, and Sebastian slumped to the ground in his customary place. Jimmy saw the man walk to the Orphanage notice board next to the warthog pen and pin something on it. He felt that he recognized him from somewhere; the way that one feels one knows public figures, beloved cartoon characters or celebrities. Jimmy scrambled up, shouldered up his bag and waved goodbye to Sebastian. Now that his pass had expired, the Sunday visits would be infrequent. But what he had just seen told him that those future visits, however rare, might be the most important in all these years he had been coming – an opportunity to talk to Sebastian.

The man who now called himself Professor Charles Semambo knew that the Jamhuri Gorilla series of lectures would attract animal science experts from the ministries, and university students – but the rest was decided by the availability of rancid South African wine, wilting sandwiches and toothpick-impaled meatballs. He had learned that the renewal of future contracts was decided in this Nairobi shark pool, and that lectures were where one met and impressed the major players in the game.

The unmistakeable smell of sweat came down from the higher levels of the auditorium where members of the public sat. The bucket-like seats comically forced people's knees up into the air – and Semambo went through the hour allocated for the lecture briskly, enjoying such minor distractions as a glimpse of red or white panties between fat feminine knees. It was his standard lecture: Gorillas 101. Habitat. Behaviour. Group Life. Endangerment.

After the lecture, he allowed the five mandatory questions from the audience. As usual, these were either of a post-doctoral nature from the front row of specialists, or idiotic juvenile comments. One man stood up and pleaded for compensation, because a gorilla from a nearby forest where he lived in Kakamega had eaten his child. He said he had voted for the Opposition because the previous government had failed to do anything about it. The people around him laughed.

Angalia huu mjinga. Hakuna gorilla Kenya. Ilikuwa baboon.

There are no gorillas in Kenya, fool. That was a baboon. The man started weeping and had to be led out. Then the last question: 'It-is-said-that-far-in-the-mountains-of-Rwanda-men-have-learnt-to-talk-to-gorillas. Do-you-think-there-is-any-truth-to-such-claims?'

Semambo felt the ground shift slightly beneath him but, as hard as he tried, he could not make out the face that had asked the question. The projector light was right in his face, hiccupping because it had reached the end and caused the words on the screen to blink. Seeking New Habitat in the Face of Human Encroachment: The Mountain Gorilla in Rwanda. 'Is that a trick question?' he responded smoothly. The audience laughed.

'If I say yes, I might sound unscientific, and you know what donors do with such unscientific conjecture, as the esteemed gentlemen sitting before me will attest.' In the front row, the museum politicos chuckled from deep inside their stomachs.

'You might have heard of Koko, the famous gorilla who was taught sign language,' Semambo went on. 'It is claimed that he is capable of inter-species communication. I think a lot of it is pretty inconclusive. So the answer would be no.'

The piercing voice floated again. Insistent. The face still invisible.

'I am asking whether you've heard of men who can talk to gorillas, not gorillas who can talk to men.'

The audience was bored now; a couple walked out noisily. Then he saw his questioner. He was just a kid, slight and lithe, about 16. Now he remembered – he had seen him a couple of times at the Animal Orphanage. (Was it possible?) Then, unbelievably, the young man took a photo of him. The angry click of the camera felt as if it was right next to his ear, and the flash lit up the whole auditorium, including a sign that read, CAMERAS NOT ALLOWED.

'Excuse me. Excuse me, ladies and gentleman. I want to allow the young gentleman the courtesy of an answer.

There might be something in what he says. I also want to remind you, young man, that cameras are not allowed in the auditorium.' There was an uneasy laughter. The herds needed their wine and pastries. Semambo hesitated.

'But since you all have to leave I will take the young man's question after the lecture.' Light applause.

Baker, the museum co-ordinator in charge of the lecture series, suddenly emerged from the shadows at the back. A naturalized citizen, he had lived in Kenya since the 1960s, and worked as a functionary of one sort or the other through three regimes. He was useful because he provided a sort of international legitimacy to the thugs who ran the government. When things swung his way, he could be a power broker of sorts, a middleman between a defaulting government and donors. He slid to the front of the podium.

'Let us give Professor Charles Semambo, our visiting expert on the African Gorilla, attached to the Museum for six months, a big hand. And please join us for wine in the lobby.'

After glad-handing the museum officials, Baker came up to Semambo, his face red with embarrassment.

'Sorry about the camera.'

'Get it,' he said tightly. He struggled for a smile then said very deliberately, 'Get me that fucking camera.'

'Charles, it's not that big a deal.'

Semambo wiped the sheen of sweat from his face. It was a bad move to bully Baker: he removed his dark glasses, reaching for a softer, more conciliatory note. 'Winslow, you have no idea how big a deal it is. I want that camera. Introduce me to the boy. I will do it myself.'

Even if it was 14 years ago, Semambo clearly remembered the day he had erased his past and come to Kenya. He had met his contact in a seedy restaurant near Nairobi's City Hall. It seemed a confusing place at first. People sat gathered around tables, wielding folders and clipboards and pens, all having various meetings it seemed. Was it some sort of game? Bingo? He met the man at the bar.

'This restaurant markets itself to wedding and funeral committees.'

'Ah,' said Semambo, laughing, 'Where the balance sheets of living and dying are produced. They are counting the cost of life. Very appropriate. Well, here is the cost of mine, exactly counted, in the denominations you asked for.'

The man looked at him and laughed back. 'I don't know why. I have to sleep at night you know? Our old man is friendly to your side. Me, I just think you are all butchers...'

A title deed, four different Ugandan passports with appropriate visas and work permits, an identification document and his new name. But hiding was not easy. There were always people looking. A couple of million dollars could only buy you so much.

When he turned away from Baker, Semambo was surprised to see the kid standing not five metres away from them. He had been mistaken – the kid was probably closer to 18. He had good teeth, Semambo saw – a rarity in Kenya. 'Have we met before?'

'No,' the boy said. 'But I've seen you at the Animal Orphanage. When you come and talk to Sebastian.' The boy's voice was a quiet whisper. 'Sebastian. The gorilla. He's dying, you know. I need to talk to him before he goes. Can you teach me?' The boy added breathlessly, 'He has maybe two months. He's old. Could even be 60.'

'Yes. I know who you are talking about. And you are?'

'Jimmy. Jimmy Gikonyo.'

'Call me Charles. Can we talk in my office? Or even better, let's go somewhere quieter.'

'Sorry, but my mother expects me home early.'

'I understand. Where do you live? Maybe we can talk on the way as I drop you off. I don't generally allow people to take photos of me.'

'I'm sorry. It's just that I thought I recognized you from somewhere. Not that we've met.'

It was two days after the election results had been

announced, and it seemed as if half the drivers in Kenya were in a deep stupor and had forgotten how to drive. Semambo counted three accidents during the 15-minute drive from the National Museum to Kileleshwa through Waiyaki Way, then Riverside Drive. They turned off at the Kileleshwa Shell petrol station and the boy gave him directions to a large, busy high-rise off Laikipia Road. Two girls loitered outside the grey building. Then a green Mercedes Benz drove up and both jumped in, waving and blowing kisses at Jimmy. The Benz almost collided with a Range Rover that was coming in. The Benz driver, an old African man, threw his hands in the air. The two young men in the other car, one white and the other Kenyan Asian, ignored him, screeched into the parking lot and bounded out of the car. They also waved to Jimmy as they passed. Semambo noticed Jimmy's hands clench into tight fists.

There was a slight breeze, gathering leaves in the now quiet front of the building. It could not, however, drown out the frantic hooting on the main road right outside the block of flats. Semambo suspected that this went on all day and night. Even from inside, one could see a large queue of walking silhouettes, probably going to Kawangware, through the hedge – a parallel exodus of the walking and mobile classes. Back in 1994 when Semambo had first come to Kenya, Kileleshwa was still keeping up appearances; now it seemed victim to all sorts of ugly aspirations and clutchings: tall ice-cream cake apartment buildings that crumbled like Dubai chrome furniture after a few years.

'Will this be fine with you? I'll wait here for the photos, then we can discuss gorilla talking lessons,' Semambo said.

'You have to come in and meet my mother. She won't allow me to spend time with you if she doesn't know who you are.'

Semambo never used lifts. He bounded up the stairs and was not even out of breath when they got to the flat. Claire, Jimmy's mother, was beautiful. A beauty of contrast

– of failure even. Lines crossed her forehead, the crumpling skin astonishingly frail. Her mouth and jaw, perfectly symmetrical, trembled with drunkenness and skewed lipstick: she seemed on the verge of tears.

'Please come in.'

Semambo could smell the whisky on her breath. The flat had an extremely low ceiling and he had to stoop once he was inside. She prattled on. He sat down and looked around. There was a bottle nestled on the cushions where she must have been sitting. There were two glasses – one empty.

'I hope you like whisky.'

The flat was crowded with triumphs of the past. There were photos of three strangers, a young man, woman and boy in different settings. The young man in the photo seemed a studious sort, uncomfortable and self-conscious, with his hand held possessively in every photo by a Claire 15 hard years younger than the woman in front of him now.

Jimmy carried both his parents' features. The world in the photo seemed to have little to do with the small flat Semambo found himself in. He could not stretch his legs and his knees were locked at right angles. Everything had been chosen to fit the flat's small specifications: the Cheng TV, the Fong music stereo, Sungsam microwave and the cracked glass table. Every appliance in the room was on; even the small washing machine in the corner.

The TV was muted. It showed a crowd of young men dancing with *pangas*, a shop in flames behind them. A washing machine gurgled as Dolly Parton sang in the background. There were two doors to the right, probably the bedrooms, Semambo thought. He could, however, see blankets underneath the other wicker two-seater where Claire was now slumped, peering at him beneath suggestively lidded eyes. 'Thank God for whisky,' she purred. 'One of the last pleasures left to an old woman like me. What you do for fun?' Her voice sounded breathy and Semambo was uncomfortable. He was no prude, but these were uncertain times, and with her perfume and cigarette smell, her drunkenness and incoherence, she promised nothing less than the loss of control.

She poured herself another shot. Jimmy appeared from behind one of the two doors. Semambo was developing a grudging regard for the boy – most teenagers would have taken on a long-suffering sullenness with a mother like that. Jimmy treated her like a slightly loopy older sister. 'Mum. The professor and I need to talk.' Her face went blank for a while, and the mouth trembled. 'I'm going to bed. You men are no fun at all.'

She went through the door that the boy had come from and slammed it. The TV now showed a soldier in fatigues creeping against a wall and then shooting down two young men.

'I need some air,' Semambo said. Jimmy beckoned and opened the other door. A small room gave on to a narrow balcony that overlooked the parking lot. Semambo crossed over into the open and looked down at his hulking Land Cruiser.

Some distance away, towards Kangemi, fires burned into the night, black smoke billowing towards the City Centre. The screams in the air were faint, the gunshots muted, as if coming from another country. Semambo looked out, listening, and shook his head.

'While some fuss about whether to eat chicken or beef tonight, many won't see tomorrow morning. We are in the abyss and the abyss is in us.'

He turned and removed his dark glasses. The face was thick and flabby, layered with dark pudge, and there were two large scars running down his neck. Jimmy felt that he needed to back away from the balcony.

'Do you think that it will get much worse?' he asked.

'Only when you see the fires in your parking lot.'

'I never thought that the end of our world could happen so slowly. This all started when Sebastian fell sick. Can you teach me to talk to him?'

'That might not be possible. His time might be nearer than we think. Just like ours. Maybe I can tell him how you feel. Let us go see him.'

Now the screams and wails began on the Langata side of the city. By the time they were near the Nairobi Animal Orphanage, their faces were lit up in the cabin of the Land Cruiser by the fire on Kibera plain. They sped down Mbagathi Way, turned up Langata Road and past Carnivore restaurant as if driving around in hell. Figures danced in the road, yelling and waving *pangas*, grotesque in the firelight. 'Hide in the back and whatever you do, don't come out. You will only excite them.'

Once they were clear, Jimmy jumped into the back seat.

'What do you talk about with Sebastian?'

'Can you imagine what Sebastian has seen of man since he was born?' They had reached the gate of the Orphanage. 'Get back into the boot and hide.'

A guard came up to the Land Cruiser smiling brightly and peered into the car. '*Habari*, Professor. What brings you here at this time of the night?'

'My old friend is dying, and I need to see him.'

'Yes, he hasn't eaten today.'

Jimmy sat back up as they drove in.

In the Orphanage, the animals' nocturnal sounds drowned out the sounds of fighting from the neighbouring slum. Then, for a while, everything was quiet.

'I don't think Sebastian has long. Living by Kibera has aged him impossibly. Nothing alive can take the past he has come from and then have to repeat it in old age.'

When they finally got to the gorilla pit, Sebastian lay on his side, heaving. Semambo rushed to where the wall was at its lowest and jumped into the enclosure, landing as silently as a cat. Jimmy passed him his bag through the front metal bars. Semambo went back to the gorilla, crooning all the while. Sebastian tried getting up. A huge light climbed up in the sky, followed by a large explosion. Sebastian twitched and lay back with a giant sigh. Semambo removed a long syringe from his bag and filled it with fluid.

'Goodbye, old friend.'

Jimmy ran to the back wall and scrambled to where Semambo had jumped down. When he hit the ground inside the cage he felt something give in his left ankle. He hobbled to the middle – Sebastian had stopped moving. Semambo removed a small razor from his bag and shaved the left side of Sebastian's thick chest.

Semambo plunged the long needle into the small, naked spot and pressed the syringe home, and in that single motion the gorilla sat up immediately. He started clawing at his chest where the injection had gone in, roaring madly and beating his chest until the rest of the animals joined in, drowning out the din of man, and fire and death.

Sebastian whirled his arms like windmills. Semambo stood without moving, then Sebastian wrapped his arms around him, roaring enough to drown out the rest of the world. Jimmy had scrambled away to the edge of the cage and Semambo's face turned apoplectic, red, crisscrossed with blood vessels. His glasses fell off, and his light eyes turned darker as the two figures became one.

Billy Kahora lives and writes in Nairobi. His work has appeared in *Chimurenga, McSweeney's, Granta Online, Kwani* and *Vanity Fair.* He was highly commended by the 2007 Caine Prize judges for his story 'Treadmill Love' and his story 'Urban Zoning' was shortlisted for the Prize in 2012. He has written the non-fiction novella, *The True Story Of David Munyakei*, the screenplay for *Soul Boy* and also co-wrote *Nairobi Half Life.* He is working on a novel titled *The Applications.* He is also Managing Editor of Kwani Trust and has edited seven issues of the Kwani journal and other Kwani publications including *Nairobi 24* and *Kenya Burning.* He is also an Associate Editor with the *Chimurenga Chronic.* 'The Gorilla's Apprentice' first appeared in *Granta* (London, 2010).

My Father's Head

Okwiri Oduor

I had meant to summon my father only long enough to see what his head looked like, but now he was here and I did not know how to send him back.

It all started the Thursday that Father Ignatius came from Immaculate Conception in Kitgum. The old women wore their Sunday frocks, and the old men plucked garlands of bougainvillea from the fence and stuck them in their breast pockets. One old man would not leave the dormitory because he could not find his shikwarusi, and when I coaxed and badgered, he patted his hair and said: 'My God, do you want the priest from Uganda to think that I look like this every day?'

I arranged chairs beneath the avocado tree in the front yard, and the old people sat down and practised their smiles. A few people who did not live at the home came too, like the woman who hawked candy in the Stagecoach bus to Mathari North, and the man whose one-roomed house was a kindergarten in the daytime and a brothel in the evening, and the woman whose illicit brew had blinded five people in January.

Father Ignatius came riding on the back of a bodaboda, and after everyone had dropped a coin in his hat, he gave the bodaboda man 50 shillings and the bodaboda man said, 'Praise God,' and then rode back the way he had come.

Father Ignatius took off his coat and sat down in the chair that was marked, 'Father Ignatius Okello, New Chaplain', and the old people gave him the smiles they had been practising, smiles that melted like ghee, that oozed through the corners of their lips and dribbled onto their laps long after the thing that was being smiled about went rancid in the air.

Father Ignatius said, 'The Lord be with you', and the people said, 'And also with you', and then they prayed and they sang and they had a feast; dipping bread slices in tea and, when the drops fell on the cuffs of their woollen sweaters, sucking at them with their steamy, cinnamon tongues.

Father Ignatius' maiden sermon was about love: love your neighbour as you love yourself, that kind of self-deprecating thing. The old people had little use for love, and although they gave Father Ignatius an ingratiating smile, what they really wanted to know was what type of place Kitgum was, and if it was true that the Bagisu people were savage cannibals.

What I wanted to know was what type of person Father Ignatius thought he was, instructing others to distribute their love like this or like that, as though one could measure love on weights, pack it inside glass jars and place it on shelves for the neighbours to pick as they pleased. As though one could look at it and say, 'Now see: I have ten loves in total. Let me save three for my country and give all the rest to my neighbours.'

It must have been the way that Father Ignatius filled his mug – until the tea ran over the clay rim and down the stool leg and soaked into his canvas shoe – that got me thinking about my own father. One moment I was listening to tales of Acholi valour, and the next, I was stringing together images of my father, making his limbs move and his lips spew words, so that in the end, he was a marionette and my memories of him were only scenes in a theatrical display.

Even as I showed Father Ignatius to his chambers, cleared the table, put the chairs back inside, took my purse, and dragged myself to Odeon to get a matatu to Uthiru, I thought about the millet-coloured freckle in my father's eye, and the 50-cent coins he always forgot in his coat pockets, and the way, each Saturday morning, men knocked on our front door and said things like, 'Johnson, you have to come now; the water pipe has burst and we are filling our glasses with shit,' and, 'Johnson, there is no time to put on clothes even; just come the way you are. The maid gave birth in the night and flushed the baby down the toilet.'

Every day after work, I bought an ear of street-roasted maize and chewed it one kernel at a time, and, when I reached the house, I wiggled out of the muslin dress and wore dungarees and drank a cup of masala chai. Then I carried my father's toolbox to the bathroom. I chiselled out old broken tiles from the wall, and they fell onto my boots, and the dust rose from them and exploded in the flaring tongues of fire lapping through chinks in the stained glass.

This time, as I did all those things, I thought of the day I sat at my father's feet and he scooped a handful of groundnuts and rubbed them between his palms, chewed them, and then fed the mush to me. I was of a curious age then: old enough to chew with my own teeth, yet young enough to desire that hot, masticated love, love that did not need to be indoctrinated or measured in cough-syrup caps.

The Thursday Father Ignatius came from Kitgum, I spent the entire night on my stomach on the sitting-room floor, drawing my father. In my mind I could see his face, see the lines around his mouth, the tiny blobs of light in his irises, the crease at the part where his ear joined his temple. I could even see the thick line of sweat and oil on his shirt collar, the little brown veins that broke off from the main stream of dirt and ran down on their own.

I could see all these things, yet no matter what I did, his head refused to appear within the borders of the paper. I started off with his feet and worked my way up and in the end my father's head popped out of the edges of the paper and onto scuffed linoleum and plastic magnolias and the wet soles of bathroom slippers.

I showed Bwibo some of the drawings. Bwibo was the cook at the old people's home, with whom I had formed an easy camaraderie.

'My God!' Bwibo muttered, flipping through them. 'Simbi, this is abnormal.'

The word 'abnormal' came out crumbly, and it broke over the sharp edge of the table and became clods of loam on the plastic floor covering. Bwibo rested her head on her palm, and the bell sleeves of her cream-coloured caftan swelled as though there were pumpkins stacked inside them.

I told her what I had started to believe, that perhaps my father had had a face but no head at all. And even if my father had had a head, I would not have seen it: people's heads were not a thing that one often saw. One looked at a person, and what one saw was their face: a regular face-shaped face, that shrouded a regular head-shaped head. If the face was remarkable, one looked twice. But what was there to draw one's eyes to the banalities of another's head? Most times when one looked at a person, one did not even see their head there at all.

Bwibo stood over the waist-high jiko, poured cassava flour into a pot of bubbling water and stirred it with a cooking oar. 'Child,' she said, 'how do you know that the man in those drawings is your father? He has no head at all, no face.'

'I recognize his clothes. The red corduroys that he always paired with yellow shirts.'

Bwibo shook her head. 'It is only with a light basket that someone can escape the rain.'

It was that time of day when the old people fondled their wooden beads and snorted off to sleep in between incantations. I allowed them a brief, bashful siesta, long enough for them to believe that they had recited the entire rosary. Then I tugged at the ropes and the lunch bells chimed. The old people sat eight to a table, and with their mouths filled with ugali, sour lentils and okra soup, said things like, 'Do not buy chapati from Kadima's Kiosk – Kadima's wife sits on the dough and charms it with her buttocks,' or, 'Did I tell you about Wambua, the one whose cow chewed a child because the child would not stop wailing?'

In the afternoon, I emptied the bedpans and soaked the old people's feet in warm water and baking soda, and when they trooped off to mass I took my purse and went home.

The Christmas before the cane tractor killed my father, he drank his tea from plates and fried his eggs on the lids of coffee jars, and he retrieved his Yamaha drum-set from a shadowy, lizardy place in the back of the house and sat on the veranda and smoked and beat the drums until his knuckles bled.

One day he took his stool and hand-held radio and went to the veranda, and I sat at his feet, undid his laces and peeled off his gummy socks. He wiggled his toes about. They smelt slightly fetid, like sour cream.

My father smoked and listened to narrations of famine undulating deeper into the Horn of Africa, and, when the clock chimed eight o'clock, he turned the knob and listened to the death news. It was not long before his ears caught the name of someone he knew. He choked on the smoke trapped in his throat.

My father said: 'Did you hear that? Sospeter has gone! Sospeter, the son of Milkah, who taught Agriculture in Mirere Secondary. My God, I am telling you, everyone is going. Even me, you shall hear me on the death news very soon.'

I brought him his evening cup of tea. He smashed his cigarette against the veranda, then he slowly brought the cup to his lips. The cup was filled just the way he liked it, filled until the slightest trembling would have his fingers and thighs scalded.

My father took a sip of his tea and said: 'Sospeter was like a brother to me. Why did I have to learn of his death like this, over the radio?'

Later, my father lay on the fold-away sofa, and I sat on the stool watching him, afraid that, if I looked away, he would go too. It was the first time I imagined his death, the first time I mourned.

And yet it was not my father I was mourning. I was mourning the image of myself inside the impossible aura of my father's death. I was imagining what it all would be like: the death news would say that my father had drowned in a cesspit, and people would stare at me as though I were a monitor lizard trapped inside a manhole in the street. I imagined that I would be wearing my green dress when I got the news – the one with red gardenias embroidered in its bodice – and people would come and pat my shoulder and give me warm Coca Cola in plastic cups and say: 'I put my sorrow in a basket and brought it here as soon as I heard. How else would your father's spirit know that I am innocent of his death?'

Bwibo had an explanation as to why I could not remember the shape of my father's head.

She said: 'Although everyone has a head behind their face, some show theirs easily; they turn their back on you and their head is all you can see. Your father was a good man and good men never show you their heads; they show you their faces.'

Perhaps she was right. Even the day my father's people telephoned to say that a cane tractor had flattened him on the road to Shibale, no-one said a thing about having seen his head. They described the rest of his body with a measured delicacy: how his legs were strewn across the road, sticky and shiny with fresh tar, and how one foot remained inside his tyre sandal, pounding the pedal of his bicycle, and how cane juice filled his mouth and soaked the collar of his polyester shirt, and how his face had a patient serenity, even as his eyes burst and rolled in the rain puddles.

And instead of weeping right away when they said all those things to me, I had wondered if my father really had come from a long line of obawami, and if his people would bury him seated in his grave, with a string of royal cowries round his neck.

'In any case,' Bwibo went on, 'what more is there to think about your father, eh? That milk spilled a long time ago, and it has curdled on the ground.'

I spent the day in the dormitories, stripping beds, sunning mattresses, scrubbing PVC mattress pads. One of the old men kept me company. He told me how he came to spend his sunset years at the home – in August 1998 he was at the station waiting to board the evening train back home to Mombasa. When the bomb went off at the American Embassy, the police trawled the city and arrested every man of Arab extraction. Because he was 72 and already rapidly unravelling into senility, they dumped him at the old people's home, and he had been there ever since.

'Did your people not come to claim you?' I asked, bewildered.

The old man snorted. 'My people?'

'Everyone has people that belong to them.'

The old man laughed. 'Only the food you have already eaten belongs to you.'

Later, the old people sat in drooping clumps in the yard. Bwibo and I watched from the back steps of the kitchen. In the grass, ants devoured a squirming caterpillar. The dog's nose, a translucent pink doodled with green veins, twitched. Birds raced each other over the frangipani. One tripped over the power line and smashed its head on the moss-covered electricity pole.

Wasps flew low over the grass. A lizard crawled over the lichen that choked a pile of timber. The dog licked the inside of its arm. A troupe of royal butterfly dancers flitted over the row of lilies, their colourful gauze dancing skirts trembling to the rumble of an inaudible drumbeat. The dog lay on its side in the grass, smothering the squirming caterpillar and the chewing ants. The dog's nipples were little pellets of goat shit stuck with spit onto its furry underside.

Bwibo said, 'I can help you remember the shape of your father's head.'

I said, 'Now what type of mud is this you have started speaking?'

Bwibo licked her index finger and held it solemnly in the air. 'I swear, Bible red! I can help you and I can help you.'

Let me tell you: one day you will renounce your exile, and you will go back home, and your mother will take out the finest china, and your father will slaughter a sprightly cockerel for you, and the neighbours will bring some potluck, and your sister will wear her navy-blue PE wrapper, and your brother will eat with a spoon instead of squelching rice and soup through the spaces between his fingers.

And you, you will have to tell them stories about places not-here, about people that soaked their table napkins in Jik bleach and talked about London as though London were a place one could reach by hopping onto an Akamba bus and driving by Nakuru and Kisumu and Kakamega and finding themselves there.

You will tell your people about men that did not slit melons up into slices but split them into halves and ate each of the halves out with a spoon, about women that held each other's hands around street lamps in town and skipped about, showing snippets of grey Mother's Union bloomers as they sang:

Kijembe ni kikali, param-param

Kilikata mwalimu, param-param

You think that your people belong to you, that they will always have a place for you in their minds and their hearts. You think that your people will always look forward to your return.

Maybe the day you go back home to your people you will have to sit in a wicker chair on the veranda and smoke alone because, although they may have wanted to have you back, no-one really meant for you to stay.

My father was slung over the wicker chair on the veranda, just like in the old days, smoking and watching the hand-held radio. The death news rose from the radio, and it became a mist, hovering low, clinging to the cold glass of the sitting-room window.

My father's shirt flapped in the wind, and tendrils of smoke snapped before his face. He whistled to himself. At first the tune was a faceless, pitiful thing, like an old bottle that someone found on the path and kicked all the way home. Then the tune caught fragments of other tunes inside it, and it lost its free-spirited falling and rising.

My father had a head. I could see it now that I had the mind to look for it. His head was shaped like a butternut squash. Perhaps that was the reason I had forgotten all about it: it was a horrible, disconcerting thing to look at.

My father had been a plumber. His fingernails were still rimmed with dregs from the drainage pipes he tinkered about in, and his boots still squished with *ugali* from nondescript kitchen sinks. Watching him, I remembered the day he found a gold chain tangled in the fibres of someone's excrement, and he wiped the excrement off against his corduroys and sold the chain at Nagin Pattni, and that evening, hoisted high upon his shoulders, he brought home the red Greatwall television. He set it in the corner of the sitting room and said, 'Just look how it shines, as though it is not filled with shit inside.'

And every day I plucked a bunch of carnations and snipped their stems diagonally and stood them in a glass bowl and placed the glass bowl on top of the television so that my father would not think of shit while he watched the evening news.

I said to Bwibo, 'We have to send him back.'

Bwibo said, 'The liver you have asked for is the one you eat.'

'But I did not really want him back, I just wanted to see his head.'

Bwibo said, 'In the end, he came back to you and that should account for something, should it not?'

Perhaps my father's return accounted for nothing but the fact that the house already smelt like him – of burnt lentils and melting fingernails and the bark of bitter quinine and the sourness of wet rags dabbing at broken cigarette tips.

I threw things at my father: garlic, incense, salt, pork, and when none of that repelled him, I asked Father Ignatius to bless the house. He brought a vial of holy water, and he sprinkled it in every room, sprinkled it over my father. Father Ignatius said that I would need further protection, but that I would have to write him a cheque first.

One day I was buying roast maize in the street corner when the vendor said to me, 'Is it true what the vegetable-sellers are saying, that you finally found a man to love you but will not let him through your door?'

That evening, I invited my father inside. We sat side by side on the fold-away sofa, and watched as a fly crawled up the dusty screen between the grill and the window glass. It buzzed a little as it climbed. The ceiling fan creaked, and it threw shadows across the corridor floor. The shadows leapt high and mounted doors and peered through the air vents in the walls.

The wind upset a cup. For a few seconds, the cup lay lopsided on the windowsill. Then it rolled on its side and scurried across the floor. I pulled at the latch, fastened the window shut. The wind grazed the glass with its wet lips. It left a trail of dust and saliva, and the saliva dribbled down slowly to the edge of the glass. The wind had a slobbery mouth. Soon its saliva had covered the entire window, covered it until the rosemary brushwood outside the window became blurry. The jacaranda outside stooped low, scratched the roof. In the next room, doors and windows banged.

I looked at my father. He was something at once strange and familiar, at once enthralling and frightening – he was the brittle, chipped handle of a ceramic tea mug, and he was the cold yellow stare of an owl.

My father touched my hand ever so lightly, so gently, as though afraid that I would flinch and pull my hand away. I did not dare lift my eyes, but he touched my chin and tipped it upwards so that I had no choice but to look at him.

I remembered a time when I was a little child, when I stared into my father's eyes in much the same way. In them I saw shapes: a drunken, talentless conglomerate of circles and triangles and squares. I had wondered how those shapes had got inside my father's eyes. I had imagined that he sat down at the table, cut out glossy figures from colouring books, slathered them with glue, and stuck them inside his eyes so that they made rummy, haphazard collages in his irises.

My father said, 'Would you happen to have some tea, Simbi?'

I brought some, and he asked if his old friend Pius Obote still came by the house on Saturdays, still brought groundnut soup and pumpkin leaves and a heap of letters that he had picked up from the post office.

I said, 'Pius Obote has been dead for four years.'

My father pushed his cup away. He said, 'If you do not want me here drinking your tea, just say so, instead of killing-killing people with your mouth.'

My father was silent for a while, grieving this man Pius Obote whose name had always made me think of knees banging against each other. Pius Obote used to blink a lot. Once, he fished inside his pocket for a biro and instead withdrew a chicken bone, still red and moist.

My father said to me, 'I have seen you. You have offered me tea. I will go now.'

'Where will you go?'

'I will find a job in a town far from here. Maybe Eldoret. I used to have people there.'

I said, 'Maybe you could stay here for a couple of days, Baba.'

Okwiri Oduor was born in Nairobi, Kenya. She is a 2014 MacDowell Colony fellow. She is currently at work on her debut novel. 'My Father's Head' originally appeared in *Feast, Famine and Potluck* (Short Story Day Africa, Cape Town, 2013).

The Caine Prize
African Writers' Workshop Stories 2014

The Lifebloom Gift

Abdul Adan

Two days ago, I was fired from my TSA job at the airport. My boss convinced some offended fool to press sexual harassment charges against me. This was like the most preposterous thing. Everyone at work knows I am straight. I have nothing sexual whatsoever for men. I know it, my workmates know it, and the boss knows it. Even the offended fool knows it. I am just not the guy to like another guy sexually. Just before breaking the tragic news to me, my cold brute of a boss (Oh my, you should see the asshole! He has this bony, unlovable nose) took pains to explain my alleged offence. He said I had a tendency to *settle* when carrying out frisk searches.

I did use the word *settle* before, that much I concede. But it was nothing as creepy as he made it out to be. It was really just a break-room joke. A female workmate from the inner city had spilled her coffee and bent down to wipe it up. She had just removed her TSA uniform and placed it in the locker. She must have already clocked out or something. Anyway, I caught sight of her dangling breasts from the corner of my eye, and there he was! In my mind, Ted Lifebloom himself was kneeling to her right and trying to get his fat hands in there. But Ted was no longer a mother-loving child at this point. He was a giant of an adult and his hands wouldn't fit into the little space between her armpit and vest. So he lay below her, arms upwards, pulled her close into a kneeling position and made the loud wish of *settling* there forever. Now, *I* didn't do any of that, didn't go for the opening, nor did I *settle* between her bent torso and the floor. I only, harmlessly, said to my friendly supervisor that one could *settle* between her and the floor. You see, it was a comment one couldn't resist, given the circumstances. As for the 'tendency' my boss accuses me of, it was only one other occasion. Not enough to justify being called a 'tendency'.

Once in a while, a traveller comes along who feels like Ted Lifebloom. He or she doesn't have to be male or female, as the particular gift of Ted Lifebloom isn't a gender-based one. There are many women and men out there who have fleshy faces, soft chests (flat or full, it doesn't matter) and round necks with those sexy, fat rings. It might sound simple when put like that, but hear me out. The particular gift isn't really in the aforementioned features themselves. It's more like the features are *qualifiers* for the gift. One has to be touched by Ted or be a student of Ted's to be aware of the gift. A great number of people out there have no idea about their special place in the universe. Thousands or even millions of Lifebloomers.

That morning, a Turkish male came through the screening door at Lambert Airport. I knew immediately he stepped up for his search that he was a Lifebloomer. How did I know? Well, let's just say he had a fleshy face and a pebble of sweet on his earlobe. Being so generous, I decided right there and then, to, in the most subtle way, have him contemplate the Ted in his heart. Often, the fleshy-faced Lifebloomers (as opposed to those with hairy arms and pockets of fat under their abdomen), possess a mole behind their knees. To get them thinking, one had to locate the mole with the right thumb and press it. Fortunately, the traveller in this case was wearing shorts, which made things much easier. All I had to do was frisk him all the way down and pause at the back of his knee. Then I would momentarily *settle* on the mole. Don't get me wrong; I realize how creepy this sounds for those who don't understand. I was smart about it though. As soon as I got to the mole, I faced the challenge of devising a time-buying trick. I needed a good excuse for a 30-second press of my thumb at one spot on the back of his knee. Not an easy task, as anyone might guess. Here's what I did: I ran my hands on his body from the shoulders down, pausing routinely at the pockets, and, on arrival at the spot where I perceived the mole to be, feigned temporary dizziness. Leaning with my left hand on the ground, my face downwards, I went into a brief ecstasy, excited by the Lifeblooming agent hidden in the mole. Like all ignorant Lifebloomers, the man jerked his leg forward to shake off my grip, but I managed to hold on for a full 30 seconds. When he complained later, it was really useless. Everyone knew about my overly sensitive nose. His smelly shoes, as any wise person would assume, must have caused my dizziness on the spot. Still, I told my stupid boss (who kept a record of the event anyway) that I was nauseated by the traveller's perfume and was nearly unconscious for a few seconds – I needed that knee for support. I don't think he believed me then but who cares really? You can't fire a man for having an overly sensitive nose, much less for being a Lifebloomer.

My own journey of self-discovery started when I was working for a medical transportation agency some years ago. I drove a middle-aged woman from St Louis to the small town of Lonely Nest, Missouri. Her house was at the end of a long street, which featured uncountable Baptist churches, at least one Episcopalian church and a post office. I wouldn't have known there was an Episcopalian church if the old lady hadn't told me about it. I unloaded her stuff and helped her into her yard where I saw her fat son of about 30 outside, napping on the grass. A greyish Akita dog slept on his chest. On seeing us arrive, he sat up and asked, 'Mum, did someone help you with the stuff?' He could see me right there! Well, at least that was what I thought. His mum asked me to shake his hand, after which we spoke briefly. He seemed interested, but kept averting his gaze. But then, his mum disappeared into the house and the fat son, whom she introduced as Ted, gave me the kindest look ever. I thought I saw the universe in his eyes – the future and the past, and most of God's holy best. His mouth was small, his nose was fleshy, his cheeks were round, his hands were hairy, and his eyes, well, watery – if one may say so.

A few days later his mum had an appointment at Barnes Jewish Hospital in St Louis. I drove down to pick her up and, Ted, against her wishes, joined us. They both sat at the back. In the parking lot, his mum told me to watch him, which, in hindsight, was very selfish of her. She didn't want him going around stimulating other Lifebloomers from their unknowing stupor. Anyway, the next few minutes gave me a first-hand idea of why I had to watch Ted. His mum wasn't gone five minutes before Ted reached over and placed his hand on my shoulder and pretty much (as I came to learn later) *settled*. I am not sure how long his hand was there because I got carried into a greenish world I had only seen in dreams until then. Everything seemed as though I was on some yet-to-be-formulated drug. It was a thing of the heavens. Let me put it this way: I heard the song of birds and sneezes of horses, smelled the fur of dogs, felt a twitch in one of my nipples which, in turn, transformed into a brown lactating nipple… In short, I understood the meaning of love – almost. And this was just the shoulder! Suppose he got to my mole! Can you imagine that? I am now like the next thing after him among Lifebloomers. Ted not only had the gift to take you to that greenish world by a touch of his hand, but could transfer some of his gifts to you. To really use it, you have to be a bearer of at least one special mole and be willing to help other Lifebloomers discover themselves.

Not long after meeting Ted, I spotted an advert in a local scientific monthly. They were asking anthropology students at universities all over the state to send proposals for articles on animal and human expressions of love. A probably blond and flat-chested student from Mizzou had an article published about bonobos settling their quarrels by having gentle sex, which, really, was some superficial crap. So I thought, why not share the Lifebloom gift? I asked his mum if I could interview Ted about his life and she said yes. She didn't ask why. She knew I was either infected or had somehow discovered my Lifebloom status. Truth be told, I had no idea I was a Lifebloomer. I just knew Ted was a very special person. Nothing, however, could have prepared me for what was to come. The following is the case study I eventually sent to the magazine. I ask readers to politely disregard any references to abnormal conditions. Some of these are conclusions reached before my own awakening. I also ask the more generous readers to interpret the conditions as side effects of being the epicentre of the Lifebloom gift. It is not an easy responsibility. Trust me.

Blooming Ted: A Case Study

Introduction

Born in Lonely Nest, Missouri in 1978, to white Episcopalian parents, Ted Lifebloom was 30 years old when I met him. His mother worked as a registered nurse throughout Ted's childhood. His father ran a Bible school at home in Lonely Nest. I came to learn about his special condition during a ride to St Louis when I drove his mother to a hospital appointment. While we waited for his mother in the parking lot, Ted placed his hand on my shoulder for what seemed like forever (although it was actually three minutes according to my watch) and informed me, without speaking, of his special abilities. He essentially sent me into a trance within seconds of contact with my shoulder, during which I learned something of the meaning of love. If only Ted's specialness was restricted to that! Ted is a sacrificial lamb of messianic proportions. The following information was gathered through a series of interviews with his parents, his former girlfriend and Ted himself.

Background

Ted lived with his mother and father until he was 20, after which his parents divorced and he remained with his mother. Between the ages of two and ten, while his mother worked as a nurse in St Louis, Ted saw her only on weekends. His childhood needs during this time were attended to by young females who came to his father's yard for their Bible lessons. His mother told me that, at one of his schools, a teacher said young Ted was too sentimental.

Whenever his mother came home on weekends, young Ted nearly always kept his hands in her blouse through the arm opening. On days that she wore blouses with loose sleeves, he was happier. He could get his hands in much easier than if the sleeves were tight and the collar was too far out of reach. He was once even said to have attempted a swift vertical reach through his mother's tight collar, during which he nearly choked her when his elbow got trapped between her chin and her neck. One evening, while his mother was away, a seven-year-old Ted had taken a pair of scissors and modified all of her tight blouses under both armpits, just so he could slide his hands in better and feel her breasts when she wore them. The manner of his touch, his mother said, was not exactly of a fondling nature. He would cup the breast in one of his palms and keep it there until his hands sweated against the breast. Sometimes he climbed into her bed while she slept and placed his hands on the narrow, smooth path between her breasts.

His father, whom I located in a retirement home in Mahomet, Illinois, admitted that he had been so fond of his son that he hadn't been able to resist cuddling him even as the boy approached pubescence.

Ted himself told me that to experience something, one had to touch it. He denied the existence of anything he couldn't touch, including air, the sun, the sky, the moon, and people he hadn't touched or at least brushed shoulders with. The untouched individual, he said, is a nonentity. To claim a place in Ted's gloriously green universe, the individual has to be touched.

Ted's former girlfriend, Elizabeth, who had since taken a job at a massage parlour in University City, Missouri, told me that Ted wasn't too different from her other lovers. 'He just touched a lot,' she said. In their love-making, she said Ted preferred the missionary position and, in positioning himself between her legs, he made such moves that I understood to be a mere settling on his part. She said she did not mind Ted's tendency to settle. Quite the contrary: she said it was the most attractive part of their six-year relationship and that, had he been more conventionally emotional, she would still have been with him. Apparently, Ted did not care much for the orgasm at the end. He simply relished every inch of the journey through her moist, corrugated innards, and stayed therein as long as he could, looking around abstractedly at the empty air in the room, and making such loud statements as 'I wish you were as big as this whole space so I could swim your entirety.'

In the light of this, I should mention that Ted has never swum in anything. I also learnt from his mother that Ted suffers from bouts of temporary amnesia that can visit him every ten minutes. Once, during one of our interviews, Ted politely asked me to offer him my head so he could stroke it and reassure himself of my existence, to which I assented gladly. The bliss of his touch is, however, something that, unfortunately, much of the world out there will never experience. It defies every adjective. All I can think of now, in my generous bid to describe what it was like, are visions of smoothness (of any surface really), of special moles found on the bodies of aristocratic females of Kazakhstan, the dreadlocks of brotherly black men, the humble delicacy of certain unreachably shy females, the freckled faces of English tourists on African beaches, the moans of Asian porn stars.

Analysis

Young Ted was severely overprotected by his father. There's no doubt about that. In fact, his father was one of those extremely cuddly people with perpetually water-filled eyes. He did not so much shake my hand as caress it when we met in Mahomet. He had a giggle about him that seemed to tickle anyone in his presence, after which he always brushed some wet residue from his eyes.

Ted's mother was a tall, brown-haired woman, with shiny seductive eyes, the charm of which she had retained into middle age. Her breasts were youthful, and her feet were small and fidgety. When she hugged her friends, it was tight but brief, almost furtive. She seemed like she was in too much hurry for her age, and she had no business being busy really. Her eyes, unlike those of Ted's father, were clear and sharp – with darting glances. She laughed often and made a joke of nearly everything, much to Ted's displeasure. Her comments about Ted were made without any discernible emotion. It was as though she were a physician analysing a remote patient she hadn't even seen yet. I imagined the ten years she'd lived alone with Ted, after his father's move back to Mahomet, to be filled with uncountable days where Ted, too heavy to keep up with his mother, sat in the middle of the living room watching her slender figure walk from one corner of the house to another. I also imagine this period to contain such little scenes as her fat son pulling his perpetually hurrying mother by the end of her skirt in an attempt to settle on some soft part of her. Yet she seemed to care for Ted, tended to his needs, but, even in my presence, pulled back her hand from him to prevent him from, as she said jokingly, 'settling on it.'

Once, when Ted was 25, his uncle visited him and asked if he might consider finding a job (for Ted was pretty much slothful). Ted didn't really understand how one went about getting a job. He asked the uncle, for instance, to tell him more about jobs, including about their colour and texture, and especially their texture. When he was told one needed hard work to attain personal independence, the already overweight Ted stood up from his seat immediately and made two circular laps around the room, before coming back to sit down, saying amid gasps: 'This is it. Hard work itself.' No matter what was said to explain to him the idea of it, Ted's hard work never evolved beyond his indoor walks. Sometimes he bent down dejectedly and shook his head, like someone in mourning, lamenting his life. When asked why, he answered that it was what distressed people did, and unemployed people were supposed to be distressed.

Ted couldn't grasp any abstractions and simply saw everything as bits to be done and lived. He would shake his head or yell to express sadness or sorrow, and would walk about to respond to such phrases as 'work hard'. I surmised that Ted's excessively cuddly father, in combination with his loving but somewhat detached mother, confused him, turning him into a cloying wreck whenever he felt positively disposed towards another. His memory lapses are results of his mother's emotional and physical unavailability. Every time he'd reached out to her for comfort and, thereby, registered inside of himself her unquestionable loving presence, she had withdrawn suddenly, and sent his collective, cuddly feelings into dispersal, leading him to question if she had been there in the first place.

Once he had an attack of his memory lapses in my presence and had to ask me to offer him an arm, a leg, a neck, or a shoulder every ten minutes. On one of those occasions, so unsure of my existence was he that he felt my arm all the way to the elbow and further up to my armpit, settling us both into a greenish trance until his mother ran in to free us by shouting, as one would to a stubborn horse, 'snap out of it!' The second time it happened, she couldn't get any response to her verbal commands and had to hit him on the ankle with a baseball bat, fracturing it. I conclude that Ted suffers from an acute case of Sentimental Languor. (Reprinted with the permission of Klaus & Debbie's Science Magazine, St Louis)

It should go without saying that, by the end of my case study, I had understood that Ted was love itself in human form. I knew also that Ted and I had a responsibility to help one more Lifebloomer at least. You see, Ted had already informed me that I was a genuine article from the Lifebloom factory that exists somewhere in the Alatau mountains and whose airborne agents make their way to a select few unborn foetuses. Both Ted and his mother agreed that Ted had at least six moles on the back of his body. The moles, said Ted, were all in special spots.

One evening, I mentioned the issue of moles to my sister, just in passing. I did not say what the moles were for. Just that some people have special ones, whereupon my saintly sister informed me of an elderly man residing in the nursing home she was working at, who had five moles on his back parts, and at least one of those, she said doubtfully, was behind the knee. Within a week, Ted and I set off for St Charles, to the nursing home where the potential Lifebloomer was residing. Ted had on a pair of khaki shorts, a white shirt, and a small grey coat he could barely wrap around his round belly. I drove the entire way to that nursing home in St Charles. I was going to park under the trees behind the parking lot (in case they had a CCTV) but Ted said we should park at a gas station a mile away and walk to the nursing home so he could feel the Lifebloomer's energy in gradual bits.

'This is it,' said Ted, a few minutes into the walk.

'What do you sense, Darlingness?' I asked. I often called him things like 'sweetness', 'darlingness' or 'sweet moles'. It is all love, really. They mean nothing, trust me. I don't ever even make fun of him.

'This is it,' repeated Ted. 'This is the man who could inherit my place. We are approaching a possible second epicentre here.'

Three days later, under the directions of Ted, we returned to the nursing home armed with four clothes pegs. The idea was that we would hold four of the moles by the pegs, while Ted *settled* on the fifth mole. So into the nursing home we walked, all smiles, pausing to greet and shake hands with some of the old ladies in the lounge. We were always civil like that, really. Our session with the special Lifebloomer (who so far had refused to speak to anyone who wasn't his family) was to take approximately three minutes. With quick steps, Ted and I, one after another, made our noble presence known to him. He was seeing us for the first time so you can imagine how *unsettled* he got. He was probably unstable too. You need not be sane to lead the Lifebloom world.

Ted was quick to take the old man's alarm bell away from him lest he called anyone. I grabbed his little wrinkly hands and told him to stay mute or face the Lifebloom wrath. That was it. We pulled down his pyjamas and set the pegs in the right order. The old fool kept squirming and convulsing so much that I had to hold him down by his back as Ted tended to each mole. Well, Ted pretty much *settled* with each press of the peg, causing much overstimulation to the poor man. But what option did we have? If he had stayed still I would have handled the pegs while Ted tended to the special fifth mole. When the pegs were in place Ted descended on the mole behind the knee with much care. Really, all he did, given the special circumstance, was suck on it to see if it would change colour. For sometimes, said Ted, extraordinary Lifebloom agents make themselves known by changing their colour. Once we were done, we climbed through the window, leaving the pegs in place. I climbed back in, seconds later, just before he got out of his Lifebloom trance, and wrote our unregistered cell number on his arm with the instructions, 'Call us tomorrow at 4pm and we will tell you all about it.'

The next day Ted and I sat in one of the bars in the Delmar Loop of St Louis and waited for the ignorant Lifebloomer's call. The hour passed and no call came. Ted kept going back and forth between the bathroom and the tables shaking the hands of perfect strangers as we waited. By sundown, it was time for Ted to express his grief about the failure of our project. I had the responsibility of leading him away from crowds so he could bend and shake his head, yell and kick pavements as necessary. Sometimes I felt so sorry for poor Ted that I had him sit down and stroked his chest, carefully staying clear of the Lifebloom agents that populated his body. Finally, he was quiet and did not say a word until halfway through the ride back to Lonely Nest, when he asked that I pull over so he could pee. He walked down through the shrubs, down the slope from the road, and, without looking back, disappeared into the darkness. It was the last I saw of Ted Lifebloom. If I had known he was going to disappear I would have pulled by the roadside much earlier, just so we could excite each other's moles and have a final swim in the green world of love, of wisdom and ecstasy. Lord, how it hurt to see him vanish without warning! I drove back to St Louis and, after a week of immersion, or rather, *settle*ment, among the comfiest of pillows, applied for a job at the dreaded TSA, where I hoped to carry out my Lifebloom duty by assessing potential Lifebloomers. And now, thanks to my brutish boss, there goes the job and any hope of locating an inheritor to Ted.

If, in my trial for sexual harassment, the soft-faced Magistrate of St Louis asks me to simplify for the court some of the grand visions of the Lifebloom ecstasy, I will give a list of images that include giant snakes slithering on bare backs of sunbathers, the kisses of toothless elderly Kazakh couples, the penetrative mouths of hyenas as they disembowel fleeing prey, the longing eyes of Akita dogs, the sweaty waists of African female dancers, the heaving chests of death-row inmates on the execution gurney, the tight jaws of some vindictive men.

Abdul Adan was born in Somalia, grew up in Kenya and lives in the United States. His work has appeared in *Kwani?*, *African-Writing*, *Storytime*, *African Roar*, *Gambit: Anthology of Newer African Writing*, and *Jungle Jim*. He is working on a collection of stories.

The Gonjon Pin

Martin Egblewogbe

You don't know Billy Holmes, do you? Of course not. Not personally, anyway, which is what I really meant. In any case, I am not going to introduce him to you. However, something happened to him which affected one of my friends, and that is the story I want to tell. Billy is not his real name, though. It's his writer's pseudonym, under which disguise he has displayed the most wretched behaviour known in publishing.

What I want to tell you about Billy is that, one fine day in late July, when the weather in Accra is quite mild and an evening walk refreshing, this man leapt over the balcony of his first-floor apartment in East Legon and fled screaming down Sergeant Adjetey Street, pursued by no-one. He was stark naked, and ran in the direction of the open-air restaurant at the end of the road, where early revellers were provided with an enhanced visual experience. This event was captured by several persons on their devices, and the video is now online.

He ran 200 feet in all before he was reached by the 'first responders', ever-concerned Ghanaians who wanted to help but also wanted the inside story – the scoop – and they reported that his first words upon being accosted, at which time he also must have come to his senses, were: 'Oh, what a shit.'

His story, in sum, was this. He was enjoying early evening entertainments after a good supper – *fufu* and antelope light soup no less – when two women came to his house and offered themselves to him. Of course, he was not entirely crazy, he was acquainted with at least one of them; yes, she was his friend – indeed, an ex-girlfriend, and they had parted on good terms etc, let me not spoil the story. In any case Billy was entirely amenable to these suggestions, but unfortunately the other woman turned out to have balls and proceeded to beat Billy while his former girlfriend laughed and fire came out of her mouth – and so he had no choice but to flee, naked though he was. In order to follow this interesting lead to the end, the concerned Ghanaians, after preserving Billy's dignity with a donated shirt, went to his apartment where they discovered nothing to confirm this story, with the exception of ruffled bedclothes, which really proved nothing. In the end Billy was advised to relax, to go to the police if he was worried, and to stop smoking 'the thing'. 'The thing', the man who proffered this advice said, could disgrace even the mightiest. I assume he alluded to a psychotropic substance.

Be that as it may, disgrace – psychotropically induced or otherwise – was Billy's stock in trade. He published a one-man online and print tabloid, issued twice a month, titled and captioned, respectively, *The (Scurrilous) Rag – No Smoke Without Fire*. Oh, what obscenities had he not published! What reputations had he not destroyed! Politicians brought down! Public officers disgraced! Marriages ruined! Secretly recorded sex videos! Occult practices of the rich and famous! Of course, all this meant that his website received hundreds of thousands of weekly hits, his newspaper was widely circulated and read, and he was hated by a few, and loved by few. Nevertheless, his business paid off, and he was rich. As the event which I have recounted happened only last week, I wait to see what the next edition of *The Rag* will publish.

But this is not really the story I want to tell. I want to tell you about what happened to my friend Kumi, who two years ago was kicked out of the University of Ghana, where he had been studying Computer Science and Philosophy. Kumi's apartment is on the same floor as Billy's. When you climb up the stairs to the landing, Kumi's apartment – A-1 – is to the left, and Billy's – A-2 – is to the right. So, you may ask, how did it happen that Kumi, whose background and family circumstances were as humble as my own, was the owner of this plush apartment in an upscale Accra neighbourhood, when he had not even completed university and was unemployed? This is an important part of the story, as you will see. Kumi had always had difficulties in school, even though he was a very bright student. He is a rather quiet chap, an introvert, in fact – a geek, if I may take the liberty – but his rebellious nature, on full display when he was forced to do things he considered unnecessary, meant that he had been dismissed from various schools and only entered the University because he passed his exams as a private candidate. So, though Kumi was my classmate in secondary school, I finished University three years ago, and now work as a radio journalist.

Kumi did not tell me why he was dismissed, but here is what I gleaned from one of his classmates. Apparently incensed by what he considered a misrepresentation of Kant's categorical imperative, Kumi had fallen into a heated argument with his professor during a lecture. What started off as a probing question from Kumi quickly turned into a curious spectacle. Kumi declared, the professor disagreed, Kumi insisted, the professor dismissed, and so Kumi rushed to the board to demonstrate a point, drawing circles and arrows on the board. The professor rejected the proposition, threw his jacket on the desk, and drew a diagram of his own. The three other students left the classroom as voices rose and tempers rose with them. The head of department, whose office was just down the hallway, was alarmed at the noise and rushed into the lecture room where he found the two sparring philosophers enveloped by a cloud of chalk dust, shouting at each other and drawing and erasing diagrams on the blackboard. The two did not take kindly to the head of department's interjection, with Kumi screaming that he was a '*dudui* element'. And so he was dismissed, the University not taking kindly to such insulting behaviour. You may ask, yes, but how does that relate to the apartment? And the answer is this: a few months after his dismissal, Kumi won a quarter of a million cedis in the national lottery.

After he moved into his new apartment, Kumi embarked upon a secret programme. Now, though I'm telling you the story, I have taken pains to conceal all identities, so it still is a secret programme, even though you know about it. It is still secret because it is so totally removed from your life that you cannot do anything about it, any more than you can do anything about Anokye. Or Babayaga.

I first visited Kumi in his apartment about six months after he moved in, on a calm Sunday afternoon that offered only the thrills of boredom. The weather in the city was gloomy from the threat of rain. There was this heavy, languorous air about the afternoon and, by the time I got off the bus to walk the one or so kilometres to Kumi's place, I was beginning to feel slightly depressed. The tree branches that overhung the pavement were dropping some tiny yellow flowers. I waited beside an old man for a sleek black Mercedes to roll by before crossing the road; he marched stiffly ahead of me, holding his umbrella like a sword.

Sergeant Adjetey Street, when I got to it, was deserted. A white Range Rover was parked outside the apartment block, but there was no-one in it. I found Kumi in the garden, sitting at a round wooden table underneath a tamarind tree. He was poring over a chess board and looked very well indeed, sporting a handsome crew cut and a sprightly air. A few pawns and a bishop lay on their sides beside an ashtray. Smoke drifted upwards from a detritus of stubs.

'Finally, we meet again,' I said, dropping into a seat opposite him. 'This is where you've ended up.'

Kumi smiled, waved a hand lazily over the board, and said: 'In three moves the white king will be in check. In two additional moves the game will be over. The white king does not know this. And so the hand of fate deals with us all.' He picked up a piece, consulted a pamphlet on the table, and said, 'Black knight to E 6.' He moved the piece across the board.

'Pretty grand,' I said, looking up at the four-storey block, the white of the walls in stark contrast to the bright reds and greens of the flame trees blooming in the garden.

'Spirits upstairs,' Kumi said, rising. 'Come on in. I have something to show you.' I followed him up the stairs, noting that he had put on a little weight, so that he was no longer lanky. On the landing we turned into apartment A-1. 'Odd neighbour I have,' Kumi said, shutting the door behind him. 'Billy something. Has orgies and such. I hear he's a writer of some sort. Aspirational stuff for you, perhaps.' Despite the air-conditioning, the room was charged with cigarette smoke, and unshaded lights glared from the ceiling, reflecting dully from the pale green tiles of the bare floor. The room was bare save for two armchairs, a piano, and a bar to which I was steered.

'Let us imagine,' Kumi said, cracking open a Jack Daniel's and half-filling my glass, 'that a man could predict the future... no, let me put it better – imagine that a man could predict future events. Would that skew the temporal trajectory?'

'Spare me the philosophy,' I grumbled. 'It's all tosh anyway.'

Kumi laughed. 'Predetermination proscribes probabilities, or does it? You believe in God, of course.'

I finished my whiskey and reached for the bottle again. It was really good stuff, so it did not bother me that I drank it neat. 'You are not normal, clearly,' I said to Kumi, 'But do give it a shot sometimes. Show me around your place. Seems like you are putting it to shame.'

Kumi ran a finger back and forth across the counter. 'You know how I won the lottery?' he asked. I looked at him. He hadn't told me about it, and no-one else had either. 'A dead man, my friend. A date of death, the number on the motor hearse. Ten digits and the remainder of my student loan. I've since wondered how could that happen, when the odds were so great. Was it in fact because the odds were so great, or because of... the hand of fate? God?'

'Satan,' I put in drily. 'God does not play dice.'

'He plays chess,' Kumi said, striking up another light and handing me the pack of Rothmans. I declined. He released a stream of smoke in my direction. 'Let me show you around,' he said, and, grabbing the bottle, led the way into the next room. There was nothing in it, and it apparently had not been cleaned in a long while, so I wondered why he bothered to show it to me. 'One,' he said, swinging the door shut and sauntering off.

'There's this thing I want you to see,' he said, stopping suddenly beside a shut door and gesturing with the bottle. 'There's only a bed and a stereo in this room... and a bookshelf. Surely you've seen these before? They look just like any other. Good. Let's go on, then.' I noticed that his hand was trembling and his breath came a little more rapidly. I caught him casting a sideways glance in my direction, and he looked away self-consciously. We stopped again at another shut door.

'This is my study. And I am working on a project.'

There was a throbbing hum coming from the room, and, with an expression on his face reminiscent of a child saying to another, 'promise you won't laugh', he threw the door open.

A rushing noise – like the sound of an industrial air blower – leapt from the room like a tiger, making me step backward. The sound was coming from the right side of the room, where, against the wall, there was a row of shelves carrying what appeared to be the biggest computer workstations I had ever seen. There were ten of them, and each CPU was about three times the size of a desktop CPU. There were network switches too, with green and red lights blinking merrily. Cool air blasted from four air-conditioners on the opposite wall, and there was a table in the middle of the room with an open laptop computer on it. A blue swivel chair was placed a little way behind the table, beside which reclined a single armchair and a coffee table. Three or four large books lay on the floor beside the table. Against the wall and behind the armchair there was a whiteboard with equations scrawled across it in blue ink.

'Goodness,' I said softly, looking around in awe. I walked slowly across the room to the window. Through the open blinds I saw the laden branches of a Yoryee tree. I turned around and surveyed the room again.

Kumi's agitation was increasing, he seemed to be bouncing up and down – but I had also been drinking, you see, so my perception of small movements could have been suspect. He was speaking, but I only caught the words: '...improving the prediction capability of repeated random events from a finite p-space by a method of reduction. How does that sound? Heh? Heh?'

Setting the bottle on the table, he lit another cigarette and began pacing back and forth. I told him I did not understand what he was saying. He farted unconsciously and, as the sad smell grew about us, he explained that he was writing software for predicting chance events which nevertheless occurred regularly – for example, floods, wars, and lotto numbers.

I took a deep breath. 'So,' I asked, 'you are building a lotto machine?'

'More or less,' Kumi said. 'But the scope is not so pedestrian – or mercenary. It can be employed for very useful things in science and engineering. Are you not interested in how it works? Heh?'

Kumi stopped pacing and approached me rather

aggressively, his forehead glistening in the bright fluorescent lighting. I drew backwards involuntarily.

'But really, think of it,' Kumi continued. 'What will next week's lotto numbers be? I cannot tell, but could I tell, perhaps with greater certainty, what the numbers will not be? What about saying that this week's lotto numbers will not be drawn next week? This is my concept of repeatability. The first step is to derive a probability function for repeatability, because with that you can minimize the sample space, thereby reducing the odds. See? I am now running a program that I wrote to mimic the wheel of fortune, generate a hundred thousand draws, then test my concept of repeatability...' here, he indicated the computers with a flourish of his right hand, leaving a trail of smoke. He sat down and leaned forward. 'Should be done in about a week. And if it works...' he began, snapped his fingers, sucked deeply at the cigarette so that the end flared up like the evil eye, and then sat there holding his breath, all puffed up and filled with smoke.

We looked at each other. His eyes started to water. The seconds ticked. The whole thing was stupefying, and I just looked at him, thinking perhaps he would start to levitate and then... something. Instead he pressed a finger on his right nostril and let flow a thick stream of grey smoke through the left, and then he gasped loudly, fell to the floor and lay there, taking great gulps of air. I suddenly felt a strong urge to shout abuse at Kumi, but all I could do was mutter: 'This is all nonsense. Just don't kill yourself.' To which he replied from the floor, weakly, 'Ahhhhh'. He seemed happy.

Now let me show you how Billy's story intersected with Kumi's. Again, I must indicate that I have no real interest in Billy's case, save for a journalistic curiosity. I have only told you about what happened to Billy because of what happened to Kumi subsequently.

Last Thursday, at 8.30pm, I received a call from Kumi.

'Something terrible has happened.' He was whispering and I could barely hear him. 'Could you come to my place at once?'

'Will you pay for the taxi?' I asked, on account of the persistent economic difficulties related to my profession.

'This is serious,' he sighed. 'Come at once.'

It was during my approach to his apartment that I met the aftermath of the commotion involving Billy. There was a small group of people talking and laughing at the entrance, so I asked them what was going on. They happily gave me details of Billy's mishap. Then I went up the stairs, and Kumi met me at the door.

He looked harassed, and asked, without preamble: 'Did you by any chance tell anyone about my... project?'

'Of course not,' I replied. 'I keep confidences. What's going on?'

'My study has been violated,' he said, a slight trembling in his voice. 'Someone broke in. And that is not all. Come.' He led me into his study. The window had been smashed to pieces, obviously by a concrete flower vase which now lay on the floor, spilling soil. A clutch of broken periwinkles had fallen just beside the window. Pieces of glass and soil lay scattered about the floor. The window was open and the blinds fluttered in the breeze.

'He came in via the balcony,' Kumi said.

'You saw him?' I asked.

Kumi shook his head. 'I was asleep. Was woken up by the crash. But there was no-one here when I came in.' Anticipating my next question, he said, 'No, nothing was taken. Nothing was touched. But...'

My eyes, led by his raised hand, followed his index finger past the table on which his laptop sat, past the shelves with the blinking servers and humming workstations, and stopped just behind the armchair, a little way to the left.

'What the hell is that?' I exclaimed.

'It's someone's balls,' Kumi said, in an apologetic tone. 'Someone's balls hanging on my wall.'

We approached the wall. The scrotum was gross to look at, with patchy brown corrugated skin and straggly hairs. The dash of talcum powder did not make things look any better.

'Oh God,' I said. Kumi could be cantankerous, but practical jokes were not his forte. This was no joke. At all. I stood there staring at the wall. I could think of nothing. Kumi was breathing heavily beside me.

'You know it is alive,' he said suddenly, breaking into my blank spell. 'It responds to stimuli. Look,' and he struck out with his pencil. The scrotal sac contracted immediately, and in my mind I heard the owner's anguished scream. An evil look crossed Kumi's face as he struck the balls again.

'Stop that,' I said.

'What do you think is happening?' Kumi asked, his eyes fixed on the dangling mass. 'I tried pulling it off... but it's stuck, truly. Like it grew there.' His words made my stomach turn.

'What are you going to do?' I asked. Kumi shrugged.

At that time it had become clear to me that Kumi had no idea of what had happened earlier that evening involving his next-door neighbour. I had already begun to connect the dots. So perhaps Billy had not been hallucinating after all, and had really been attacked. I told Kumi what had befallen Billy.

'And so you think,' Kumi begun, 'that this chap attacks Billy, Billy jumps down and runs away, and then he comes here through the window. Why? To escape, or to... do the same to me?'

'Escape, most probably. This is not likely to be about you – you do not have enough enemies, Billy does. But Billy said that there were two of them, a man and a woman. Most likely they heard the crowd bringing Billy back into his apartment, so they rushed in here, hoping it was vacant, and then they heard you coming...'

'...and then they touched the wall and vanished. Except

that the man left his balls behind. You know, that's a silly story,' Kumi said. He struck the balls again, rather absent-mindedly, and then began to pace.

The doorbell rang. It sounded far off, and must have been ringing for a while before we noticed it. Kumi went off and soon returned with a tall, burly man in a black suit. His round head was clean shaven and polished so that it shone under the fluorescent lighting, and he had a severe expression on his face, accentuated by a heavy – though well-clipped – moustache and beard that made his lips look like small animals in a forest. He had this nonchalant air about him, accentuated by the seriousness of his black bow-tie. He paused for a moment at the door and surveyed the room slowly, his right hand in his pocket.

'This is George,' Kumi said to me, and George spared me a nod. He looked like the MC of an awards event, plucked right off the stage.

'Are these the balls?' he asked, and bent to examine them. After a few seconds he straightened, turned, and walked to the window, carefully avoiding the debris on the floor. He gazed at the window without a word, and then came back towards us, paused at the whiteboard, picked up the eraser, and cleaned off Kumi's equations. Then he drew a large question mark followed by a line that travelled diagonally across the board, ending with an arrow head pointing at the offending scrotum.

'At this time, somewhere in Accra, or Ghana, there is a man walking about without balls. These are his balls.' George pointed. 'Let me tell you what has happened. This man – shall we call him "X" – has vanishing juju. This type of juju is quite well known. However, something must have gone wrong, and X vanished and left his balls behind.'

Kumi stared at George in stupefaction, his mouth hanging open.

'Do you expect me to believe this stupid...' He seemed lost for words, and it was a few seconds before he completed his sentence: '...shit? I am a rational man. Take a look around the room, there is science going on here, man! And you want me to believe... this...?'

'What?' George asked. 'It is right before your eyes, the balls. I do not ask you to believe it, I am offering you an explanation. It is very rational. Am I not making sense?'

'Not at all,' Kumi replied. 'What is "vanishing juju"? How can a man just vanish?'

'It is right before your eyes,' George said. He seemed to be getting annoyed, his eyebrows had dipped lower, and his mien was increasingly menacing. 'Call it what you will,' he said. 'You like science? Why is it not possible? Consider it in terms of quantum entanglement. A warp in spacetime. Science can always propose something.'

George turned back to the whiteboard. He made a list in large letters: '1 Call the police. 2 Alert the scientists. 3 Get the spiritualists. 4 Cut off the balls and throw them away. 5 Do nothing.'

'Cutting off the balls is out,' George said, and drew a line through the words. 'There will be bleeding, blood all over. And X might perhaps die. That would be murder. Don't involve the police – this matter will enter into unimaginable absurdities if you do. Likewise the scientists, though I rather fancy that option. The police would get involved then, as well. Now to the spiritualists. But which? Do we go to Master Hindu or to Al-Zimbirigu? You see those adverts in the papers every day. But there's too much mumbo-jumbo and really they do not know what they are about – you don't think so? And now consider the last item, which is to do nothing. This seems best. X, seeing a patch of concrete wall where his testicles used to be, should be even more worried than you are. It's his problem mainly. He will solve it.' George put a big * beside item 5.

George's line of thought seemed quite reasonable to me, though I believed that the spiritualists should still be considered. Then maybe a juju man would have to be brought on site, fly whisk and bells and cowries and all, in which case, would the man have to come back to fetch his balls, or could he have them remotely returned? Despite the seriousness of the situation, a small laugh bounced about in my belly, but I did not let it out.

Kumi was standing behind me and I turned around to look at him. His face was creased in an angry frown and his Adam's apple worked up and down. I could see he wanted to talk, but it took him a little while to calm down sufficiently. When he finally spoke, his hands were trembling and his voice was hot with anger. 'Do nothing? Am I to live with someone's testicles hanging on my wall? Oh, the very thought!' Kumi shouted.

George looked at Kumi, his face expressionless. He raised his right hand and stroked his moustache. This seemed to infuriate Kumi further. 'I cannot stand this!' he shouted. 'Your premises are faulty. All your thinking can only lead to a wrong conclusion! There is a rational explanation for all this, we can understand it all without recourse to magic! That's right. There are no balls on the wall! It's just some sort of a mirage, a trick of the lights – or perhaps the periwinkles are exuding some hallucinogens... I cannot accept what you are saying!'

'Will you behave yourself?' George asked sternly. He was clearly out of patience and his jacket tightened across his chest as he flexed his muscles.

'Look, Kumi, take it easy or we'll just leave,' I said. I did not like the way things were going at all. Kumi had a wild look in his eyes and his breath was coming in short, loud bursts. He looked on the verge of a hysterical breakdown.

'Well, get out, then, get out! I'll take care of it myself!' Kumi shouted, and fell backwards into the armchair. 'Go!'

So we left, George and I, leaving Kumi fuming in the armchair with the balls dangling behind him.

'He's a peculiar sort of asshole,' George said to me as we went downstairs. 'But I'm sure he'll come around.'

There was a dark-grey Jaguar X8 parked on the street just outside the apartment block. George walked slowly to the car, got inside, and drove off. The bastard didn't even bother to give me a lift. I went home by bus.

Who was this George character? So well educated, well dressed, rich, odd. Where was he from? I do not know. I'll ask Kumi, of course. It is an important item that I must include in the story. But all sorts of other events have since occurred, and as I sit here writing this I have still not asked Kumi about George. In any case, let me tell you what happened next, and you will see why I forgot to ask him.

Today is Saturday. Seven hours ago, at 11.40 in the morning, I received a call from Kumi. He did not bother with greetings.

'Oh God,' he groaned. There was a depressing weariness in his voice.

'Take it easy,' I said.

'I've been arrested by the police... They want to search my house.'

'Wait... The police? What happened?'

'This is not the time!' Kumi screamed.

'Then when is the goddamn time?' I shouted back. 'Give me some...'

'OK! OK! I threw the thing over the Adomi Bridge... and then there is this man behind me and he says we've got to talk... and he's a policeman... and I asked that you be there as witness... so we're coming to your place...'

'What? You're bringing the police here?' I was more amused than alarmed at this twist.

'We're outside your frigging door!' Kumi screamed.

I went outside. Kumi's Range Rover was just pulling up under the large neem tree outside my house. I live in a compound house at Adenta, and my neighbours, two of whom were playing draughts on their veranda, were staring at the resplendent item of luxury and casting glances in my direction as well. There was a man in the front passenger seat and as I stepped forward he got out and walked towards me. It was the policeman. He was in mufti, and well dressed at that. With his white shirt, rose-coloured flying tie, black trousers and leather shoes, he could have been a business executive. He held out his hand, stopping me in my tracks. I shook it.

'Detective Nketiah, Police CID,' he said. 'I believe you know Kumi S--- ?'

'Is anything the matter?' I asked, looking at Kumi, who had placed his head on the steering wheel, the very picture of dejection.

'We have a standing warrant to search No 102 Sergeant Adjetey Street,' the detective replied. I noticed that the detective's lips were unnaturally black, much darker than the rest of his face in fact. He went on: 'We've been monitoring a lot of suspicious activity there. I wanted to have a word with your friend at home – to ask him a few questions, informally, you see. He requested your presence. Shall we go right away? We may not need you for long.'

'Doesn't he need a lawyer?' I asked.

'He declined. This is informal, really. Just a few questions. But if he refuses, I'll arrest him and we'll have to go through the formalities at the station.'

The whole thing did not seem threatening, so I shrugged and said, 'Oh well. Let's go.' I was not doing anything serious at home and could spare the time. In any case I was really curious as to where this was going, and wanted to be part of the action. I went back inside, locked up, and returned to the car after about five minutes. Inspector Nketiah was still standing where I had left him, a little way from the car. He came up to me and whispered: 'But your friend, is he correct?'

'Most of the time.' I replied.

We got into the car. Kumi whispered a greeting to me in a cracked voice. He avoided looking at me, but I saw in the reflection in the driving mirror that his hair was uncombed and he was covered in grey dust. He was wearing the same clothes he had been wearing when he threw George and me out of his house. He smelled of sweat and tiredness.

I found out during the drive that Kumi had pretty much told the detective everything that had happened, and in the ensuing conversation I also got to know the circumstances of his arrest. He had been picked up a few minutes after throwing 'what appeared to be a heavy weight' over the railings of the Adomi Bridge. Though the action was not very suspicious in itself, Kumi's haggard looks and guilt-ridden demeanour made the detective pull him in. It turned out that Kumi had been tailed from his house – apparently, the police had put the apartment under surveillance. Perhaps Billy was involved in something shady, and the eyes of the law had turned in the direction of the occupants of No 102 Sergeant Adjetey Street. After days of struggling with himself about what to do, Kumi, in a fit of suicidal desperation, had gone and bought a hammer and a chisel and proceeded to remove the section of the wall to which the balls were attached, which he succeeded in doing after about three hours of work. Exhausted, he had fallen asleep and woken up at dawn today. Then, still covered with dirt and stone chippings, he had put the thing into a bag, jumped into his car, and driven off to dump it into the Volta.

When we arrived in Kumi's study I saw that there was a hole the size of a football where the balls had been. It was like an ugly scar in the smooth tan of the wall, with rough and jagged edges. Loose chippings and dirt were strewn all over the floor close to the wall. A large block hammer and a concrete chisel had been tossed carelessly aside.

Kumi poured himself a large whiskey and lit a cigarette, obviously in an attempt to calm his nerves. He sat in the armchair, staring blankly at the computers that went on running whatever program it was he had written, calculating his 'prediction capability of repeated random events from finite p-space by a method of reduction'. Detective Nketiah walked around the room, examining each item carefully and writing things down in a small notebook. He asked few questions – obviously the facts seemed to fit the story. Then he sat down in the chair behind the table and asked Kumi for a cigarette. It was at this time that I got the suspicion that his unnaturally black lips were due to heavy smoking of marijuana and tobacco. I had noticed this before in a few other smokers. Besides, the way he handled the cigarette, running his thumb lovingly along the length before putting it into his mouth, made me even more convinced. Anyway, Kumi had offered him an expensive brand, right from a carved wooden case.

The detective smoked in silence, his left hand hanging over the side of the chair. His eyes were closed and his face expressionless. I stood leaning against the door post, while Kumi sat in the armchair with his head in his hands. The roar of the computers seemed to grow louder with every second. Nketiah smoked slowly and with relish, letting the ash drop on the floor, and for the next four or so minutes he did not open his eyes. But then he stopped smoking, pinched off the lit end of the cigarette, and dropped the stub on the floor. He brought his notebook and pencil from his pocket and scribbled something, tore the sheet out and placed it on the table, weighting it down with the lighter. Then he rose, looking intently first at me, and then at Kumi.

'You young men should be careful, you know,' he said. He turned to Kumi. 'I'm not going to take your statement, you're no longer under arrest... so far it all looks OK. Quite crazy, but not too much, so it's fine. I'll be on my way now. Good afternoon to you.'

Detective Nketiah paused when he got to the door, and he looked straight into my eyes. Then, thrusting his left hand into his pocket, he walked out. His footsteps receded down the hall, and I heard the front door open and shut.

Kumi remained where he was sitting, his head still in his hands. It sounded like he was crying.

I went over to the table and looked at the note the detective had left behind. There was a single telephone number on it, followed by the words: 'Call me if you get your machine to work. H. N.'

Martin Egblewogbe is the author of the short-story collection *Mr Happy and the Hammer of God and Other Stories* (Ayebia, 2012). He has also co-edited the collection of poetry *Look Where You Have Gone To Sit* (Woeli Publications, 2010). He is a co-founder and a director of the Writers Project of Ghana, a literary organization. His hobbies include still photography and astronomy. Martin is a lecturer at the University of Ghana and lives in Accra with his wife and two children.

As A Wolf Sweating Your Mother's Body

Clifton Gachagua

Katia is quiet upstairs. I'm not sure if she's sleeping. All her days are nights now. When I go up the stairs carrying a bowl of salad – *insalata caprece* – she asks me for the time. I place the bowl down and ask her to ring the bell if she needs anything. As I turn around to leave, she asks for some morphine; she's seen me use it on different occasions. Her voice is soft and low; I can tell it takes a great deal of strength to talk. I tell her I don't have any left. She'll have to win back my trust if she is to receive any special favours, especially after she broke my nose the last time I opened the door. The bedroom has been apportioned so that she hasn't much space to move around. She's been on a diet of green vegetables and oranges, having recently decided that she's a vegetarian. Sometimes I cheat and make her white meat, pili pili and a mushroom sauce just to see if she is serious. In that small space she cannot afford to dictate terms. I make all her food in my small kitchen, where we have on many occasions kissed each other goodbye.

When I go back up again her feet peep through the small space where the plywood almost touches the lozenges of the parquetry. I smile, but only because she cannot see me. I would not want to give her the satisfaction of knowing she has given me what I need most. I bend down and touch those feet. I can feel her blood turn cold under my touch;

it must take a lot of courage for her not to jerk. I bend even lower and feel the soft skin on my cheeks. I tell her not to move a muscle as I run down the stairs for the kit. I run back to her. I ask her to drop her feet into the mix of warm water, bath salts and egg yolk. I let them soak. To pass time I tell her about my new creations. I recite the names slowly: tender imitations, slight variation, night out, starry night, duchess of kink, mist in her eyes, happy Byzantium, raspberry seed, hot firebrick, cold sienna. She doesn't say a word; I can't tell if she's even awake. She has a pulse and that's good enough. After the soaking I cleanse her feet in a fresh basin of water.

'Want to guess what secret fragrance I added to the water?'

No reply. I wish she would say something; it might make her stay with me more comfortable.

'If you guess right I'll get you some morphine.'

No reply.

'Peppermint.' I offer.

She adjusts her right leg. She always likes me to start with the right leg owing to the scars on the left one, never mind I cannot see that far up her legs. I squeeze her leg in anger; it gives too easily. She's not putting up a fight. So she has been ignoring me, now my morphine is not good enough for her? I want to run out of the room. It seems now, in retrospect, that I have always been overwhelmed by the urge to run out of a room whenever Katia is present. On second thought I decide to stay; there's a bigger war I'm fighting. I begin work on her toes.

I paint women. Not in the grand way of those who have come before me, my father having become famous posthumously for his untitled nudes, but in a more genteel way, by which I mean that I polish women's nails, with a predilection for toes. My father grew up in the country and came to the city a young man, in defiance of his own father's wishes – he was to marry the daughter of a rich landowner. He opted rather to roam the streets of Nairobi, disinherited, clueless, without any useful talents, and hungry. He finally managed to find a job in an Indian shop under the watchful eye of a second-generation Gujarati proprietor. No-one knows much about his time in Nairobi except the many women he loved, and me. I know his history because he told me in those last days when he came home to die. Maybe it was a way for him to say he was sorry. Maybe it was his love language. Maybe, and I'm more inclined to believe this, he had nowhere else to go. He told me he'd been a painter, showed me a life's worth of sketches. When I asked to see the paintings he gave me the address to a gallery on Dennis Pritt Road. After his death I took a trip to the gallery only to find out all his nudes were of Gujarati descent. His critics have found different ways to theorize why his paintings only feature Gujarati women, especially in a time when the Indians lived behind high walls and only came out to buy orange, yellow, red and green bell peppers at the market.

My women are more varied, although more and more now I tend to veer towards light skin. Not to say I don't have a soft spot for Indian women. On good days I have rich customers, willing to pay thousands for a good job, but on most days I am glad to roam my own side of the city. The women all have my number. They share it among themselves when they happen to meet. My work is better than anyone's. I'm not so inclined to the politics of women and fashion but I do know about colours and feet. And nails. Toenails. Fingernails.

After I'm done with Katia I go downstairs and rest. The nail polish kit is right next to me, the bottles of darks and lights separated, from the reds and pinks to the neutral and cream, every fine hue right where it belongs. The colours are slowly settling in the cold bottles. The women will love these new combinations, they will have to. I have worked too hard for them. Every once in a while I will surprise them with some new hues.

There's a copy of *Playboy India* on the table – I can only

masturbate to Indian women. A bird tries to get out of the bedroom, banging its body against the mirror. I want to help it but it will mistake my intentions, then its own panic will kill it. I let it be. The faces of Indian women remind me of my favorite colour; they make me want to say *burgundy*. No, maybe something more, maybe *sweet sweet burgundy*. The fine granules of white sugars roast in the pot; the heavy smell makes my nostrils itch.

A bloody serviette on the table. I've been taking so many anti-histamines I have run out of saliva. I thought I was dying when I discovered this. It turns out I only need to take a sip of water every ten seconds. When I told Katia I'd run out of saliva she called me a lying bastard, said it was the most elaborate and stupid lie she'd ever heard from a man to get out of kissing her. I laughed and asked her how many men had refused to kiss her. She broke my dinner plates. We have different sensibilities and senses of humour. In the end I told her it wasn't the kissing I was avoiding, that the idea of going down on her without saliva in my mouth made me scared for my life. She left me. Her loss. Wait until all the saliva comes back.

Katia is silent now. She's upstairs in what used to be my bedroom. She cannot hurt me from there.

I pick up magazine cuttings of Indian women's feet. *Indian women's feet*. I think about their feet a lot. None of the critics and scholars who have been studying my father's painting have picked up on this, but there is a certain afterglow in the feet of the nudes, a certain lingering of his brush, in the way sometimes a child will become obsessed with a toy he is seeing for the first time. I'm convinced he was also obsessed with feet. I think about non-black shades of feet. Nail polish looks good on them, and here I'm thinking something like amaranth or amethyst. Or something more sassy and playful like bright cerulean or daffodil. Hands are interesting too but, when it comes to absolute intimacy, handling feet offers something even more than the picture of a healthy infant suckling at his mother's breasts. One almost feels where feet have been and where they want to go, all the places they go to in their dreams. It takes a great deal of control to stop myself from licking them. I always ask them to come in with their shoes on. I want to take off their shoes myself, bow down to them as they come in, place each foot on my knee simultaneously. And I take my time, I linger. I want to know whose shoes fit and who got a size smaller or bigger. Then I take out the big book of nail and feet care. Business is good because I massage their feet too, perhaps better than their lovers ever have. Katia doesn't like it when I massage her feet. I think that might have been where our problems started.

When I first met Katia she was fresh out of campus, having worked only two months as an intern at the gallery on Dennis Pritt, owned by my father's biggest collector, a rich Gikuyu who in his younger days wore square-rimmed glasses and printed nationalist propaganda for certain banned groups. There's a portrait of him at the reception. Katia was full of a certain kind of energy that I had only seen in my father's nudes. She was nervous, impatient to succeed, always at the heels of the gallery owner, would do anything to get ahead in the art world, as small and insignificant as it was. She was small-bodied, moved about nervously, at once wary of where she was and still lost in her own thoughts, so that she walked – darted, really – like a small animal in a dark cage. I sensed her anxieties at once and was surprised when she made the effort to talk to me, a stranger.

'You don't have to stand so close to the nude.'

I turned around to meet her gaze. She wore hoop earrings too big for her face, a long hippie-like skirt and more bangles on her wrists than was necessary. I imagined she wore beads around her waist. She was smiling.

'It's rude to stare.'

I swallowed hard. She was beautiful. Not in the way of magazine girls. More like the idea of beauty I get on a sunny day in the country, reading erotic verse next to a pond, watching dragonflies mate.

'I want to smell her.'

She smiled and turned her attention to the nude.

I paint feet because I don't imagine I'd be able to handle painting lady parts. When Katia talked to me I was standing in front of Untitled #3, looking deep into the woman's parts, trying to smell the paint there. Untitled #3. The Indian woman sits on an antique chair, one leg resting on the arm of the chair so that it's barely possible to discern the place between her legs.

'She's probably long dead by now.'

'Not the paint.'

She smiled and walked away. I did not realize it then but I wanted her to stay. I was cranky for the rest of the day without knowing what was bugging me. Now I know I wanted her to stay. I have always wanted her to stay. She has to stay.

I stayed away from the gallery after that first encounter. I had my own women to paint. At the time I was doing my work mostly for bridal parties. There was always a wedding going on somewhere. I had to turn down a few customers. When more than one bridal party called I asked them to send pictures of their feet. They sounded unsure after the request, a short pause during the call as they thought about it, finally giving in – they'd heard the kind of work I could do and they were not going to let a good thing go because of their petty inhibitions. I stuck the pictures of feet up on a board in my bedroom, examined the feet, finally choosing the bridal party with the highest score – 1 being worst, 10 almost close to perfection. But even with my diary so busy my mind was still on Katia.

In the end I admitted to myself that I wanted to see Katia again. I went back to the gallery. I'd been away from the gallery for two months. It wasn't until three further visits that I saw her again, in the same hoop earrings and smile.

This time I caught her standing very close to Untitled #3. I tapped her shoulder. She turned with a start, almost crying out. I heard a few murmurs from behind us.

'Don't do that.'

'I'm sorry.'

She turned back to the painting. I was hot with shame. In my fantasies our second encounter was picture perfect: I was supposed to turn up, save her from some kind of armed bandit, and in return for my heroism accept her undying devotion and love. I wanted to run out of that gallery as fast as I could, to run and never come back, to forget her. She turned around, as if sensing my shame.

'You like sandwiches?'

'I don't mind them.'

In the garden, surrounded by the violet flush of jacarandas, she took out what would become the best sandwiches I have ever tasted. She had this smiling way about her, as if she knew something the rest of us didn't, as if when she went home every evening she'd find God there waiting for her. It unnerved me that she could just sit there and smile with everything going wrong in the world. I wanted to reach over the table and strangle her. I wanted to reach over the table and kiss her.

'Why are you interested in the nudes?' I asked.

She smiled and took a bite of her sandwich, breadcrumbs falling on her chest.

'Golgotha makes it hard to turn your gaze from these women. He obviously spent a lot of time on them. I'm just not sure if he loved them or hated them.'

'Maybe both, with equal measure?'

'It's almost as if he's a predator. A wolf. There's fear in the women's eyes.'

It wasn't the sandwiches or her knowledge of the mood in the nudes that made me like her. It was her feet. I could see them through the open sandals. For a moment I did not listen to her, preoccupied by them.

'It's rude to stare.'

They were simply the most beautiful feet I'd ever seen, with a score of around 9.2.

***

When I first painted Katia's nails she was asleep. We'd had an argument the previous night and slept mad at each other, so that, when I searched for her body during and after a nightmare, she turned away to face the wall. In the nightmare, which is a recurring one, there's a wolf chasing me. We fought because Katia was convinced I was seeing someone else, owing to the fact that I always found an excuse not to touch her in the waking world. This was four or five months after we had started seeing each other and whenever a chance came up to get naked together I came up with some silly excuse. I did not want to tell her I had my own anxieties about being seen naked: no-one had ever seen me naked as an adult. My mother used to wash me in front of the entire neighbourhood and everyone who passed by our house took a second to offer their opinion on the direction my member faced. I did not want Katia to know I was a virgin. She took my excuses as insults to her womanhood. That's how we ended up fighting. I woke up the following day and painted her nails, I'm not sure if it was an apology or another insult – that I could only get intimate with her when she was half dead.

Painting a sleeping woman's toenails presents certain challenges. Inclinations change. And, given that Katia was a violent sleeper, I was, for that one hour or so, scared she'd kick me in the face. Her reflexes were scary. I learned to be wary of certain things when I painted sleeping women. It had taken me a lot of self-control to stay away from her feet. I had long luminosity dreams about them, just myself and them, walking under a starry night in a faraway place. Her right thumb nail is the best I have ever had the pleasure of painting. Perfect how it makes the bend down to the cuticles. The left thumbnail is a bit of a mystery, being the only nail that has lost its symmetry: the left edge of the nail makes a sharper bend compared to the right edge. It's not too obvious, but it's definitely there for the discerning eye. I had on many occasions woken up in the middle of the night to study her toenails, taken photographs and measurements. It took me a while to convince myself to paint her. I could tell her feet in my sleep from a million other pairs. The previous night's fight presented a perfect opportunity for me to induct her into the school of women painted by me.

When I opened the bottles of nail polish they gave off the stinging smell I like so much, a good way to invite morning into my house. I had neutrals and a pastel blue. She stirred when I touched the edge of a nail. I sat still. I took her smallest nail – I always work my way from the smallest to the biggest.

In less than an hour I had painted her feet. In that hour she had tossed and turned, kicked and groaned, smudged some polish.

When she woke up she did not notice the new job. Even after she took a shower. I wanted to imagine she was doing this on purpose. By now she still didn't know what I do for a living; she had stopped asking. From her guesses, I've been many things, from a freelance journalist to a thief. I served her breakfast, waiting for her to say something about her nails. If I didn't think too much about that one left lopsided bend in the toenail I thought this might be my best job yet. I was so anxious for her to notice that I put sugar in her black coffee.

'You know I don't like sugar in my coffee.'

'You're right.'

That was not what she was supposed to say. My right eye began to twitch.

She ate her breakfast slowly, smiling. I fumbled with my French toast – I didn't toast it to the best shade of brown.

She left the house without a word. I could imagine her

ungrateful face, her victory walk, smiling all the way down through the stairs. I put on her underwear and masturbated.

For the rest of the day I was a mess. I didn't make small talk with the women. They noticed this and gave up. I did my job, collected my pay, turned down offers of tea and offered no goodbyes when I left. I carried my heart heavy in my kit. It was the lowest I'd been in a while. I don't know what to do with myself when I'm like this. Alcohol has never helped.

When Katia came back that evening I made sure she would never leave my house again.

***

Visits to the gallery are now fewer. The images of my father's women are now fast fading, and, in a way, therefore, so is the memory of my father. Thinking of it now, he's never been more than one big cloud of memory, a false promise revealed when the strong wind scatters the cloud and the edges of my vision are nothing more than air and a vast nothingness. Those nudes meant a lot. When they talked about him in the papers I felt proud. Not any more. I no longer love him posthumously. I have my polish, my playthings, I have myself to play with, I have Katia who has tried to help but there's only so much she can do when she is up there all tied up. I go up there every day to take her supper and we talk. She still wants to become a gallery owner some day. She's too tired now to scream. I lined the house with blankets and mattresses, sealed the openings in windows and doors with masking tape, played music loud. In the beginning, she screamed even knowing that no-one would ever hear her. I suppose I would scream, too. She owed it to herself not to give up too easily. When I take her supper I make sure my footsteps are heavy on the woodwork as a way of announcing my arrival. Now that she is in a small space, her reflexes have become worse. She slid me a note after a month, asking me to announce my arrival from the bottom of the staircase. I wait as she eats. Even now she is trying to help me out, talking to me about how my day has been and if I still have those nightmares. She's a lovely and gentle soul.

I'm not in any way prepared for the scene waiting for me upstairs. I carry a tray of food up the stairs. There's a strange smell in the air. I switch on the lights and slide the tray towards her. She doesn't pull it in her direction. I knock on the wood three times. No reply. I switch the lights off and begin my descent.

'Golgotha.'

I turn around. It's the first thing she's said in weeks. Is she confusing me with my father?

'Gogol?'

It's me she's after. I can imagine her stupor. I switch the lights back on. In my excitement I hit the bulb with my head and for a while the room is filled with a shifting amber. I steady the warm bulb. Katia slides her feet through the opening. They look like a lemon herb hummus pizza that has long gone bad. She has chewed off all the nails; she has been eating her flesh. Her toes are a mix of pale red, brown and dark green, the same colours my father used in his nudes. My first instinct is to run for the morphine. But halfway down the stairs I catch myself, I turn around and go back up.

'Show me your hands.'

Her hands are just as obscene, the gangrene much worse.

'I did this for you,' she says.

I can imagine her smiling behind the plywood.

'But you're vegetarian.'

I get her the morphine, careful not to give her enough for an overdose.

Later that night I get a call from the gallery owner.

His house is a big mess of mismatched furniture. He comes to the door when I ring the bell. From the glass I can see his huge body walking towards me. It would be unsafe to sit next to him: he looks like he might topple over and fall any time. If it isn't the arthritis, it will be the obesity.

'I know, you don't have to tell me, my weight scares people.' I must have been staring.

He takes out some whiskey – single malt – and, without asking, pours me a tot in a stout crystal glass with the initials GG on the side. We toast to better times.

He has that patronizing air older rich men have when they talk to much younger men. He's seen me in the gallery a couple of times and wants to know if I'm a painter. I tell him I'm not. He decides I must be – after all, I'm Golgotha's son. I want to know how he knows but he dismisses me. His questions are long and invasive, circling vultures, my answers short and to the point. I'm not sure why I'm here although I'm dying to find out. I don't make this obvious.

A few more tots later – my head feels light – he gets to the point. He takes off his glasses, his eyes fixed on mine. He wears the impression of a general about to die.

'My wife will not shut up about what you did to her.'

This time I pour my own tot. The initials on the glass have merged into one blurry smudge of black; my vision gets worse the more I drink.

'She says you've done to her what no other man ever has.'

I tell him I have no use for compliments.

'You young men, you're too angry.'

He stands up from his seat and lowers his body near mine. The French armchair almost gives under his weight.

'I know you're wondering why I called you here.'

When I got the call and noted down his address I remembered immediately that I had been to the same address. It was a part of the city I never visited, apart from the visit to his wife. It was where all the richest lived. Very few Indian women live here, I imagine.

He has to move his entire body, this sea lion of a man, to get to the whiskey. I let him struggle to and fro a bit, watching the disgusting blob. He's too big to stretch all the way to the whiskey, which must be a foot from him. I want to laugh, to go to the middle of the room, right under the big chandelier, and laugh – the kind of derisive laughter that starts with pointing fingers and ends in tears. After a while I get him the whiskey, pour him his twelfth tot.

'It might help if you were not too angry, you know. The system' – he makes air quotes – 'as you call it, is not against you. You are the system.'

I bet he has had to deal with struggling artists before, young angry men and women. He imagines I am one of them.

He tells me he was once young and angry, in those days of the nationalist struggle. In the end he discovered it didn't matter how you made it, your hands would remain bloodied either way. He opted for capitalism and trophy wives in the end.

'My wife is not here tonight.'

What's your point, old man?

I tell him I have to go. I know Katia is waiting for me, she needs her supper.

The man disappears into a white room, locks the door behind him. It seems each step is his last. Then he makes another step and I'm truly sorry, for him, that he has to be trapped in that body. Listening to his footsteps feels like waiting for the world to end.

When he comes back to the room he is in flip flops and a long gown. I cannot tell if it's the same gown his wife put on during that first visit. He pulls a chair in front of me and shows me his feet. This act of lifting his feet towards me shocks me. It is the ease with which he offers his feet that makes me move back in my seat. He offers them to me with an air of entitlement, a certain way that says he's offered his feet to others like me, better than me, and I have no option but to accept what has been so generously presented to me. On any other occasion I would have marched out of the room. But there's a glow in his feet that makes me stay.

On closer inspection I find that his feet are much more beautiful than Katia's, than all my father's nudes. I'm convinced that I will never see feet this good. They are so beautiful that I sober up. I immediately take out my kit and get to work. No words are exchanged. I tell him I like to work in silence. He lets me lick his feet. I cover his toes with my tongue as one would with a damp towel. I run out of saliva. He mentions he wants baby blue and laughs like a wolf in the night. I'm anxious and eager as I work on him, sipping on orange juice, making sure I get everything right. I want to hug his feet and never let go. As I work on him I decide I'll have to get rid of Katia and make more room upstairs: a big man presents certain challenges.

Clifton Gachagua is the first winner of the Sillerman Prize for African Poetry 2013. He has recently published a volume of poetry, *Madman at Kilifi* (University of Nebraska Press) and appears in a chapbook box set, *Seven New Generation African Poets* (University of Nebraska Press). He was recently selected for Africa39, a selection of the most promising 39 authors under the age of 40 from Sub-Saharan Africa and the diaspora. Clifton works at Kwani? in Nairobi, Kenya, as an assistant editor.

Pam Pam

Lawrence Hoba

Pam Pam stayed alone. To those who knew him, young and old alike, he answered to the name Mudhara Pam Pam or simply, vaPam Pam. And to strangers he gave the name Pam Pam. It was not a usual name, so we all thought it was not his real name. We spent hours speculating where such a name could have come from. Could it be the sound his pata pata made as he made his way to the communal bathroom? Pam pam pam. Or the sound his mouth made as he chewed a succulent paw paw? Pam pam pam. When we ran after him, shouting 'what is your name?' he would answer 'Pam Pam'. And we would jump up and down. He never grew tired.

My father, who said he had access to all camp records, even checked his file at work and told us the inevitable. All his papers, even his signature, bore that unimaginable phrase. Whatever it was, we would soon grow tired of all the talk about his name and each take to our daily tasks until a new family came to the camp and we had to convince them that Pam Pam was his real name. My father would again go and check on the records and jot down every little detail, in scrawny little handwriting that revealed all his efforts at wanting to appear educated – even though he wasn't.

So, we had grown tired. And for a long while no-one sat down to their usual meal of sadza and green vegetables (or the occasional kapenta) over that name. Maybe that was also because no new person came to live in our section of the camp for a while. But one summer Saturday morning, all that changed. We suddenly wanted to know his name.

Saturday was the day everyone didn't wake up to go to work or church. Everyone except the soldiers on guard duty, the canteen storekeeper, the Seventh Day Adventists and the clinic nurses. But these were people who didn't stay in our section of the camp, so they could as well have been dead to us anyway. In fact, as my father would put it, they died to us when someone introduced a caste system in the camp and moved us to the oldest section of the camp with tin houses and communal toilets. He would take every new arrival into our section, along with my brother and me, to the brick houses section and show us all the houses he used to stay in, 'before some idiot decided that only real soldiers could stay in those nice houses and us in those sheds'. But the army camp was really no-one's inheritance. We came from all over the country, made it home for a while and left when we had to leave.

But it seemed no-one knew when Pam Pam had first arrived in the camp. My father said it did not say in his records when he had come. So, nobody could tell us where Pam Pam had come from, or if he had always been alone. So, we grew tired. And that particular Saturday morning as we lay in bed late into the morning, my brother and I dreamed that nothing would make us discuss Pam Pam's name again, at least not with my father, or make us take the trip to the new camp.

But the noise outside pulled us out of our blankets. It started as a low hum, and grew slowly until it made us want to see what was causing it. We scrambled outside, my brother not minding the big wet patch on his shorts. He wet himself and everyone knew, because we always took the blankets outside to dry. Outside, people were scampering towards Pam Pam's paw paw tree, and we had almost missed the beginning of another harvest ritual. We ran after them.

Saturday mornings were sunbathing mornings. We – men and children – gathered at the centre of our houses where there were rocks, while the women did the chores at home. We basked in the sun, talking about anything and everything. It was when we got to hear the weekly updates of camp gossip. Only Pam Pam never came to these unofficial indabas. He only availed himself when it was a camp-sanctioned meeting where the Base Warrant Officer almost always imposed a new set of tighter rules governing our continued stay. Then, even the women and the little babies were required to be there.

Pam Pam stayed alone. His life revolved around things one could count on one's fingers: work, home, cooking, washing plates, washing clothes, sometimes going into town, and eating paw paws. In fact, he rarely washed plates since he worked in the Officers' Mess and had most of his meals there. It was this last activity that made him an enigma in the old camp. He loved paw paws and ate them every day when they were in season.

Our section of the camp, which we were supposed to keep to as much as possible, had very few landmarks. Besides the indaba place, the pine trees in which we trapped doves and played hide and seek, and the little hillock – which was mostly out of bounds to us because of the guard camp at its summit – there was one other unusual feature. It was behind Brighton's house, towered above all the tin roofs and could be seen even from the indaba.

A paw paw tree.

Once upon a time, Pam Pam lived in Brighton's house. That was before Brighton's family came to stay in the old camp. The queer thing about Pam Pam was that he stayed alone. Although he was not a young man any more, no-one ever came to visit him. Every day after work he tended to his little garden, taking out weeds with swift but tender movements.

Then one day he planted three tree seedlings behind that house, where his little garden was. After two seasons only one was alive and he looked after it until it was tall and sturdy. We followed the growth of the tree, wondering how someone could care so much for a mere plant.

For a while the tree did not bear any fruit, and we thought he would curse it as in the Bible. But Pam Pam was not a church-going man and even the Jehovah's Witnesses who bothered just about everyone knew not to knock on his door or approach him while he sat outside in his folding chair, wearing underwear-sized shorts and slippers, humming an incongruous tune.

It was in the year Brighton's family came that the tree first started showing signs of bearing fruit. By then, Pam Pam had been moved out of the house because it was meant for a family and not bachelors. The Base Warrant Officer, a man whom we all knew for his ruthlessness, came himself, accompanied by three soldiers carrying rifles, to tell Pam Pam to clear out. Someone had warned the BWO that Pam Pam had said he would not budge an inch.

For three months thereafter, Pam Pam and Brighton's father argued about the garden behind the house. Not that Pam Pam ever said a word to the other man in spite of the gossip of the other man's wife. After taking over the house, Brighton's family had thought it only natural to take over the garden as well since it was behind their house. Everyone did that. Even Pam Pam had taken over the patch at the house to which he had been moved. But when Brighton's family refused Pam Pam access to their garden, all the plants, except the paw paw tree, wilted one night and later all the vegetables the new tenants planted would not grow. At last they agreed to split the beds with Pam Pam, and only then did Brighton's family manage to rear anything in that piece of land.

That was when we knew the second queer thing about Pam Pam.

He was a juju man.

This was the only other thing we came to know about him, besides his name: the fact that he had no known religion and seemed to have outlived everyone in the camp. Some people said that he was from a region outside the country, but that was only speculation based on the queerness of his name, and not in any way supported by his tone of speech or by the records my father had access to. That he never went away made that assertion harder to believe.

So Pam Pam got the patch with his paw paw tree and Brighton's family's vegetables grew. But Brighton, even at that young age, took it worse than his parents, and vowed the matter would not just die like that. Whenever he passed by Pam Pam, he would spit on the ground and say in a low voice only we could hear, '*pfutseki Pam Pam*' (get lost Pam Pam).

But when, after Pam Pam was forcibly rehoused, the BWO's wife had two miscarriages and the officer himself was temporarily admitted for a minor case of insanity, we all began to fear Pam Pam. So when the paw paw tree bore fruit, no-one and nothing would even dare touch them. He'd let the first fruit ripen until we thought he wanted to punish us for something.

Now, the old camp had many fruit trees, oranges, peaches, paw paws, apples, mulberries and grapefruits. We competed for their bright fruits with birds, which almost always knew how to find the ripe fruit faster than we did.

We were kids then, and we would steal from any tree. We stole from our neighbours, and we stole from the soldiers. We stole from the BWO's house, and even from the trees by the aircraft hangars, from where we always came back with our stolen fruit and three lashes each on the backside from the soldiers on guard there.

But we watched Pam Pam's paw paws from a distance. Even the birds and little moths that spoiled fruit seemed oblivious to the succulent, ripe, yellow paw paws.

Then, one Saturday, when the first fruits were ready, the harvest ritual began. It was exactly three o'clock and the paw paws looked like they could never get any riper than they were. Or, perhaps, it had to do with the sun which was hitting them at all the right angles, making them shine above the roofs. We were just gazing at the paw paws when someone pointed to us something that had been seen only once and never again in the camp. Paw paw trees were the least strong of all trees we knew, and did not have branches one could step on. Thus climbing them was not only considered dangerous, but stupid as well, especially after Trevor tried to climb one a few years back and we almost had a funeral for him. Since then, Trevor was never quite right in the head.

Pam Pam crawled steadily up the paw paw tree, a small bag strapped to his waist. At first the women gasped, making loud gawking sounds like those made by ducks. When the initial shock of thinking that Pam Pam wanted to kill himself by throwing himself down the tree wore off, we all gazed in awe as the man plucked one paw paw after another and tucked them safely in his bag.

When he was done, he made his descent, expertly sliding down and landing softly. We had all gathered around the tree, and we made way for him as he strode to his house. Later that day, we met at our secret base in the pine trees and laughed at how foolish Trevor had been to have fallen off a paw paw tree when it was that easy for Pam Pam to climb. It was also the Saturday Brighton started talking nonsense about how Pam Pam would fall off that tree one day and I told him to shut up. Had we not seen the man just climb up and down the tree? And the tree had not so much as swayed.

But Jabulani listened to Brighton. And when I left them, bored, and afraid my mother would ask me where I had been, they were still talking animatedly, with Brighton making Jabu chant a series of litanies that he said would be the death of Pam Pam.

Even though he was young, Brighton was never one to be begrudged without seeking revenge even for the least of issues. We always thought he would one day end up in trouble, but he was wily enough to do it unnoticed if it was someone who had power over him.

Everyone in the Old Camp already knew that when the BWO's house was stoned in the middle of the night, Brighton had something to do about it. That was after his father had spent the night in the camp prison cells for threatening to kill someone in a drunken brawl at the common beerhall. It was the BWO who had hauled the man in the middle of his family supper long after the incident and thrown him outside into the camp police van.

But two nights later we had woken up to loud calls from another indaba, with the BWO and the Base Commander threatening to chase all non-soldiers out of the camp for the damage, but no-one had volunteered to suggest if they suspected anyone. The work had been so discreetly done that the military police failed to identify the culprit.

But it was Brighton's persistent growling '*vakamama*' which made me first think he had something to do with it. And when I told Jabu my suspicions and he just laughed, I knew it was true.

It was this aspect of Brighton that always led to my mother telling me that the boy would be my downfall. It wasn't really that I had climbed anywhere to warrant the word downfall. But I was a bright child and, over the years, Brighton's notoriety had grown, including for swearing at the priest in the most vulgar terms, that many an adult now knew just about enough not to cross his path. Being intelligent, and well-brought up, it had to be within my scruples to know that Brighton was not good news at all.

So we were quite surprised that Brighton had let Pam Pam get away with the issue of the garden behind their house, even when he still growled '*pfutseki Pam Pam*' all those years later. But then, Pam Pam was scarier than anyone we knew in the camp and I would not expect anyone to do anything to him.

Not Brighton at least.

He had seen what the man could do. He himself attested to this loudly.

Now, on this particular fateful Saturday, which was two years after the first harvest, the paw paws were again unnaturally ripe. They looked as if they were in it together with Pam Pam to punish our sticky staring eyes and yearning hearts. So we waited for the ritual as always, knowing it would surely happen. We were with Brighton, who kept saying '*nhasi muchaona, nhasi muchaona*' (today you shall see).

We had made our usual circle around the tree and garden when Pam Pam arrived, his bag strapped to his waist and in his usual Saturday shorts. He neither greeted anyone nor did he answer to the children's usual cry of '*mhoroi vaPam Pam*' (hello, Mr Pam Pam). I had made myself outgrow my enthusiasm for greeting him, but my brother still shouted along with the other children and Brighton.

Pam Pam just circled the tree once, as he always did, and, seeing nothing unusual, he moved closer to the tree. But suddenly he retreated, as if suddenly unsure whether he really wanted to go up.

Retreating from the tree, he circled it again, before returning to the same position he had been in before. Moving even closer, he clasped the tree's trunk in his arms. Pam Pam made the climbing of the paw paw tree look like such a passionate affair that the women couldn't help but murmur 'Aah! Ooh!' as if he were embracing one of them. We had learnt of these moans in the soldiers' Single Quarters.

Brighton, Jabu and I had begun to sneak up on the soldiers, curious to see what the women who often went in and out were going there for. We had been shocked at what we saw at first, but soon we understood. Now, we wondered if all these women wished Pam Pam was holding them instead of the damned paw paw tree.

And, if Pam Pam heard them, he did not show it, for he started slowly to make his ascent up the tree, doing so in rhythmic motions that reminded each of us of what we had seen in the Single Quarters. When he was halfway up the tree, Pam Pam stopped and looked down. It was a windy morning and the tree was swaying a bit more than usual. But the old man resumed his climb, inching closer to the fruit and rising high above the roof.

He was reaching for the first paw paw when what we had always feared started to happen. Each season the tree had grown taller and older, taking the paw paws a little higher than the previous season. I had said to Jabulani that if anything were to happen to Pam Pam, it would be because each year the tree was growing weaker.

Maybe inside us we had all, without saying it to anyone, hoped that one day he would fall off that tree. So when it started to happen, we gasped, and started cheering, and then, realizing the folly of what we were doing, we all moved away from the tree, not wanting to be crushed either by Pam Pam or the paw paw tree or both. Aided by the wind and Pam Pam's weight, the tree had started to break right at the base. But it was unusual for a tree to give in where it was strongest. I looked at Brighton, and he had the widest grin I had ever seen on him or anyone.

Brighton was mean, real mean, like his father – and maybe the BWO – and sometimes I regretted being his friend. But we had come this far, and I was not one to turn my back on anyone, especially one who knew how to keep sparks flying. Brighton and Jabu knew just how to do it well.

But, if anyone had thought of rescuing Pam Pam, the tree had no time to waste on such ventures. It was as if it were rushing to prove a point. No sooner had the initial stupid applause died down and a faint '*maiwee*' been uttered by the women, than both tree and man came tumbling down.

All we heard from Pam Pam was a groan, then blood started to flow out of his mouth and nose. Jabu and I were among the first people to run away, too scared to see a man dying, but elated all the same at what might have happened. Jabu kept shouting: '*Brighton akapenga. Brighton akapenga*' (Brighton is badass). And no matter how much I insisted on making him speak more, nothing more would come out.

Later that night my father insisted that none of the paw paws had smashed on hitting the ground. But Pam Pam was surely a mess and most women and children had fled when blood started flowing from his nose and mouth. When the clinic paramedics arrived, they insisted on asking Pam Pam his name over and over again, not believing anyone could be called such a thing. So it was that Pam Pam died shouting 'Pam Pam!'

Lawrence Hoba (Zimbabwe) is an entrepreneur, literary promoter and author. Hoba's short stories and poetry have appeared in *Writing Lives*, *Laughing Now*, *Warwick Review* and *Writing Now*. His anthology, *The Trek and Other Stories* (2009) was nominated for the NAMA 2010 and went on to win the Zimbabwe Book Publishers Association award for Best Literature in English.

Lily in the Moonlight

Abubakar Adam Ibrahim

A fruitarian. That was what she said she was. If he had not known her by then, had not been inside her and heard her talk, he would have thought she was being fanciful, flippant even, like some of the other university girls who occasionally walked the nights.

They'd met in the harmattan haze, in a night of restrained revelry. He hadn't wanted to go out but Abbas had insisted, dragged him even as he sat trying to write a love poem, or a poem about love. They were two infinitely different things; a love poem and a poem about love. He'd never written either of those before.

It came to him naturally, now and then, this flow and ebb of words. Titillating sometimes. Grim and unredeeming at others. But that night he had been fiddling with his iPad, thinking of words, of their cadences and nuances. Love poems seemed clichéd to him, mostly. Apart from Neruda and Rumi. Perhaps it would be easier if he was in love. That was what Abbas had told him.

'Love is an emotion you can't fake, or Rank Xerox. It has to come from inside.'

'What do you know about love, or poetry?'

'I will tell you what I know; you need inspiration. And I know where to find it.' Abbas smiled and Al Sahir imagined the smile to be one of those little emoticons. Innocent but full of implied meanings.

Abbas was driving, so Sahir pushed his head into the headrest and took in the street lights that looked like a string of golden beads flung into the night sky. Until Abbas made a sharp turn and drove down a lane with little traffic, with girls standing under the lampposts, thumbing the few passing cars.

'What are you doing? No, no. Please, no prostis.'

'Don't worry. I've got condoms. Enough for us both.' Abbas waved away his protest, negotiated with three girls. Sahir did not look at them until they got to the hotel, when Abbas was paying for the rooms.

They were a fairly decent human buffet: different shades and of varying degrees of endowment. They looked clean, not like the proper ashawos, with unevenly bleached skin and obvious skimpiness that suggested overuse. These ones were young and smelt, not of cheap perfumes, but of stalled dreams and suspended ambitions.

At the bar, Sahir watched as they drank and talked and flicked fake hair away from their faces. And then Abbas went off with the two buxom ones.

'So what do you want to do?' said the one he got left with, the one with modest breasts and reserved demeanour.

In the room, when she came out of the bath naked, he was sitting on the chair with his clothes still on. She knelt before him, wondering if he was a kisser or a rammer. She tried to kiss him but he pulled away. She reached for his zipper, pulled it down and felt him hardening in her hand. A rammer then.

When he said, 'Can you lie down for a bit?' and gently freed his hardness from her grasp, he did not strike her as one who had paid for her services; the sort who came to women like her because their wives or girlfriends were doing the wifey or girlfriendy thing – being prim and proper, bereft of imagination.

A voyeur? Would he want her to touch herself – something she didn't like doing in front of others – or would he be a talker, one of those men who just wanted company? His hardness suggested otherwise.

She reclined on the bed, positioning herself so her curves showed, so he could see the mounds on her chest, the flatness of her stomach and her belly button.

He observed her, like a painting, with the eyes of an appreciative artist and when he pulled out his iPad she wanted to tell him: 'No pictures, please.' But instead he started typing, frowning, looking up at her every now and then, pausing reflectively. Finally, he shook his head and put away the device.

'I'm ready now,' he said.

She had imagined he'd say: 'Open up, brace yourself, I'm coming in', like the character in a novel she had once read, the title of which she couldn't remember. She would not have liked him then, she would not have minded if he didn't use a condom. But he made love to her. And if she had known he was a poet then, she would have known that he made love like he wrote poetry, in embellished verses and measured cadences. In a way that made her feel as if she were the one paying for his services. She turned her face away so he wouldn't see the tears in her eyes.

'I thought you were a rammer,' she said when they were lying next to each other.

She liked the way his thick eyebrows rose in question and how he smiled when she explained that rammers were men who rammed into women, without consideration or foreplay.

It was when he called room service to order food and drinks that she said, 'Oh no, I shan't be eating anything.'

'Are you afraid I will drug you, do some weird ritual stuff with your corpse?'

She would have given a callous answer if she didn't think that perhaps, in another life, she could have loved a man like him. 'I'm a fruitarian,' she said.

'What on earth is that?'

She only ate fruits. It was a decision she had made impulsively, as she occasionally did, after she ordered at a restaurant and felt there was something not right when the steaming eba and egusi was placed before her. All that meat and cholesterol. And she needed to manage her health anyway. She got up and walked away. Since then she'd eaten nothing but fruits for two years.

He looked at her with renewed interest, not with the eyes of a poet seeking inspiration in the female form, but with those of a man truly seeing a woman for the first time. Her eyes enchanted him.

'What name do you call yourself?'

'Lily,' she said.

'You are a weird one.' He pulled up the sheets. 'What do you study at university?'

'How did you know?'

She was polished, she was smart and looked clean. Mid-twenties, most likely. And he knew sometimes the university girls did runs, to augment their resources. Abuja was an expensive city and there were many randy rich men looking for young girls to spend their money on – of course, in return for some services. She was pursuing a degree in pharmacy.

She thought he didn't seem like a pervert. Did he get a kick watching her naked on the bed?

'I am trying to write a poem about love, or a love poem,' he explained.

She wanted to see so he showed her. Three lines on the screen, like an interrupted reverie.

Shrouded in folds of mystery
In scented dreams
Of intangible essence

'For your wife?' she asked. 'Girlfriend? Men hardly write these things for their wives.'

He was a poet. Of modest fame. He didn't tell her that, of course, because then she would start asking questions and, some day, perhaps say she'd slept with Al Sahir, the enigmatic poet. And then she would want to know his real name.

How it weighed on him, his real name. How it opened doors and encumbered. How most times he preferred to remain Al Sahir, whose poems that probe, and give offence and hope in the same breath, turn up in anthologies, newspapers and magazines. Al Sahir, whose début collection *Children of Dust* had garnered acclaim and won awards. Awards for which he never turned up, heightening the mystery around him.

Their parting was without commitments or melodrama, but with a seed sown. Such that two weeks after, with his experiment with love poems, or poems about love, still a substantial failure, he asked Abbas if they could return to where they had picked up the girls.

She was not there and he had no interest whatsoever in the new girls Abbas found.

'The vibe isn't right. My muse doesn't speak to me through them.'

'What's with you, dude? Why this obsession about love poems? They were never your thing to start with.'

Poor Abbas. What did he know about poetry, about the muse and the creative process? Or the desperation of a poet to spread his wings and not be categorized simply as 'an angry poet', 'a poet of protest'.

He was important though, Abbas. He was the one who turned up in place of Al Sahir when his presence was absolutely essential, to receive awards and the occasional cheques – only the substantial ones. There wasn't much money in poetry, or prose for that matter. But there was fulfilment, and, for him, that was all that mattered.

He was 32, without obligations and without the need to make a living. His life was mostly devoted to the pursuit of excellent poetry.

The next time they went, he saw her negotiating with another client. She had got into the man's car already so he got out of his and raced to the other car's window.

'Sorry, Mister, this lady is unavailable tonight,' he said

to the man. 'Kindly make a choice from the others and do accept my profound apologies for the inconvenience.'

After she had pleaded with her client, she got out of the car smiling. 'What are you doing? Why are you doing this?'

In the hotel, he loved her with a passion that comes with longing, with waves of eagerness lapping the shores.

As he slept, she stood at the window and wondered what the breeze would feel like on her face if she jumped. But there were burglar-proof bars on the window and they weren't that high up anyway. Third, fourth floor? She might probably break some bones. Nothing more.

She pulled a chair and sat, looking out at the street below, washed in the silvery light of the moon.

When he woke and saw her caught in a streak of moonlight, he picked up his iPad and started writing. He stopped when she turned to him and smiled.

'You seem sad, Lily'

'I'm fine,' she said.

It was bad for business, she knew, to start talking to clients about her troubles; about the ailing grandma who brought her up when her parents died, who was ill and kept asking for money – as if Lily didn't have to source funds for tuition and living expenses herself, as if she had a job, as if she enjoyed being treated like a thing because some men thought they had bought her dignity because they had paid for her body for a while. Like the man, two nights before, who had tried to shove his foot into her because he saw someone do it in a video. Or the other one who pounced on her and took her with such violence, because his fantasy was rape, bruising her before she had the chance to get wet. All for how much?

She started crying. When Sahir came to hold her, she broke away and ran into the bathroom, where she remained for a while.

'You never told me your name,' she said when she came out, a towel tied around her waist, her skin still wet.

He looked up from his iPad. 'Bashir,' he said.

'Is that your real name?'

He smiled. 'You'd never know, would you?'

That was all she needed to know. She might not have heard of Al Sahir, but she might some day. But with her, he was Bashir, the name his late father gave him.

She said she was sorry and kissed him. She pressed him to her and wondered how to explain that it was the humiliation that gnawed at her. The thought of what her father, a man of significant pride, would have said if he saw her then, if he knew what she did occasionally to get by. Full-time student; part-time ashawo. The other girls rarely viewed it that way. They said they were just having fun and making some money while they were at it.

But wasn't it his fault, her father? If he had not tried to be a hero and got himself killed instead. If he had not insisted on publishing that story about the Head of State, whatever it had been. She had been young then, seven or eight, when soldiers had come and taken him away. Two days later, they had asked her mother to go collect him.

Her mother had thought she would just need to sign some papers to get him out so she had gone with her daughter. Lily had seen him then when, without preamble, they had brought out his corpse instead. His face had been bloated and caked with blood. She had been horrified. She hadn't realized it was her father until her mother had started wailing.

She was never the same after that, her mother. When she died three years later, those who knew her said it was from irredeemable heartbreak.

Lily pressed herself harder against him and he held her: no questions asked, no judgements.

He took her phone number and gave her more money than she'd hoped for, since they hadn't negotiated – enough to last a month. They never negotiated fees after that.

Some nights they made a symphony of sensations at his posh apartment. On others, they went for walks. Sometimes they whispered in the nights, in each other's arms. Sometimes they talked about the little fundamentals of life, of the things that young men and women dream about. Sometimes he read her some of his poetry, or some Rumi, Neruda or Tagore. Even though poetry wasn't her thing, she listened with interest. She loved the sound of his voice. Sometimes they just enjoyed each other's silences; as they enjoyed the obscurity of their false names and half-concealed identities.

It was the day he told her he was working on an entire collection of love poems, or poems about love, that he asked her to stop seeing other men.

'I'm not yours to be kept,' she said.

'I'm not trying to keep you, Lily. I just know this is not the kind of life you want for yourself. I see it in your eyes.'

He offered her a substantial monthly allowance. In his eyes she saw that he had thought it through.

'You ask me to depend on you and I don't even know you. I don't know your real name or what you do for a living.'

'You know my name. Bashir. I'm a poet. That's what I do.'

'And all this money you spend, all you are offering me, it comes from poetry?'

'I've been fortunate.'

'Don't lie to me.'

He sighed. 'It's true, I have won some awards, some good money.'

'I've never even seen a book you wrote!'

He sighed. 'You call yourself Lily, and I know for certain that's not your name. How can two people know each other so much, and not know each other at all?'

'My name is Ene.'

Did that make any difference, the name? Did it matter what she was called? Was it not what she was that mattered? Should matter?

He didn't push because he knew she would push back, wanting to know more, asking questions he wasn't ready to answer.

But it hung between them, this unfinished conversation. And even though he didn't think she saw other men – she wasn't a proper ashawo anyway – he knew that as long as there was no accord, she could still go on runs and he would be powerless to do anything about it. Did that mean that he loved her; this desire to have her, to possess her? Or was it just a chivalrous endeavour to protect her dignity? To what end? Did he not feel empty without her? How did Rumi put it?

The soul sometimes leaves the body, then returns. When someone doesn't believe that, walk back into my house.

He brought her a copy of *Children of Dust* and said, 'I write under a pen name.'

'What does it mean, this name?' she asked, running a finger over the raised prints.

'The Magician. Or The Sorcerer. From Arabic,' he said. 'Now you have seen the book, will you stop this runs girl life?'

She saw how it hurt him that she had to do that, but she still resented the idea of being his responsibility. Nevertheless, she hugged him and kissed him. 'Let's see how things go.'

Armed with his pen name, she googled. Over 1,900 entries, but not a real name, not a face. There was a Twitter account and a Facebook fan page. But no idea about who he was. That was when she knew with absolute certainty that there was something in his name he didn't want known.

When he was inspired, he would sit down to write while she watched TV or read her books. Sometimes while he wrote, she would sit by the window contemplating jumping, falling. It was mostly on the days she went to see her ill grandmother. The old woman would ask for more money and grandchildren, as if these things were cultivated in gardens from which one could pluck them gingerly, singing a happy song. And then she would talk about Lily's parents and curse those who caused their deaths. On such days, she loved how sometimes he would turn and smile at her, how he would squeeze her shoulders reassuringly, how he regarded her with respect and held her protectively.

'I have a good feeling about this collection,' he announced rising from his laptop.

She kissed him. 'And I assume I will be the inspiration for this one.'

'I remember you by the window, with the moonlight streaking in, catching you in its subtle glow. You seemed so sad and so at peace. I will call this collection *Lily in the Moonlight*.'

'I love you,' she said, hugging him. She started crying. He couldn't understand why but he held her and told her he loved her too. And he felt it coming from his heart, those three little words.

It was those little words that mattered on the day he poked his hand in her purse and found the bottle.

They had gone shopping at Sahad and, with her hands full with their purchases, she had asked him to fetch keys from her purse. That was when he felt the little medicine bottle. He looked. A bottle of ARVs.

'Found it? In the little pocket.'

'Yes.' He handed her the keys and they went in. He sat down looking into the bleakness before him.

'What is wrong?' she asked, kneeling before him, holding him.

'You never told me about the ARVs, Lily. How could you not tell me something like that?' He got up and left.

For two days, his phone was switched off and she couldn't find him anywhere. Not even his friend Abbas. Her days stretched into a vast dreary field and she felt, as he had said, like a body without a soul. She thought of throwing herself in front of a bus. Or taking a fatal sip of Conium in the lab at school. She would have, but she wanted to explain to him, to tell him she would never expose him because she loved him.

When he knocked on her door three nights later, she held him so tightly their hearts, emptied by separation, melded.

'I needed to clear my head,' he said.

She told him then about the boy she had fallen in love with when she was 17. She had been naïve to sleep with him without protection.

But Bashir loved her. So it didn't matter what she had done, anyway.

'We shouldn't keep secrets, Bashir,' she said.

'I know,' he said.

'Is there anything you want to tell me?' She pulled back to look at his face.

'Perhaps some day. For now, I want you to love me for who I am.'

She wondered again what he was fleeing from. But she felt obliged to give him time, as he had given her, without judgement. So they carried the weight of half-disclosures like a burden that only love could lighten. He wrote his love poems, or poems about love; she studied her chemicals. He ate his food, she ate her fruits. They quarrelled sometimes. They made up. They made love, did things that people in love do.

But she found out eventually. She was having her shower, preparing for her evening lectures, when he called out that he was going for a walk. By the time she was dressed and heading out, she saw a green passport, which must have fallen out of his pocket, lying half-hidden under the bed.

That was where she saw his name. Bashir Maigogul. She sat down on the bed, certain that only one family bore that name. That was when it began to make sense to her.

She walked in from the rain that night while he was at his computer, pouring out his masterpiece, his love poems, or poems about love.

'How was school?' he asked, as he hugged and kissed her.

'Fine.'

She changed and made him coffee.

'Thank you, love,' he said.

Her coffee cup trembled in her hands while she sat by

the window, looking at the deserted street below as the rain slicked off the blacktop.

'Come, let me show you something,' he said, holding up a book.

She didn't move. 'I know who you are.'

He turned to her.

'It all makes sense now. The fact that you don't do any work but can afford an expensive place like this. The pen name. The hypocrisy of your incendiary poems that burn those who have plundered this country. Your father. That bloody tyrant.'

She watched him slide off the chair onto the rug, the book he was holding falling beside him. He tried to reach for her. 'I'm not proud of my father's reputation,' he said, breathing heavily. 'Help me up, please. I don't feel so well.'

'I saw my father's corpse after your father's dogs were done with him,' she walked slowly to him. 'I was seven, I can never forget. My mother died because of it. I walked the streets because of it.'

His eyes bloomed with questions.

'I put Conium in your coffee.' She held up a little bottle.

His body would shut down, his mind would remain clear. Soon his respiratory organs would collapse. She dabbed his eyes when tears ran down the sides of his face towards his ears.

'For my parents,' she said, 'for me.'

'But I love you,' he said, his eyes turning sideways, desperately. Was it the book he wanted? She dabbed his brow, his tears, ignoring hers. But his eyes were impatient. She picked up the book. *The Rumi Collection*. On the marked page, the text was underlined with a pen.

If anyone wonders how Jesus raised the dead, don't try to explain the miracle. Kiss me on the lips.

Like this. Like this.

When someone asks what it means to 'die for love,' point here.

Finally, he was at peace; with a smile on his face. And

from her eyes too gushed a rivulet of lost love. She kissed his lips. *Like this. Like this.* The emptiness inside her echoed back. What was it he used to say about souls and walking back? She raised the little bottle to her lips and laid her head on his chest.

Abubakar Adam Ibrahim has been named on the Africa39 List of the most promising 39 African writers under the age of 39. He has also been shortlisted for the Caine Prize for African Writing for the title story of his début short-story collection *The Whispering Trees*. A winner of the BBC African Performance Prize for Playwriting and recipient of the Gabriel Garcia Marquez Fellowship as well as the Civitella Ranieri Fellowship, he lives in Abuja, Nigeria, where he works as a literary journalist when he is not cavorting with riverine witches and sirens.

Running

Elnathan John

Your mother says fear is a killer. You believe her in the tentative way that you believe new information – the health pages you surf on the internet, for example, that tell you how palm oil, consumed copiously by your grandparents who died in their late nineties, is an evil cholesterol-packed killer. Or the other pages that say dragging a towel down your face makes your muscles sag, or that masturbation causes mouth odour.

These days you catch yourself saying it: fear *is* a killer. You are afraid of believing things about the universe which may turn out to be false. Still, you leave a trail behind, of beliefs you have abandoned, some thread connecting you to things you have sworn off, just in case they turn out to be true, just in case they may save you. You are afraid of becoming like your mother. Of not caring if your wrapper is skewed at the edges. Of not bothering to wear a bra when walking out to buy bread or Indomie in the morning. Of summarizing the world in catch phrases.

Dawn comes early. You feel tired these days – you wake up feeling like you need to rest from sleeping. You roll out of the depression your body has made; your mattress is getting soft. This year, you have sworn not to buy the cheapest items on sale. In the end you always regret it – the hand dryer from a new manufacturer that cost almost 10,000 naira less than the others in its range, which works only once every three times you try to use it; the car you bought cheaply from a colleague who was leaving the country, which is now in its fifth month at your mechanic's junkyard; the mattress which has lost all its firmness after barely one year. You end up feeling like exactly the kind of sucker you are afraid of becoming.

Before you returned to Abuja from Christmas in Gombe two days ago, you used to heat water for your morning tea in the microwave. Now your father, having read of its many dangers, has sent you a three-page document explaining how microwaves cause cancer. Sodangi told you he got one from him too – and another explaining why he should never put cellphones in his trouser pockets, on his lap or in his chest pocket. When you asked Sodangi the reasons the paper gave, he laughed: 'Kawai, the thing said the waves damage you: everything from messing with your sperm to cancer and heart issues.' You laughed and told him: 'Abeg, don't put your cell phone in your pocket o. You don't want anything to mess with his chances of grandchildren bearing his name.'

Now, every time you try to use the microwave, you think of cancer – malignant tumours taking over your organs, your father staring down angrily but with concern in the hospital, his eyes telling you: Asabe, na gaya miki! I told you!

With the index and middle fingers of your left hand, you feel your right breast for lumps as you get the miniature water heater from the overhead cabinet in your narrow kitchen. Lying down is how you should do it, you tell yourself. You started doing this when you visited Uju in the hospital after her operation. For weeks after seeing the huge bandage where her breasts used to be, you would wake up in the middle of the night, panting and unable to go back to sleep. Uju held your hand the day you were escorting her home from the hospital and told you: I don't feel like a woman any more. You squeezed her hand and gritted your teeth to hold back the tears. How does one reply to that? you asked yourself.

Sodangi is the one who never screwed up. The one you

always wanted to kick into the well or lock up in the water drum so he would suffocate to death when you both played hide and seek. The one you always wished would not recover from his frequent bouts of malaria. Because, growing up, it was clear to you what your father's preferences were: that he planned for Sodangi to inherit the empire. Sodangi was that brother – six years younger – who became the man of the house when your father was not around.

These days you love Sodangi because he grew up, unlearnt how to be the head of the house and learnt (you have told him this is the smartest thing he has ever done) how to let you be his big sister. And that is why he is the only one you let call you at 7am.

'I fit show later later. You cook?'

'I be your wife? Where are all those girls you have been toasting around town? Where is... what is that her Igbo name again?

'Akachi... Sis, leave matter. That one is old story sef. But I told you about the new one na. If you follow these girls, you will age faster than a military pensioner in a queue for his pension.'

You laugh, wondering where he gets his crazy metaphors from.

'Kai Soda! Which new one again?'

'Her name is Mouzayian. Her mother is Lebanese. Her father is from Abakaliki. I told you na.'

'Ha. Igbo-Lebanese. Moving up in the world, are we?'

'Go jor. Should I come later or not?'

'Oya now come. But not too late *o*. Come around eight. I would have come back from my evening walk.'

Your eyes hurt from soap as you wash your face in the bathroom sink. A couple of seconds is the maximum amount of time you can keep your eyes shut without feeling your heart stop and your nostrils block and your whole body go into spasms. Blindness is the scariest of disabilities for you. As a child you would never shut your eyes completely during your father's long morning devotion prayers. Especially after watching the movie where a little girl woke from sleep and suddenly couldn't see any more. Your father beat you and called you a rebel child fighting against the influence of the Holy Ghost, but there was nothing he could do to make you shut your eyes completely.

***

Tweezers have a way of disappearing when you need them. As you examine your face in the mirror, you notice two thin hairs on your chin just where you pulled some out a few days ago. You move closer and try to pinch the hairs out with your fingers. You laugh as you see the silly expression on your scrunched-up face.

***

The people in your Karu neighbourhood are all outside shouting Happy New Year to each other. You hear Mama Oyiza's husky voice in the background. You shake your head. She wouldn't know happiness if it hit her in the face like a brick. She is probably the most joyless person you know, fighting about everything from the way a person looks at her, to a shop owner giving her son the wrong change. You will not step out until it is dark – you are not in the mood for pleasantries and pretend-happiness.

It is 2014 yet you feel stuck in 2008, the year you started your first job. You are in the same two-bedroom flat your father rented for you. The traffic to town is better than it used to be before the road construction, but it is still a nightmare early in the morning and at the close of work on weekdays. Your room is arranged in the exact same way, the only new additions being the LG refrigerator you got as a birthday present from your fat bald boss who has been trying to convince you of the benefits of sleeping with him, the split unit AC you got from your cousin who left the country two years ago to be with her British husband, and the paintings from Muyiwa, your artist ex-boyfriend. Your wardrobe is bursting with clothes you will never wear again. Mostly hideous colour combinations that you were required to wear at least once, because all the people your age have been getting married for the past seven years and whoever is refusing to buy the ashoebi will automatically be termed 'bad-belle'. You do not care that people wonder why you are still single in Abuja. But you do not think you can bear people saying you are jealous of those getting married, although, in truth, you cannot stand all the happiness at weddings.

Perhaps you might have said, like Ada your troubled colleague always says, that you are *a little depressed.* However, you cannot say you really know what it means to be depressed. Ada is not someone you can compare yourself to. *Ada is really fucked-up*, you remind yourself whenever you are tempted to use the word depressed. She spends half her break periods crying in the bathroom, shows up with cuts on her arms and throws up food two out of five times that she eats. You do not sit up all night crying or have thoughts of killing yourself or anything dramatic – you just know that at least once or twice every week you feel like the world is crashing down on you.

Lying back on the bed, you remind yourself you must change this mattress and buy something proper that won't sink when you sit on it. There are cobwebs on the ceiling, but you are too lazy to get up now. You will make Sodangi do it when he comes. This is what you like about him. He seems to like being told to do domestic work. He would have enjoyed cooking if he knew how, but your father messed with that part of his life in his attempt to forge his regent into a man.

Now that you are lying down, you feel your breasts again for lumps. You begin moving the three middle fingers of your right hand in small circles on your left breast. *What if I actually find something?* You stop. After a little while you begin to tug gently on your nipple with your index finger and thumb. Changing hands you use your left fingers to roll and pull your nipple. Your right hand slides down your flat belly, into the loose trousers of your pyjamas, beginning the circular motion that makes your feet twitch and your toes curl up. It is Mr Bassey you think of as you breathe harder: his pink lips and his hands that look like baby hands, his neck and his white shirt and the way he always looks like he just came out of the shower when he walks past your table at work. As you spread your legs wider, you see his face. He is lying on top of you, his mint breath all up in your face like a fresh breeze. You like his weight on you. His fleshy baby hands have replaced your slim hands and his fingers now stroke harder and faster in the same circular motion. Your toes curl up even more and your muscles tighten and you whisper the name of this 45-year-old assistant-manager-secret-crush of yours who smells like mint and chocolate wine.

Mr Bassey, you whisper because the Mr makes it all formal and taboo and thus turns you on even more.

After the spasms, you instinctively blow some air from your mouth into your nostrils. There are no odours. Only the mint from your Close-Up toothpaste. You avoid the mirror when you walk into the bathroom to wash up. It feels like stepping out of heaven right into a pile of shit. *Not on the first day of the year*, you tell yourself as you run the shower.

New Year resolutions are for losers, but you make one as you squeeze some lavender bath gel into your right palm. This is the last time, you tell yourself. The last time you were with someone, the night you decided to break up with Kasweh, you remember feeling nothing, just counting the minutes until it was over so that you could go into the bathroom, shut the door and run the shower to block out your moaning while you did what your boyfriend couldn't do.

The shower does not wash away the terrified thought of ending up alone at 45 being the only one who can satisfy yourself in bed. You stop for a moment, wondering what answer you would give if someone asked why you masturbate; whether it is because no-one has been able to satisfy you or because you masturbate so often that no-one can satisfy you. It is possible to answer; it dawns on you that you do not know why. You just do it.

You pick the book you started last night and open to the dog-eared page where, in Prophet Revelations Bitchington Mborro's church, Darling, the main character, talks of a baby with 'crazy bullfrog eyes' whose face looks shocked, like he has seen the 'buttocks of a snake'. You feel as though you shouldn't laugh, like infants are off-limits, like it is bad karma to laugh about evil things being said about helpless, ugly babies, but you do. You drop the book, laughing so hard that a tear rolls out of the outer side of your eyes. It is just page 33 but already you think: this NoViolet Bulawayo, more African writers should help us enjoy their fiction like this. Most of them are all too busy trying to show off and make some goddamn point as spokespersons for Africa. You are happy that you took this book from Andrea, who fancies herself a writer even though her blog is unreadable. The book puts your fear of becoming a single, forty-something-year-old wanker on hold.

***

When you feel like going at it again only five hours later, when even Bulawayo's gripping prose cannot distract you, you turn to the drawer where Uncle Sam's prayer books are. He is a knight in the Catholic Church, and he dumped all the books with you when you admitted to him that you hadn't been to church in some time. These days you do not admit to being Catholic in public. You are tired of defending the abuse scandals and you think the stand of the Church on contraception is not valid for the world in which you live. But, really, it was Father Ignatius who chipped away at your faith. When it was discovered that he was indeed the father of at least one child in his parish, he was transferred to a parish in some remote town in Bayelsa. That was when you stopped going for confession.

***

It is niggling pangs of hunger that nudge you awake at 6pm. The power is back. You need to take two bowls of soup out of the freezer so that they will defrost fully before Sodangi comes at eight. There is just one apple left and the space where you keep red wine is empty. You do not understand why people say red wine shouldn't be refrigerated. The last time Sodangi mentioned it you gave him a piece of your mind.

'That's all pretentious nonsense. I prefer my red wine cold *jare*. The *oyibo* people who say you shouldn't refrigerate it, they have cool cellars where they keep their wine. Their countries are temperate. Is it in this tropical heat I will be drinking hot wine? If you want hot wine, go buy your own...'

The red apple is as crunchy as you want it, but it is its coldness that does it for you. You drop the two frozen bowls beside the kitchen sink and sit in bed with the apple in one hand and your iPhone in the other. There are dozens of generic New Year messages in your inbox. At least two people have sent you the exact same message: *Let's ring this new year with only good things: wish you a happy new year.*

What a stupid message, you say out loud.

Only Mr Bassey's message stands out:

Asabe, I hope you get to rest well this holiday season before we get back to the discomfort of making money for someone else. Happy New Year.

You lie back on the bed and smile, digging your teeth into the cold apple. The biting, sucking and chewing sends you into the space you have resolved not to go into again.

Fuck it, you say, dropping the apple, licking your three middle fingers and letting them travel between your legs.

At seven, when Mr Bassey and the spasms have gone, and you have cleaned up the mess, the air in the house starts to drive you crazy. The walls of the flat seem to be closing in on you. Very quickly, like someone trying to escape a collapsing building, you put on your shorts, make your braids into a ponytail, step into your running shoes and head out. You are on auto drive, briskly taking turns and footpaths and shortcuts, trying to focus on something else, anything but Jesus and guilt and contrition and damn prayer books.

In a dark alleyway between two blocks of flats, you see the glow of a cigarette. The glow rises as you approach, intensifies, and flies away into the gutter to the right. As you get to where the glow was, a slim, tall man emerges from the shadows moments before you feel his bony hands grab you, first around the stomach then over your mouth. A long knife emerges from godknowswhere, hovering dangerously beneath your chin.

You freeze. The same way you froze when Salma's bag and phone were snatched and you could not run or scream for help. Instantly you are ejected from your body and become a spectator of all that is happening. He turns you around. You look in his eyes with a blank expression in yours. In his eyes you see hunger and fear and desperation, someone who will stab you if you make one false move. He lowers the knife and grabs your breasts, squeezing them hungrily. Pulling you close, he rolls up your top and tries to unclasp the bra hooks. He struggles with it, grunting. With the knife he cuts it loose and pulls it out of your sleeveless top. He holds you tighter, breathing his Tom-Tom mint and tobacco breath into your face as he tucks the torn bra into his back pockets. You feel his penis hardening as he rubs against you. He kneads your breasts like he is trying to burst them open. He has started pulling your shorts down when he stops, realizing that you are just standing there, not struggling, not crying, not kicking. He grips you by the arms. You see a huge penis, like a long cassava tuber hanging out erect through his zipper. This is the first time you are seeing an uncircumcised black male. Apart from your panting, which is from brisk walking, no sounds leave your mouth. He slaps you, hard across the cheeks.

'Won't you struggle, Bitch?'

His shrill, almost effeminate voice pierces your ear. You put your hand over your cheek where he has slapped you. Tears roll out of your eyes without notice. You wipe them as they come. He is panting too, his nose flaring, eyes shocked. In a few seconds his penis starts descending, going limp. He tucks it back in his trousers and runs in the direction from which you came, pulling his zipper, grunting.

For the first time, you are glad Sodangi is an hour late.

***

You are still in the bathroom absent-mindedly scrubbing your body when your brother lets himself in.

'Hello hello!' he shouts, breaking you out of your trance. You turn and the first thing you see is the black polythene bag that contains your t-shirt and shorts. Tomorrow it will burn.

'Have you come? Take food from the bowls in the kitchen and microwave it. I am coming.'

Hot water has long stopped coming out of the shower head but the wall is warm when you lean your back against it for balance. Your calves hurt from standing so long. You can still see your frozen body. You slap your forehead several times, to pull yourself back to the present, to ask yourself the questions you know your mum would ask you if she knew. Why did you walk through a dark alleyway alone, that late, dressed like that? Why didn't you bite, kick, scream?

You stand in front of the mirror to examine your breasts. There is the thin slight swelling of a scratch beneath your right breast. You touch it to see if it stings. It doesn't. You pick up the polythene bag and dump it in the bathroom bin.

It is fear that makes you force a smile when you step out.

Your mind is on the man who tried to rape you – if he will keep your bra, if he is now at home, holding it, thinking of you and what he could not accomplish, or if he dumped it somewhere nearby. You think to walk past the area in daylight to see if you will find it lying in some gutter or by the road.

Sodangi asks what is wrong with you when you do not laugh at his jokes and when it takes you longer to respond to him as you curl up in the single sofa. You say it is your walk that made you tired and that you think you might have sprained a muscle in your calf and was he not supposed to come earlier, much earlier than this? He returns to mixing rice and beans with stew. You have told him before that he has temporary ADD when he has not eaten.

While Sodangi munches away, you struggle with how to say what just happened to you. Even though he is perhaps the only person you can share this with, in your heart the decision is shot down, for fear of how he will feel, of what he will think of you, his big sister just standing there letting a strange skinny man fondle you and strip you almost naked in a dark alleyway. Just like you have never stopped wondering what Salma thought of you as you stood frozen, almost like you were the partner of the young man who snatched her phone and purse.

'How is Mouzayian?' you ask.

'Sis, don't ask. That Lebanese blood affected only her skin and hair. She behaves like she is from a rice farm in Abakaliki.'

'You are just so foolish, I tell you. You didn't see all that when you were shagging her abi?'

'Haba sis, who said anything about shagging?'

'Sorry, you were doing Bible study. Or is it choir rehearsals?'

He laughs.

It is when the remote control falls from his hand to the floor that you realize he has fallen asleep on the settee. He does that – falling asleep in the middle of a conversation. You tap him awake and ask him to move to the bed in the other bedroom. He mutters something you do not hear as he drags himself to the room. In your head he is seven, reluctant to leave the TV in the living room when your father declares lights out. As he bumps through the door, you smile, sure now that you will never tell him.

'Thanks for coming,' you whisper, knowing that in the morning you will only meet the made bed, the cleared table and the clean dishes.

***

On the first day of work after the holidays, you will be glad not to have run into any of your superiors as you reach your desk, 30 minutes late, panting and cursing under your breath.

Ronke will be her usual excited self. From where she is making photocopies across the open office she will call out to you.

'Happy new year o! See how you are looking trim when the rest of us are looking like fattened cows.'

'Ah, you look smashing yourself, Ronke, in fact to me you look like you have lost weight.'

'Really? Thanks!'

You will see her stomach which she struggles to hide and the folds of her neck and her fat greasy cheeks and her massive calves which remind you of an elephant – you will wish you didn't have to play 'lie to me'.

'Who dropped the sweets on my table?' You will stare at the Tom-Tom mints.

'Is Oga Bassey o, he gave everyone,' Ronke will say.

Mr Bassey will walk past, smiling at you, wishing you a happy new year, asking if you travelled, and why not, smelling of the same perfume he has been using since you met him.

You will answer in monosyllables that shock even you. And when later that evening at home, lying flat on your bed, you try to conjure the image of Mr Bassey, your body will refuse to respond or recognize his image as anything but a middle-aged man who is too stuck in his ways to change his perfume.

Elnathan John is a full-time writer who trained as a lawyer in Nigeria. His writing has been published in *Per Contra*, *ZAM Magazine*, *Evergreen Review*, *Sentinel Nigeria* and Chimurenga's *The Chronicle*. He writes political satire for a Nigerian newspaper and his blog for which he hopes some day to get arrested and famous. He has tried hard, but has never won anything.

The Murder of Ernestine Masilo

Violet Masilo

Few people had ventured out into the mid-morning heat. Here in Masvingo, Zimbabwe, the villagers of Zaka were wise to the harsh habits of the sun. The locals arose early – at times as early as 4am – to get their chores and errands done, as they knew all about the inexorable midday heat. The lone figure of a woman carrying her child on her back appeared like a mirage amidst the waves of heat, before she was swallowed by the horizon as it gave way to asbestos rooftops, which were part of the growth-point the woman was walking towards.

Ernestine Masilo entered her local police station. The grey paint on the dirty walls was peeling and the wooden benches for the public were rickety and worn.

It was only 10.30 in the morning, but sweat was dripping from her brow, her armpits were soaked. There was a queue. She joined it by wedging herself into the little space that was left on the bench.

'God help me; I am so tired!' she thought to herself. Her torn vagina throbbed, not making the day any easier.

Ernestine wiped her brow before bending over to untie the baby on her back. The baby was 18 months old, but looked a lot smaller due to his Failure To Thrive Syndrome. He let out a hearty wail as he was released from the comfort of his mother's back. Ernestine took out an old plastic bottle which had a discoloured liquid in it and gave the baby small doses of the lukewarm water to sip. This stopped the baby's wailing. For a moment the mother and child were lost in each other's eyes. Ernestine almost smiled. She had miscarried her first pregnancy. Her son was the apple of her eye.

'Next!' The police officer staffing the charge office at the growth-point that day wanted to clear the queue as quickly as possible so that he could go and sit under the cool shade of a Musasa tree and smoke a cigarette.

Ernestine slid her small buttocks across the shiny wooden bench, wincing quietly. There were only six people left in front of her. She looked anxiously at the clock on the wall – it was now 10.45am – she had to get home before noon, and the walk to the station had taken her an hour or so.

'I wish he would hurry up,' she thought, while watching her baby marvel at the long fluorescent light on the ceiling.

'Next!' She cradled her baby in her arms and proceeded to the imposing charge-office desk. Her heart thumped as she stood waiting for the officer to address her.

'Why am I afraid?' she asked herself. 'I have not committed any crime.'

She wondered why she was still not being served. After all she was finally 'next'. It was already 11.25 – time was not on her side.

The officer completely ignored the drab and sweaty woman in front of him. He was preoccupied with the local businessman Mr Jaravasi, who wanted extra security at his nightclub later.

'We'll be there, Chief.' He grinned amicably. 'Just make sure that our usual arrangement is there, hey! It will be me and six of the boys on duty today.'

'Don't be late; the gig starts at 5pm. We expect to finish very late, probably early morning. I will have your beers and food by the time you arrive. Of course, I will give each of you something for coming.' The short, plump businessman caressed his belly as he spoke in a futile whisper.

'No problem, we will maintain peace and order throughout.

That is our job exactly.' He waved Mr Jaravasi off. 'We will be there very early, sir, around three.'

As he turned to face the woman, his grin vanished. 'What do you want, lady?'

When the police officer at last addressed Ernestine it was 11.31. She would never get home in time.

'Sir, please, it's my husband,' she began.

'What have you done? Killed him?' He barely looked her in the eye as he addressed her. He was busy counting how many people were left on the bench, calculating how best to get rid of them so that he and his peers on duty could make their way to Mr Jaravasi's.

'No, no, no!' said Ernestine, distressed. 'I would never do such a thing, how can you...'

'Get to the point, lady!'

'*He* wants to kill *me*. He always does after one of his drinking binges. You see, he is a builder and sculptor. Yesterday he sold some of his soapstone sculptures and then he came here to the growth-point to drink. Every time he gets drunk he comes home and he...'

Ernestine's story was interrupted once again by the officer as he hollered at one of his workmates who had just wandered in.

'*Shamwari* John. Don't forget about the gig at old man Jaravasi's place today. It's on on! Same payment arrangements as last time.' The last sentence was a whisper to his colleague.

'Super!' Constable John had a swagger as he made his way behind the desk to stand next to the officer. He was a tall, lean young man who seemed to have a lot more energy than his grumpy workmate.

'Let me help you clear the desk so we can lock up early.' The two men grinned at each other as Constable John called out:

'Next!'

The officer turned back to Ernestine.

Ernestine had used the interruption to put her hot and

restless infant on her back once again. It just made this whole situation more manageable for her if she did not have to coo at his baby antics.

'What exactly is your point, madam? I don't think describing your husband's social habits is getting us anywhere. Has a crime been committed and, if so, what is it?'

'When my husband drinks, he becomes an animal. From the minute he walks into the house he insults me and then he passes out.'

The officer frowned. 'Well, that's not a police matter. You can report that to the Chief's court and it can be dealt with there.'

'*Hanzvadzi yangu!*' Tears rolled down Ernestine's cheeks. How on earth could she make this man shut up, pay attention and LISTEN to her for just five minutes? 'It's when he wakes up that the trouble starts, because he starts drinking again! Immediately! And then and then...' Ernestine sobbed.

For a split second the officer felt something for her. Not sympathy or empathy; he just felt pity for women like her. How did these women honestly expect to keep a man when they were so unkempt? The girls in the growth-points where their husbands drank were clean and fabulously dressed. They always smelt fresh, with a distinctive aroma of camphor cream and bath soap. He imagined the one he was going to grab tonight, a nice high-maintenance growth-point tart. After all, Jaravasi was paying. Having been a police officer at this growth-point for the last five years, he was tired of these rural women and their marital complaints. To make matters worse, very few of them were properly and legally married.

'...he beats me!' Ernestine shrieked the police officer back to attention. 'He beats me with his fists, with his boots, with an axe handle, with pots, with pans and with sticks! He beats me with anything he can lay his fingers on and he throws me against walls!'

There was a moment of grave silence in the station. People in the queue had long since pricked up their ears to hear the juicy details. Though they were observing with interest, they would never get involved in a story like this. Too messy. It was none of their business. However, they would have something to talk about for the rest of the weekend at the dusty growth-point. The eavesdroppers suspended the reality of their own misery and focused their attention on this haggard young woman.

'He tramples on my head until I feel like my skull is going to cave in. He kicks me in the stomach until I can feel my uterus throbbing. He beats me until I can only see darkness and a few... few stars... far... far away. That is why I am here. I've left him sleeping and when he wakes up I DO NOT WANT to be beaten. That is what I want you to understand. I am tired, I am sore and I cannot live like this any more. If he beats me today he is going to kill me. All I want is to go to my mother. She is in Bulawayo. That is why I am here – so that you can help me.'

The officer cleared his throat. Why was he feeling embarrassed? He had done nothing wrong; he was just doing his job.

'Well, unfortunately we are not able to extend any welfare to people. We cannot assist you to get to Bulawayo. I am sure you know our government is broke.'

Ernestine stood her ground. 'Sir, by coming here I am already in so-o much trouble. You do not even want to imagine how much trouble I am in! I cannot go home; he will beat me. I just need the bus fare to get to Bulawayo. On the radio they said if I am abused I must report the issue to the nearest police station. That's why I am here.'

The police officer chewed on his pen.

Michael Madzimure was a builder from Masvingo who had come to Bulawayo to work on a contract basis. Ernestine had fallen hard and fast for the good-looking and charming man.

She knew that he had no formal education or qualifications. She knew he was from Masvingo and therefore was Karanga while she was Ndebele, a fact that elders from both families would most certainly frown upon. But she believed he was obsessively in love with her. He would occasionally slap or kick her if he felt she was misbehaving. It was all out of love, she told herself. Ernestine adored Michael. She had great hope for a simple, if cash-strapped, love-filled future with him.

For Ernestine 'O' levels had been a struggle and, after she achieved five passes, her mother, Gogo, had insisted she at least try doing A-levels. Her mother had a lot of hope for Ernestine's future – she was her only child, no father had ever been identified to anyone.

'I want you to get a degree, Ernestine,' her mother would often say. 'I want you to be the best at whatever you choose to do.'

Ernestine's mum did not want her daughter to fall prey to the mistakes that she had made. Her daughter was going to be someone in life. Not a shebeen-queen like she had been at her age, hanging out in unlicensed, seedy bars, sleeping with many many men for very very little money.

When Ernestine was born, Gogo prayed and prayed that her daughter would be HIV-negative despite her own positive status and God had answered her prayers. He had also been merciful enough to keep Ernestine's Gogo fit and well, with close friends and neighbours at the clinic commenting on how well she was doing on the Anti-Retroviral Therapy. Gogo was now a Peer Counsellor and was not ashamed to reveal her HIV-positive status.

'My daughter is my reason for living,' she often told fellow patients. 'She is the reason I take these awful tablets every day, twice a day without fail.'

Ernestine felt overwhelmed by the 'A' level arts subjects she was reading for. It was all so complicated and she felt she was really in over her head. The more Gogo pushed her to read her books after school, the more she hated school and her mother. Instead of concentrating on improving her academic record she fell into the trap that had tripped up many other girls before her... Men.

Michael was a welcome distraction from the stress of school work and the pressure that her mother put on her to succeed. Sooner rather than later, Ernestine was pregnant and she was forced to drop out of school – much to her relief.

Gogo was overwhelmed by shame and anger over the pregnancy and expulsion. Michael further humiliated her by refusing to pay any *lobola* for Ernestine.

'Yes, I am responsible for the pregnancy but what *lobola* can I be expected to pay for the daughter of a retired whore, who was no virgin when I met her, clearly demonstrating that an apple does not fall far from the tree.'

Ernestine's mother's heart bled but, being the survivor she was, she decided to take control of the situation. She would never throw her only child out onto the harsh, male-dominated streets of Zimbabwe. Her daughter, after all, was her *zai regondo*, the egg of this eagle, and she would fight to the bitter end for Ernestine to have a better life than her. Gogo decided that Ernestine would have her baby. Once the baby was born she would look after her grandchild while her daughter went back to finish school and attain that all-important degree.

It was not to be.

In the darkness of the night one day, Ernestine left. A friend of Michael told her he was leaving Bulawayo to return to Masvingo as his building contract was complete. Ernestine arrived at the bus terminus with a school satchel full of clothes and her rapidly growing belly.

'What the...' Michael was shocked to see her. He had done his best to slip quietly out of town. Ernestine had been a welcome distraction – great sex – but he was not willing to be tied down by her and her bump.

'You are not leaving me here alone, without you,' Ernestine passionately declared. 'The love I have for you will enable us to overcome anything and everything!'

Ernestine had not forgotten to ask about the state and quality of the love Michael had for her; she had an ingrained thought that the feeling was not so mutual. 'He will change and grow to love us,' she lied to herself.

That was how she had ended up in a rural police station on the other side of the country, where she had no family, no friends and no allies. Her life was hard. Food, money, love and happiness were scarce in her home with Michael. Her in-laws hated her. They never visited, nor did they invite. Her mother-in-law spat loud whispers in the community – saying that Michael had brought home a Ndebele whore – and ensured that the Madzimure family never accepted her.

'That stupid Ndebele leech will be your downfall!' his mother often screamed at him.

At first Ernestine had ignored the spite, hoping it would eventually go away, but things only got worse. Being literate and yet isolated, she was always alert and hungry for news and information about what was going on in her country. She heard about a new law to protect women like her.

The officer was not moved. 'Lady, you are now getting in the way of other people who need to be attended to. This Domestic Violence Act is not very clear to us and anyway the Officer for Public Relations who runs the Domestic Violence Unit and could perhaps assist you is away in Harare for a course. So come back Monday if you want. She'll be back then. To my eyes, no crime has been committed yet so there is nothing we can do. If and when a crime has been committed you can come back.'

He turned away abruptly. He knew very well about the DVA that had been enacted in Parliament to protect all

Zimbabweans from physical, emotional, sexual – even financial – abuse. He could not be bothered, truly. This women's rights thing was not something he personally believed in. Culturally women were very junior partners in a marriage. He felt no guilt, no shame, as he turned away.

Ernestine could barely see the path as she walked out of the station. She did not bother to hide or wipe away her tears. They continued to roll into the sand as she walked back to her home. It was boiling and the sweat on her back made the baby fidget constantly. Her vagina throbbed and ached with every small step. The officer had said she should come back on Monday; the lady officer would help her to get money to go back to her mother in Bulawayo. Her mother was not wealthy but Ernestine longed to be in the comfort of her mother's humble home. Her mother would always love her, care for her and her baby. Her mother would forgive her foolishness.

Her mother had warned her. 'Who will help you when you have problems in a strange and faraway place?'

Never would Ernestine have thought that her Michael would evolve into a husband who deprived her of even a cent for her own use. He kept the money, he drank the money. He only bought the groceries and everything else she requested as and when he wished. Even the money from the land she tilled day in and day out was his to keep and control. She had nothing.

As she approached their humble and unhappy homestead, Ernestine decided she would lie to her husband for the first time in their three years together. She would tell him that she had rushed with the baby to Mai Agnes, the kind village nurse, but had not found her at home. The baby had had a fever, she decided.

Ernestine unhooked the homemade wire-and-wood gate. As she latched it back on she hoped her husband was still asleep. Perhaps if he slept off his concoction of marijuana, homemade brew and semi-legal spirits, today would be different.

Ernestine made a conscious decision before opening the front door. She took her baby off her back and placed him under the big mango tree on a reed mat to sleep in the cool shade.

'He is safer there,' she thought as she entered her home, a hollow pit of fear in her stomach. Her hands were cold, clammy and dripping with sweat. Her heart was racing.

Her fears were justified.

Unlike on TV and in the movies there were no Crime Scene Investigators to attend to the scene of Ernestine's murder. Instead her body, found by a thirsty passerby who had sought water from the abandoned homestead, was carried out wrapped in a grey, worn-to-the-thread blanket. It was carried at the back of a police vehicle that was driven by the same officer she had spoken to. He was hung over and tired after a night at Mr Jaravasi's club. He truly could not care less and failed to see how his individual actions had led to this event.

There was no post-mortem done on her body, as there were no doctors in attendance at all the surrounding hospitals. They were on strike.

CSI and post-mortem examinations would have shown that there could have been several causes of Ernestine's death.

It could have been blunt-force trauma to the head. The pots and pans would have done that. *She felt metal cracking her skull and was too shocked to feel the pain.*

It could have been strangulation. His hands would have done that. *When he wrapped his rough builder's hands around her throat, she felt the pressure building as she desperately struggled to find a way to breathe. Her mind became a hazy grey. She felt as if she were watching her own movie.*

It could have been the broken ribs that punctured her surrounding organs. His boots would have done that. When he loosened the grip on her throat it was to stand up and get a good, vicious kick into her ribs. *Ernestine felt her ribs crack and an intense stabbing pain overcame her chest area. She needed to just breathe but, every time she tried, the pain intensified and blood slowly seeped from her nostrils and mouth.*

It could have been cardiac arrest. Her own body could have finally given up and caused that. *Ernestine felt her eyes rolling back in their sockets, she desperately tried to refocus them so she could at least see each punch, each kick as it came but her eyes were now in complete darkness. Each time she tried to breathe in, a strange sound of liquid and air could be heard.*

There was no investigation into the conduct of the police. Who was poor little Ernestine Masilo to try and break the brotherhood of man?

There *was* a manhunt to catch her husband, perhaps to save face. That effort came too little too late. He had jumped the border into South Africa within 48 hours of committing his crime. He had left his son crying under a tree and his wife dying in the house.

There was no press conference, there was no urgent summit. No-one called for dialogue, no new treaties or laws were signed. No human-rights advocates came to assess the situation; Ernestine was after all just another Zimbabwean woman. No social, political or economic significance.

Only two people remembered and swore neither to forgive nor forget: Gogo and her grandson, Ernestine's son. He had survived under the cool shade of the mango tree; the police and social services worked diligently to ensure the child was placed safely with his grandmother, all the way in Bulawayo.

As death began to engulf Ernestine, she mercifully felt no more pain. No physical pain. No emotional pain. No more sadness. No more humiliation. Just a beautiful serenity.

Violet Masilo was born in Harare, Zimbabwe, in 1974. She was educated at Dominican Convent High School and Gokomere High School, both of which are Catholic schools. After her A-levels she went on to study Psychology at the University of Zimbabwe. Her passion for writing began in primary school where she began contributing articles to a children's magazine. Her first novel *The African Tea Cosy* won a Zimbabwean National Arts Merit Award for Best First Creative Published Work. She is married with five children and juggles work, motherhood and writing. She writes under a pseudonym.

All the Parts of Mi

Isabella Matambanadzo

Miteuro landed in Beijing in the heart of a skeletal winter. The trees were naked. Frosty. No fruit or flower spawned from them. Only long bony fingers of brittle ice hung like arthritic limbs. Haggard. Even with their warm feather coats, the birds were in hibernation. She marvelled at how the traffic here was different from the city she had left half a day ago. It was busy and urgent. At once. As if time was about to come to an end.

Then there were the buildings. They appeared as if they'd been assembled for giants. Tall and thick. So much so that when they spoke to each other the clouds trembled a fraction in reverberation at the orchestra in the sky.

The apartment she was shown, carved out of boulders of glistening marble, sat at the very top of a skyscraper, the turreted peak of which held up the bottom of the clouds. She looked out at the nothingness in the air through windows barricaded with stainless-steel rods. Unable to see, she put her right hand between the security grilles in the hope of catching a crisp gust of breeze. She felt nothing – neither draught nor wind. Just deadness. It was as if she had walked through the massive unknown cemeteries of the guerrillas buried and forgotten along the way.

That omen should have been enough. In her disorientation she pushed it aside, looking instead at the photograph. It had an old-fashioned white border about half a centimetre thick. They stood together, the two of them. Shoulder-to-shoulder. At least 180 centimetres tall. The photograph showed a woman of striking beauty and force who appeared to match the man in every imaginable way: attitude, opinion and demeanour. They were smoking hand-rolled cigarettes.

She'd come to China to think, to make a fresh start. Or so she'd reasoned with herself. In truth, she'd followed the man, Ding Bang Dai. She snuck the photograph into the seam of the gilded mirror. It stood flanked by two frozen imperial lions, ivory fangs agape in false ferocity.

The photograph flipped her mind. His voice took her back to the place where it all began, his grown-up face becoming young and warm.

The comrades' camp was in Tanzania. There, where the lukewarm water of the Indian Ocean licks the shores of the port lazily, leaving a salty layer of crust on the rim of Dar es Salaam. The sweet fragrance of new fruit, ripening under the easy-rising East African sun, clings steadfastly to the seaside air.

Zawadi Afaafa, a third-generation indigenous businesswoman, curls the hood of her sunflower-yellow *kanga* around her head. Her hands are ornately marked with henna tattoos. When she holds her palms together in prayer, they bear the words crafted at the Organization of African Unity's 1963 conference in Addis Ababa. Her proclamation to the angels and deities for her people's freedom.

She scythes open a kinky-haired coconut with one deft blow and swallows the luxuriant milk as if her life depends on it. She unfurls giant mangoes, exposing their fleshy essence. She tears at the thick skin of sticky sugar cane stalks and rolls back the bumpy leather of a jackfruit, revealing, at its heart, a decadent mass of dripping sweetness. Bees buzz berserk delight at droplets of intense juice: orange papaya, golden pineapple and crimson watermelon. She stands back and admires her feast of fresh fruit, calling out '*Karibu Chakula*' to the day's first passers-by.

Next to Zawadi is her long-time friend and confidante,

Aziza Nchimbi. She stokes the charcoals in the *jiko* stove to a simmering glow with the damp finger of a knobbly baobab tree. She peels and pounds garlic and ginger into a sticky paste, mashing in the hot seeds of the notorious dwarf *pilipili*. She stuffs the little spice parcels into the still warm guts of the catch the fisherfolk have brought in for the day, drizzles with lemon and garnishes with generous handfuls of fresh coriander. The seafood treats are slow-fried into a stew that is served together with bowls of aromatic rice. It is the harbour city's most desired dish. Its surprise is in how the evenly grated meat of the coconut (whose milk Zawadi has earlier downed) dissolves the tang of *pilipili*.

There are no scales to measure portions or amounts. The two women use the expert judgement of their passions. They are known locally as Dada Zaza and Dada Ziza.

A tall Chinese man steps off a rickety dhow into these scintillating flavours. Dawn shimmers him inland from a rusty ship with no name. No other known cargo. Or so it seems. He stands, sure-footed on the sand, taking in the pong of moist dung. Where he comes from there are no big-horned cows with bells clanging around their necks. He watches them plod carefully over freckled shells crocheted in a net of green seaweed that has hauled them out of the ocean.

Sizzling ginger and garlic in oil, tastes he knows well from his mother's kitchen in his distant homeland, greet him. The smell of purple onions punctuates the void. It is a flavoursome welcome. As he's been told to do, he steps up to Dada Zaza and Dada Ziza, whom many first-timers mistake for siblings. He asks them for a very specific order of *Kachumbari,* the rehydrating tomato, onion and coriander salad of the East African coastline countries.

'*Asante sana*,' he says, receiving the bowl and water to wash his hands from the duo. They give him a seat facing a makeshift football pitch.

'*Kuja hapa, kuja,*' shout the pubescent voices of the young men, calling for their share of play. '*Haraka we we* Pele! *Cheza! Cheza nzuri,*' they egg each other on, laying claim to the beach. Their laughter is young. Spontaneous. Uncontaminated by life's debilitating failures. As the ball rises, it sprinkles sparkly sand into the air. They kick, tackle and race, tumbling cartwheels into the nearby ocean, leaving a jovial spray of rainbows.

It's a money game. The rules are simple and fair. The winning team takes the glory but everyone shares in the spoils of a collective victory. The nerdy boy's job, the one who wore thick spectacles, is to receipt the money. '*Moja, mbili, tatu…*' he counts on his fingers as shilling coins chink into his palm. Later, he buys and evenly distributes the prize. Cherry-flavoured lollipops and envelopes of pink sherbet.

The school bell rings three strikes: '*kengele, kengele, kengele,*' warning of the beginning of assembly. '*Twende shule*': the boys bellow their delight at the day's next adventure, this time behind a desk. Beating their bare chests before buttoning on their khaki uniform shirts, they tip sand out of their shoes, put their socks and laces on. They head off in single file. Singing the anthem of their continent in voices both broken and still unripe.

Mungu ibariki Afrika
God Bless Africa

At the gates of David Livingstone Mission School they file off to their different classrooms.

The Chinese man wipes his mouth with a rectangle of *kanga* cloth cut into a napkin. His next destination is written on it: Morogoro.

Dada Zaza and Dada Zizi are expecting him. They work for Tanzania's intricate underground. Mwalimu has made the country the capital of liberation struggles. Every Tanzanian knows about Africa. A solidarity movement, with its nodes of carefully layered cells, runs across the length and breadth of a continent whose people are determined to extricate themselves from servitude and penury. And from her shores, on both the east and the west, is a coiled umbilical cord that gets its firepower from Beijing. China is backing the guerrillas with training, ideology and provisions.

The Afrikan Tsar Princess, or just ATP – for that is her war name – is sleeping against the trunk of a heavy acacia tree, frankincense seeping out of its sides. Her soldier's cap is lowered over her eyes. She is on night watch when the Chinese comrade arrives at the camp. Her dreams are always in her own language.

Ishe Komborera Africa
Ngaisimudzirwe zita rayo.
Inzwai miteuro yedu.

She is lulled out of her snooze by the echo of a different voice singing the same chorus:

Mungu ibariki Africa,
God Bless Africa,
Ishe komborera,
Isu, mhuri yayo.

She looks at him with a snarl, annoyed that he has usurped her dream. The scowl on her face does not deter him. He extends his hand in well-mannered greeting. 'I am Ding Bang Dai, from People's Republic of China.'

'Major General Mukundi,' is her sole reply, ignoring his hand. She doesn't give him the liberty of using her guerrilla title, ATP.

The left-handed Afrikan Tsar Princess, a Cuban- and Soviet Union-trained combatant, is fluent in six languages. All self-taught. She drives her troops, excelling at both strategy and tactical formation. She has an affinity for gruelling martial-arts exercise routines. And meditation.

Her father is unknown, possibly of colonial pedigree, the murmurs whisper. She squashes these at their every utterance. Refusing to endorse any possibility that, just because she was fair-skinned, her oppressor's heritage might be hers. Her mother has raised her with the fire to fight. As she slithered, a tough first-born child, out of her mother's thumping womb, a shrill oath was heard throughout the land declaring this child, '*Mukundi*, defeater and destroyer of all the enemies of her people.'

So strong are her irises that their power empties the contents of your soul. The comrade from China, who knows the lyrics in her tongues, is mesmerized. She gets under his otherwise impenetrable skin.

Their love is as fierce as her fight for the birth of a new homeland. On the battlefield, and in bed, when there is one, they compose a tomorrow of togetherness.

She has taken lovers before. Both in Russia and in Cuba. She felt nothing for them, the men she had trysts with. Her body had an ache, more for her country than for them. Her mind was curious. Would it be the same? She wondered. Did the shaft of his manhood curve to the left or to the right. In Russia it was dull. Mechanical. In Cuba, she felt disappointment. All the pent-up anticipation of hip-thrusting Latino lovemaking went of in a deflated poof. After that she has taken to pleasing herself. The quality of her own contentment is far superior.

After Ding Bang Dai's arrival, ATP begins keeping her hair shorn close; just like his. Camp gossip attributes the smoothness of the cut to his steady hands. It is how they relax, with him sculpting her hair using his shaving blades. They study the thoughts of Commandante Che – on a screechy tape recorder when they have batteries, or from photocopies of hand-scrawled notebooks and transcripts.

Her breasts, untamed by a constricting bra, make

Ding Bang Dai's eyes look down reflexively. There is no embarrassment between them. An unexpected desire is his response. His enchanted gaze remains intense. Looking deep into the pith of her unusual face.

The clock ticks. Faster than she wants it to. Reports from home say her leaders are in talks. The comrades, scattered like seeds popping from a pod ahead of the rains, are twitchy to get back to something familiar, something comfortable. They want to head home. Daily updates in the nasal tones of the BBC shortwave radio, interrupted by the squawk of transmission feedback, promise an easy return. And then the bitterest betrayal happens in southern Africa. A nationalist lawyer and several others are killed in an apparent car bomb in Zambia. The game changes. As do its leaders. Tension flares amongst the ranks. Everyone suspects everyone. Food served by the camp chefs goes untouched. There are leaks about who might be the next hit.

A programme of elimination is under way. The credentials of children who have become women and men on the battlefront of their independence war begin to be questioned. Her male comrades, respectful of her on the battlefield, start speaking to her in the singular peculiar to men who see women as 'these things'. She does not know who to trust, the Afrikan Tsar Princess.

Her Chinese Man is recalled to Beijing. His duty fulfilled. 'We can go to-get-her,' he tells her in his Chinese English that drops the wasteful *th* for a simple, clean *t*. He has the inflections of someone who has learned his English in the African bush. 'I can arrange every-t-hing.'

She goes to China out of love. And yet, in China, she feels odd. Obvious. Her skin sticks out. On the streets of Beijing, people stop to look at her and, even more bravely, or brazenly, touch her. She feels invaded and prohibited all at once. Her hair starts to thin and fall out in tufts of worry and panic. She unravels a faded *kanga,* saved from her Tanzania stock, and makes a turban for her head. Her mind swivels.

Swirls. She thinks longingly of her Africa. How to return to her own source. The hymn that has become a continent's anthem loops ceaselessly in her ears, pulling her homeward.

Zita rayo Ngaisimudzirwe
Africa Komborera Ishe
Inzwai yedu miteuro

She jumbles the words in confusion. It is 1980. Her country is buoyant. There are parties everywhere, celebrating, swapping the Queen's flag for one in which the red symbolizes the blood of a struggle she has failed to forget. A prince with no surname comes and collects the remnants of his crown's gluttonous occupation. All this she sees remotely, on a small television that pronounces it a victory for socialism.

Her Chinese man is now busy with his own revolution. He's been made a General, following a lavish ceremony with a pig on a spit. The title has been bestowed for his valour at home and in foreign lands. It is accompanied by brass badges, salutations in the media and a change in him. He is impatient and irritated by everyone.

He no longer looks at her with longing desperation. His lovemaking is staccato. *Ka ka ka-ka ka.* Like a short-range rifle. Always in the same position. Most times he keeps his uniform on, not giving her his smooth skin to caress. He doesn't wait like before, for her arousal, but spears into her. Her delicate skin scorches and tears at his inconsiderateness. And, as he puts on his boots and leaves, saying, 'I go back to office now', her soul splinters.

She misses her Ding Bang Dai. She aches and howls for how he was in Tanzania. Singing her tongues in her dreams. The ideology of revolution according to Commandante Che that they shared on a stretched cassette. Under their waterfall, he cupped clear river water in his palms, funnelling it along her bare body. She had gushed with delight until she begged him to stop, her legs trembling with ecstasy. And he would not listen. His desire was inexhaustible. He tugged at the wool between her legs until she was swollen and bruised with elation. He was fascinated as much by her mind as he was by her taut soldier's frame. He played with the dimples in the small rise in her back. Kissing her blissfully. At first she was shy, but she became the one who led his tongue to play endlessly with her sap, spending all of her warrior's stamina.

She wasn't alone in her obsession with him. The other troops had been taken completely by him. He knew how to keep them mesmerized with his offers of dragons as dowry for their sister. They had wondered about this fire-breathing horned monster from the high hills of his land. Comrade brother-in-law they had called him.

In Beijing, she had expected to discover more of his complex threads and layers. Instead, with the passage of time, he'd pulled further and more stealthily away from her. Leaving her isolated. Disgraced. How had she, an élite guerrilla, failed and folded herself in conquest?

He keeps a uniformed man at the front of their palatial apartment. Another trails her every time she tries to go out and explore Beijing. She turns into herself and withdraws deeper into the vacuum of their ornate bedroom, fearing curious fingers and eyes will touch her, stroke and poke. She is taken ill. Her whole life, she has been the picture of remarkable strength and fortitude. Her sickness is in itself a stab. The Expatriate Doctor is called.

A man with clammy, small hands, and no words, he observes the symptoms. An elevated temperature and fever, she is lethargic, constantly exhausted. Her head pounds persistently. Unable to eat anything other than a small bowl of tasteless, weak gruel, she has become unbearably thin. Her stomach is bloated.

He asks her for samples of her fluids – blood, saliva, urine that has long lost its acidic sting. He is preferred, this Expatriate Doctor, because of his confidentiality.

The Chinese Man is suspicious of his own healers. The unexpected diagnosis causes her so much anxiety that she has to be confined to her room, her enormous empty bed. She is a woman who has never wanted children. Her way of coping with the belief that she was barren.

'Yes,' the Expatriate Doctor says, this time he is certain. 'There are two separate heartbeats,' he explains to her in the tone of one used to delivering bad news with calmness. In other countries where he has worked, this diagnosis is met with jubilation. Only here is there sorrow, as if a funeral has befallen the family.

As the General's Afrikan Tsar Princess, it will be impossible for her to break the Family Planning Policy that permits only one descendant per couple. Her resistance will be treated as defiance. An intemperate nature will not be tolerated. She will 'be imprisoned, one of the babies suffocated as an example of the importance of utmost obedience, of patriotic adherence. And so too,' says the Expatriate Doctor in his measured manner, 'will anyone who tries to help.'

Defiance has defined her birth and life. She does not understand how now, at this moment, she should be required to conform. The Expatriate Doctor, a man of much experience in these situations, whispers under the breadth of his stethoscope, 'We know a way. We can help you.'

And so it was facilitated. A trip to a less-than-welcoming London. A London dusty and glum with the threats of coal miners throwing soot in strikes, calling on an iron-hard Prime Minister to give them a living wage.

Her children are born. So alike, so similar, only one is a boy and the other a girl. She names her daughter Miteuro. It is a small signifier of her African roots, a prayer to come home. She kisses her hard and whispers 'my daughter of the soil', before swathing her in the final *kanga*. On her chest she presses, face down, the photograph. She hands her over to the expectant hands of an elderly couple who have paid a hefty fee for the uncomplicated backstreet adoption. This child of Afro-Confucian ancestry will spend her whole life hidden by an obscured identity.

With the little boy she returns to Ding Bang Dai's Beijing in December 1988. Her heart colder than the snow that clings like steel daggers to the trees on a boulevard overlooked by a portrait of the country's mighty Mao, whose eyes are everywhere. Looking, looking, looking.

Now an adult, lured to southern Africa by the whispers of her unknown ancestors, Miteuro would step off the *Kilimanjaro II*, a double-decked ferry that shuttled passengers to and from the mainland, with hope in her heart. Echoes of a brokenness that was not quite hers, but simmered still, had stopped a troubled bubbling.

She rewound the reel of her contentment. Taking in their every detail: their alikeness; the matching of their recently tanned complexions, the fall and style of their hair. Even the co-ordination of the khaki and blue in their His and Hers wardrobes; They could have been siblings, she deduced. A blush rose to her brown face as she thought of the sprouting romance between her and the unlikely man she had met through work. He would hold her hand. Knead at the knot in her shoulder. He had put surprising effort into a proper courtship to win her caged heart.

He'd told her of how he had grown up in a place where he only half belonged. With a busy, disciplinarian of a father. An only child. A mother no-one spoke of. Mostly boarding schools.

It had been easy and spontaneous. They shared so much. They were both of mixed race. Looking for something friendly and familiar. She had spoken of her parents. Survivors themselves of a small incident that had happened on a tiny insignificant island protectorate, leaving very few behind to tell the story, they had lived a quiet, stable life. On another island. In another place. Undisrupted by any nostalgia of a previous and idyllic being. They had been brown enough to cause no suspicion. Their hair kinked sufficiently to agonize an afro comb. They shared the unspoken trust of a quirky couple that had nothing else. A couple that, through no fault of their own, or negligence of anyone else, had lost and buried several children just as they were entering that age of promise.

Miteuro and her suitor were the image of the new perfect imperial class. Early thirties, and tasting success. Well schooled, professional and ambitious. They were part of the have-it-all generation. Back and forth they had moved. Circling in each other's stories.

Their courtship was disrupted by a heavy phone call. Of illness and a request to hurry home to London to her fretful parents. She arrived in the week that they both died, one of age, the other of a broken heart that could not pump without its partner's. She was the sole heir to a neat and organized estate. Not that Miteuro needed any of it. She had built her own substantial wealth speculating on the hyper-inflationary property market of a small landlocked southern African country.

There were requests in the will for her to make significant, yet discreet, donations to several institutions and individuals in southern Africa and in China that did not quite make sense to her, but that she honoured fastidiously. She was asked to check in regularly on an old doctor who lived comfortably in a retirement home. He rambled on every time she saw him about 'the other one. Two, there were two.'

Her final business was in a sealed envelope at the solicitor's. A hand-written letter. Precise and polite. With it was an old photograph. Cocooned cautiously in fragile layers of a faded *kanga*. Elaborately stitched into it were the words Ding Bang Dai, Beijing, China. It had the heavy weight of a family heirloom. And smelt curiously of unwanted clues.

That is how Miteuro, who had never had any interest, passing or real, in China, ended up sitting here, looking into the man's face with new knowledge of her inside self.

In the letter, he tells her of how, in rising, he had lost it all. He speaks of a sorrow, a sour grief he holds alone. He conveys it in a posture of measured dignity and order. There has been enough disruption. There is to be no more. He says her name. Mukundi. The shaven-haired African Tsar Princess, Major General and mother. One she would never know.

She conceals her emotions tastefully before this stranger, the solicitor, with a small, neat swallow of the saliva that has gathered at the base of her throat. He shows her another photograph where he holds, this man, the tiny hand of a small boy who looks exactly as she did when a toddler. Tears rise unexpectedly to her eyes. She has come face to face with herself. From the depths of her beginnings has emerged an unimaginable surprise. This is her father. There was a mother. And a brother. A twin. The man to whom today she is betrothed.

Their separation at birth had stabbed hard at the heart of a mother who was divided. A mother who gave up one child so that both might live. A mother who, on the fourth of June 1989 hurled herself, head first, beneath military tanks commanded through Tiananmen Square by her revolutionary partner and equal. Her lover, General Ding Bang Dai.

Isabella Matambanadzo is a Zimbabwean feminist activist. She was taught to read and write by her maternal grandmother, who until her death, was a primary school teacher in rural villages in Zimbabwe. Isabella's writing is influenced by the various experiences that women have of life and living across the world. And by the stories women tell.

Blood Work

Barbara Mhangami-Ruwende

Lady Braeburn is looking at me. I know this look, because it is the same look that dressed her pallid face the day she said clearly, like a ventriloquist, without moving her flaccid lips, 'I don't like black people.'

I know that look because on that day, she was irate with me for putting on white latex gloves before I evacuated her bowels and washed her soiled bottom. On that day, she cried out of one eye. A single silvery stream down her craggy face because I refused to share communion with her when Father Antony came to say Mass in the parlour.

That same evening, Lady Braeburn flung her supper tray off her lap with a force that sent her Waitrose Shepherd's Pie – with mushy peas – flying through the air, to paint an abstract piece on the wall opposite her antique armchair. I decided to leave her sitting in that armchair all night, staring at her creative effort on the wall, while I went to bed.

I resolved to leave the next day. I was furious. There was no way I was going to continue to stay under the same roof with the cantankerous old woman, with her asymmetrical face and one eye that occasionally took naps of its own volition, while the other one followed my every movement, in that house that smelt as ancient as she looked. There was no way that I, a political administration graduate from Solusi University, would continue in this thankless task of cleaning shrivelled-up bodies and manually evacuating bowels that were too old and too exhausted to expel their own contents. There was no way that I, Nothando-of-the-dancing-backside

Dube, would put up with this sort of humiliation.

I am somebody where I come from. I am *MaPretty* with the street smarts of an alley cat. I came first in all my classes from grade 3 to form 4. I achieved the highest O-level grades in our district: six distinctions and one pass. For A-levels I snatched three distinctions in history, literature in English and religious education. At Solusi, the prize for best student of the year was mine three years in a row and, by the end of my third and final year, I had two suitors proposing marriage. I had dreams of a Masters in international relations from Cambridge and a DPhil from Oxford. There was no way in hell that I would become like Rudo, existing in an alcoholic haze, jumping from train to train, creeping from house to house, seeing variations of the same depressing circumstances. No way.

I did not leave.

Rudo calls this job blood work for blood money, selling your soul for the British pound. She drinks away her earnings from her live-in care job when she goes to London. The wardrobe in her bedsit is choked up with clothes, shoes and bags. She has bought every kitchen utensil and gadget that has so far been invented: automated tin-can and wine-bottle openers, casserole dishes, china tea sets 'to decorate the display cabinet in my matrimonial home', baking trays, decorative place mats, cake mixers, non-stick cooking pots ('no overnight soaking of the *sadza* pot'), silverware, juicers, blenders, automated chopping and dicing devices, rice cookers – two, 'in case one stops working' – and cookbooks ('to prepare delicious meals for my family'). All this hoarding is in preparation for her future marriage to her future boyfriend and a beautiful future life full of future children.

For now, she sleeps with a bottle of Smirnoff vodka on her night stand. She says it is for calming the night madness. I laugh and ask her what she means, and she says it is a kind of madness that besets her around the hour when it is darkest. She lies wide awake and the voice in her head heckles her because she cleans old white people's shit from their rear ends while she swallows their verbal diarrhoea every day with a smile.

Now I understand what she means.

Rudo introduced me to this job. She works for an agency that does not ask too many questions about things that do not concern them, like where you come from or if you have papers that permit you to be in Britain. That is for the immigration department to worry about. The agency just wants to know if you want to make money quietly.

'Here is an NI card,' she tells me as she hands me a small card. We are on a train to a place called Slough, where the agency is.

'You are Stephanie Edwards. That number there is your NI number and you live in Peckham, London. Use it to fill in your form when we get to the agency.'

I giggle at the absurdity of using someone else's name.

Rudo snaps her chewing gum, grinding the sweetness out of it, her jaw muscles flexing.

'It will be very useful to you. Make sure that you answer to that name without fail when you get your assignment. Also, ask to be paid in cash, not by cheque.'

She snaps her gum again, chewing hard, looking out of the window.

I want to ask her more questions, like whether the NI card I am going to use belongs to the Jamaican friend who helped her flee from her cousin. Instead, I think of the money I will soon be making. Finally, I will be making money after being an unpaid housemaid for my mother's friend, Lucia, for seven months. I am glad I bumped into Rudo on the tube and ran away from Lucia, her overstuffed apartment and her mirage-like promises, which were always on the horizon, perpetually on the verge of becoming real.

We get off the train into the pale watery sunlight and I see the agency ahead: 'Angels of Mercy Assisted Living.'

Lady Braeburn has a lopsided face, the result of a stroke

that left her with a face pulled down on one side and lips that do not move. When she smiles, only one side of her mouth lifts upwards and one eye glistens. The dead side of her mouth has a continuous dribble of saliva down to her chin. When she cries, she has drool running down one side of her mouth and tears trickling out of the eye on the opposite side. She cries often, but always silently.

She looks at me as though I were someone else. She has told me snippets about her horrific experiences at the hands of another black care worker; a nightmarish tale of abuse and neglect that occasionally yanks me from sleep. The girl did not give a hoot if the old lady's bowels were stuffed to bursting point. She would sometimes leave the old lady to marinate in her own excreta for a while, before hosing her down in the bathroom with bitingly cold water, until her wrinkly buttocks had a bluish tinge to them. She would get in the lady's face and tell her that no-one loved her.

She would tell her that her son, George, had just been over to give her wages and that he had not even asked how his mother was. She would tell the lady that George could not wait for her to die so that he could get his hands on all the money she was so stingy with. She would tell her, with a smirk I imagine, that he did not put her in a proper nursing home because it was more expensive than having the Angels of Mercy take care of her. That way there would be more money left for him after she kicked the bucket. Sometimes she would stare at the old Lady, put in her earphones, turn on her iPod and blast her brain with potent beats.

Lady Braeburn is still looking at me. This is the same look she has when she listens to Mozart's Requiem Mass in D minor. It is that same look she wears as she, with a shaky hand, shovels bland, tepid and textureless food into her mouth. She sits hunched over her supper tray performing the monotonous task of giving sustenance to a body that is done with living. The look says: I am lonely and tired. Day after day, she goes through the motions involved in this business of survival, as do I. I look at her wispy halo of silvery purplish hair, the lilac cardigan thrown over her scoliosis-bowed back. Something about her frailty tugs at my conscience and makes me feel like a bully. I am not able to sustain any resentment.

On some mornings, I take her silver-handled hairbrush and, with gentle strokes, I brush her hair while humming 'Amazing Grace'. I think of gogo MaSibanda, my own grandmother, back in Silobela and how I would sometimes oil her scalp, give it a good massage and plait her hair for her. I imagine that it is she who is emitting jagged sighs and occasional grunts of pleasure as I rub Johnson's baby lotion on fragile disintegrating skin. I am careful not to rub too hard or apply too much pressure, the result of which would be the instant appearance of an angry bruise. Gogo MaSibanda drinks her tea gingerly, as though her cup is a holy vessel. Lady Braeburn sips her tea in the same reverent manner. I often sit and watch this with fascination and think that perhaps, with age, tea becomes more than just hot water infused with the essence of some dried leaves. Or perhaps the experience of drinking a cup of tea becomes a treasured experience.

Sometimes we sit in companionable silence – together yet apart – watching *EastEnders* or *Coronation Street*, munching on Brie and crackers. When she chokes, thanks to her spastic oesophagus, I pat her firmly on the back and give her a sip of water. At moments like this a feeling threatens to overwhelm me. It is a feeling that propels me to take her cold hands gently into mine and to rub their leathery skin to stimulate circulation. I use camomile lotion. I rub in circular motion, carefully, because her fingers feel as though too much pressure will cause the bones to disintegrate with a definitive crackle. We go for snail-paced walks, sit on the grass by the pond near Salisbury Cathedral and feed old bread to the ducks. Lady Braeburn turns her face to the anaemic sun and she smiles her lopsided smile. One might think she is asleep but she is alert to all the sounds around her. A twig snapping under someone's foot will cause her to open her good eye. The other eye might open slightly a few moments later, or not at all.

On occasion I find myself telling her – unbidden – about my family in Silobela. I tell her about Suko, my brother, who crawls in the dust because his feet face backwards. I tell her how everyone in the village said he was bewitched and that the local witch, Mayibuye, was responsible. Mayibuye was responsible for many calamities in our village. When they discovered the body of Dumi, the goat herder, floating in the only drinking well in our village, they said Maibuye's assistant *tikolotshi* – a creature part human, part animal – had pushed him in. When they found out that his grandmother, his only surviving relative, had died three days before, they said that too was Mayibuye's handy work.

I don't know if Lady Braeburn is listening, but I tell her anyway. My mind wanders as I look out of the kitchen window, hands busy washing dishes. Suko comes after me. Then there is Khumbulani, my sister who stopped talking the day she came home in a blood-stained skirt and with teeth marks across her chest. Her mind fled her ravaged body and has never returned. Suko is 17; Khumbulani is 15 years old. Then there is my mother, who has a Singer sewing machine and is the only seamstress at the growth-point. It was her sewing that paid for my secondary school. I got a bursary to go to Solusi University because I was very intelligent.

I perceive alertness in Lady Braeburn as she turns her head towards me from her comfortable sun-kissed spot at the dining-room table. Timid rays peek through rolling grey clouds. I am momentarily preoccupied with the stubble-like tufts of brown grass outside, on which a couple of frisky squirrels chase each other round an empty flower bed. Her gaze intensifies, and I turn to examine her. I am not familiar with the look on her face now. It is a penetrating look, a look pregnant with knowledge. She trains her good eye on me and lets it rest on my face. I notice her faint beauty, a shadow hovering behind the asymmetrical, wrinkled features to which I applied powder and lipstick that morning. She is 96 years old, a treasure trove of stories that neither I nor anyone else will ever hear. I am filled with a deep sense of loss. My eyes come to rest on her hands covered with liver spots, the fingers knotted with arthritis.

I have told her things I have not told anyone since I came to Britain. I wish she could tell me what her life was like as a young woman. I long to find out from her if she had ever had to do things she would never have dreamed of doing in order to make life liveable for another. I wish I could ask her whether she had ever borne a mantle of responsibility so heavy that her soul buckled and groaned under its weight. What was it like for her to fall in love, get married, have a child, become a widow and have her only son be so cold towards her?

I sigh. I tell Lady Braeburn about how I jumped at the unexpected opportunity to become a *Diasporan*, one of the élite who hop on planes to London, America, Indonesia, Australia, New Zealand, Poland, China and any other place on the planet geographically and economically far flung from Zimbabwe. Hunger had driven us in huge numbers out of Zimbabwe, like rats on a sinking ship, plunging into an unfamiliar ocean. Many of us were treading water; some had drowned while others swam happily. I did not have a plan when I left home, pushed by what seemed to be a biological imperative to get out. To survive. Anything I would encounter was going to be better than what I had experienced at home. Of this I was certain. The whole country was winded. The yonder was better. It had to be better. Or so we all thought. I would make money. Lots of money for my brother's surgery, for Khu to see a psychologist to bring her mind back into her body, and for me to further my studies.

I tell her of my dream of becoming a politician, in order to use my education to full effect – for the benefit of my country. I share with her my dream of doing a Masters at Cambridge and a DPhil at Oxford. I tell her how the old grey heads have to leave so that new blood can take over and rid the country's institutions of corruption. I speak passionately, louder than usual, and as I come to the end of my political speech, I notice Lady Braeburn studying me. Her demeanour reflects what I have been feeling but have been unable to articulate. It comes into sharp emotional focus with a rapidity and force that wrings tears from my eyes: both she and I are stuck in a place we would rather not be. Somehow life has brought us together, a highly unlikely meeting under ordinary circumstances.

My instincts tell me that Lady Braeburn desires the rest that comes with death, when everything stops: the heart, the lungs, the kidneys, and the blood coursing through vessels like plumbing in a house. They all stop toiling. Forever.

I pine for home, for the sunshine, and for boiled sweet potato and sugary black *Tanganda* tea out of an enamel mug. I long for a bed I call my own, not the different beds this job will subject me to, in different houses with different smells – all unfamiliar.

Lady Braeburn is tired of the manhandling hands, different hands: some gentle, some rough; some cold and some warm. She is tired of the words trapped in her head, the feelings caged in her heart that she has limited means of expressing. She is tired of the dependency that has stripped her of her dignity, the dignity that comes with only you knowing the colour of your bodily waste and the state of your private parts.

But we are here in Salisbury, on a bleary autumn day, surrounded by antique artefacts from an era I have only ever read about in history books. Here I am before her, the embodiment of a country that she recalls as part of the great British Empire. An empire that has slowly been eroded, country by country, until all that is left is the tiny British Isles, now dependent on natives of the former colonies.

Lady Braeburn signals for a glass of port. We share a drink in silence, save for the sounds of her swallowing. Then she dozes in her chair. Her chin rests on her chest and she snores lightly, clutching the empty glass in her good hand. I walk over and dislodge it from her grasp. She does not stir. I take the glass to the kitchen and place it in the sink. I reach into my skirt pocket and pull out the prescription refill which George handed to me when he came to pay me. I finger the wad of money in the other pocket of my skirt; five hundred pounds bound together with a rubber band. I am glad I have my pay. Now I can send some money home. I read the name on the vial of pills and the name of the drug is unfamiliar. I walk to the lady's bedroom and look at all the vials sitting on the dressing table. This drug is new. I am uneasy because she has not been to the doctor recently. Only he changes her prescriptions.

'Make sure you give her this medication along with the others tonight,' George had said as he handed me the vial. I put the vial back into my pocket and leave the bedroom.

I walk back into the parlour and adjust Lady Braeburn's cushions. I am startled when she says thank you, with a deep voice that seems to project to the back of her throat rather than out of her mouth. I thought she was fast asleep. She takes my hand into her good one and asks: 'What is your real name?'

I am so shocked at the question that I forget to lie. I tell her that my name is Nothando Dube. Immediately I feel sick.

She nods her head slowly. My heart beats fast, sending blood rushing into my ears, the sound of the ocean. My skin is prickly and itchy all of a sudden. A headache starts to hammer away at my temples. My mouth is dry and tastes sour. Fear squeezes sweat out of my pores, my armpits are moist. I am going to be deported. I think of rushing upstairs, packing my bag and disappearing into the anonymity of crowded London, before she tells her son, or Father Antony. I can't move.

She looks at me for what seems like a long time. I cannot swallow but my throat feels as though it is closing up.

'A beautiful name: Nothando. Sounds like music.' She smiles, a solitary tear rolling down one cheek.

Barbara Mhangami-Ruwende was born and raised in Zimbabwe. She currently resides in the United States with her family. Barbara's background is in public health – epidemiology. Her short stories have been published in the anthologies *Where to Now* (AmaBooks) and *Still* (Negative Press). She also blogs on social-justice issues, among other things, at onbarbsbookwriting.blogspot.co.uk She is currently working on a novella and a collection of short stories.

The Sonneteer

Philani A Nyoni

He had got up to receive her, leaving Hummond playing his harmonica in silence. Hummond was no ordinary man by any account, but, for now, let's talk of his physical attributes. He stood tall as royalty and mischief always rippled the surface of his watery eyes, which had drowned many women. Men dared not look into them for they were as mesmerizing as a python to an antelope. Hummond was a Matshobane of a man. The eponym derives its weight from a man whom history remembers on two accounts: first as, relevant to the context, he was exceptionally handsome; and second, he sired Mzilikazi, the founder of the Ndebele State.

With Hummond neat in his corner, dreadlocks thick and wild as the aerial roots of a fig slung over a shoulder, the man raced downstairs trying to straighten a posture which had been crooked by his occupation. He was conscious of his physiological and cosmetic deteriorations.

When she looked at him, for the first time in five years, despite her exhilaration she noted, with justified alarm, how the bird of eternity that bathed in fire had grown into a hooded vulture. *We all have to grow up* she thought, but that was easily the lightest surprise that encounter had to offer. She walked up the dark corridor, a bolt of excitement flaring through her arteries. The walls were defaced with age as though rebelling from form and assuming a new one: that of abstract time-painted graffiti chronicling histories of disappointment and neglect. If she hadn't romanticized it so, it would have been a dingy hall.

He led the way up, straight through a niggardly-lit corridor, turned left-right-left. It all felt like a labyrinth of movement meant to conceal the residence of a terrorist. He opened the door and her gaze collided with a ruder scene. I would have said 'atrocious' but that would ruin the story. The walls were mostly blue, and they would have been completely so had it not been for the streaks of black owed to the leaking roof. The water had poured through the fissures in the asbestos onto the chipboard ceiling, which hung in places like a full diaper the colour of a used teabag. When the ceiling could not contain it, it poured over the edge, down the wall, discolouring it like that election poster she had seen opposite the black-glassed National Art Gallery. It was a bespectacled simian portrait, grinning with the aggressive intention to fight another round. Faded in the rain, it looked like a correction of a photograph by God, and, if a photograph is a captured day, time stilled, the image of a moment, God must have been saying some things should not be around.

They walked in and Hummond walked out.

She wasn't used to such sights. Where she lived on the 40th floor was heaven compared to this. If she had paced the room, it would have been nine wide steps by six. Her estimate was not far off.

He grinned. There were two cane chairs in the corner close to the full-length window, which was directly opposite his food corner. In the food corner were a fist-size plastic bag of rice; a 750-ml cooking-oil bottle, which had a couple of tablespoons, three days' worth of oil at most; a 250g packet of salt; a five-kilogram bag of mealie-meal half-emptied, folded down neatly and stuck with a peg. That is how she knew there were cockroaches pestering him.

'Please take a seat,' he offered, fumbling with a chair which at some point he managed to drag on the polished floor toward her. She thought the polish made the whole room smell purple. Of course, she couldn't smell colours but she expected something that smelled like that to be purple.

She sat down with abandon, stretched her lips and a row of pearls peered between. How often had he seen that mirage in the heat of a daydream? Now the oasis was before him. He felt his tongue dry immediately. *Sweet nun on a candlestick*; what would he say to her? He licked his lips and stiffened in his seat.

'Good to see you!' she remarked first. What was on her tongue was *you look good* but she didn't say it. It would have been a lie.

He didn't look good, he looked the opposite of Hummond. Hummond the beautiful man, who stood in posture like an exclamation mark where the man was crooked, hunched slightly from crouching like a question-mark over his keyboard, or pen and paper. Even now, as if by instinct, he leaned forward and clasped his hands between his knees. 'Good to see you as well!' He grinned like a kaffir nodding at a baas. He was genuinely elated but also tongue tied, so for a while all he did was grin and nod his head while his brain tried to adjust to the excitement thumping his chest like an elephant stampede. He looked to her face and, dazzled like a Damascus-bound Saul, turned away. She had a face made for photographs, the type one could look at all day, but he couldn't look too long; ironic considering the history between them: she was the virgin he had deflowered, the thinker he had flowered.

When he turned away, his gaze collided with a cockroach scampering across his one-plate stove toward the soot-coated premier stove (he kept the latter in case he ran out of prepaid electricity and didn't have money or in case of load-shedding). He shot up immediately and crossed his legs. Smiled at her. He wanted to grin.

'So how have you been?' he asked.

They fumbled at conversation for a while. Soon the silence grew thick as fog; he was about to talk about the weather when she said she was thirsty. He was pleased to get up and pour her a tumbler of water from a 20-litre bucket.

When he dropped the lid in place and slammed it shut, an adolescent albino cockroach fell out of the handle-socket and scampered in the wrong direction from safety, into the open where she saw it fluttering about like a rooster trying to fly, scampering rather, like a madman chasing his shadow. They both watched it for a few moments until he jumped on it. She gasped.

'Oh my God, it was so pretty!'

'It was playing in my mealie-meal.' He wanted to add, 'that's why it's white', but of course she had seen it was white; why else would she think a cockroach would be pretty?

She didn't say anything; she took the tumbler and he watched that throat, silken with beauty, waving the water down. Her head fell forward and her dreadlocks drizzled over her face. With a gentle backhand, she drew them over a tri-pierced pixie ear studded with a coat-button and laid the tumbler down. Her lower lip was stamped purple where she had drunk.

'Your water is good. In Pumula the water is terrible.'

His only response was a smile. Of course, she was the girl who lived in Pumula, and got teased in high school because there was no electricity in the suburb. He wanted to speak but his tongue was paralysed on the floor of his mouth.

She was nervous too but she hadn't expected to be doing most of the talking. The way she remembered it, he would take control of any situation. In high school he had been the captain of every mutiny. The being beside her poorly mirrored the boy she knew. Perhaps he had grown up, but the growing up hadn't been kind to him. His vulture neck seemed in dire peril, propping up a lollipop head shaven clean. She thought he had devolved into a Mahatma Gandhi from a Che Guevara. In her fantasies they had met and embraced to lock tongues and dreadlocks; in reality he was bald and they hadn't even hugged a hello. His stringy biceps peeped out of a yellow but whitening t-shirt, the right slightly larger than the other, betraying his right-handedness. She looked away, beyond him – how ridiculous he looked clean-shaven, like he was permanently pouting.

Away from him, in the opposite corner, were two suitcases. One was his bedding, the other his wardrobe. She didn't know that but I have authorial privileges. She could easily have guessed, but her attention was captured by his other wardrobe, hung away from view from most of the room by a pillar. There was a long roofing-nail protruding from the wall with four dress shirts hanging there as stiff as the death penalty. From the hems at the bottom of the foremost, the sharply creased turned-up ankle of black formal pants stuck out. That is not what struck her but the hat that hung above like the bowed head of a crucifix. It was made like a Dobbs, but a scrawl that could have been a signature said Robert G Mugabe in gilt embroidery. Startled, her gaze fell away from that corner to the one across; she made out the two stoves and the meagre provisions and her eyes kept falling backward until they reached a thermal flask – beige, brightly stamped with an image of that face, spectacles and all, printed onto it in a square. Of course, she couldn't see the back, but if she had she would have seen The Ruling Party's logo in black, complete with the conical tower of Masvingo, Madzimbabwe, the Shona for 'House of Stone'. That would have mortified her, considering that after she saw the face on the flask and her eyes skipped back towards her, they fell on a downturned mug with the same portrait as upside down as she perceived the country, then ricocheted onto the face again, this time on a ceramic plate surface. She leapt as high as he had to kill the white cockroach, composed herself after two steps and stood by the window to shield her face, rippling back to calm from his view.

He was surprised but quickly calmed as he watched her from behind, uninhibited by her face – like a tiger that prefers to stalk humans from behind. The soft fabric of her pants waved in a breath of air like a ragged flag, making the hieroglyphs (like Matopo rock paintings) on them dance. Even a housefly, he thought, if it would overcome its reverence for her skin, would dance a hallelujah on it. How well formed a physique; Da Vinci would have multiple orgasms on the tip of his brush.

'Come see this,' she said, hanging onto the burglar-bars and leaning down for a better view.

He got up and stood beside her. She was nasal euphoria, he didn't get too close though; he smelt himself and she smelt him too. Unlike him, who perceived it a stench, she cherished it; it was the smell of sweet memory.

'Look!' she pointed. It was a tailless skink chasing some insect around the ledge. It turned awfully in its manoeuvring after the adroit prey until the insect flew beyond its sniper tongue's reach. Wobbling, the failed predator disappeared from the frame. Exit skink.

Her sight through the pane of glass skated the surface of the ledge and fell onto the asphalt of the road, which began after the straight line where the ledge ended. From there, the green extended into a bush veined with muddy pathways toward an ancient block of flats which stood like red-brick matchboxes. On washing lines hung cloth nappies, bleached white as clouds. Their cleanness made a curious paradox juxtaposed with the state of the bush, littered with, among other things, poorly disposed-of disposable diapers. Still, the grass, like nature that tries when humanity errs, attempted to swallow up the shit in its happy greenness.

She came out of her reverie to feel him next to her; they weren't touching but their auras were intersecting. It was just like old times, watching the world with the perspective of an eagle, or a god learning the body language of people. He had taught her that when people became characters, the characters would become people; he was sharpening her writing instinct, he had said. Creators were gods, he had said once, in the hazy golden glow of a glorious sunset from the top of a skyscraper after an hour of Physical Anthropology (an exclusive module in the custom-made writing course he was giving her), before they kissed like dawn and dusk at the end of time. In her mind they were two pieces of celestial flint, colliding to ignite a sun. She smiled, he smiled back; their eyes were too transparent to conceal a similar thought.

She remembered how they had written graffiti on the walls of government buildings, with a cardboard stencil and a spray-can, the same message even on the police-station walls: THE BUCK KEY FOB. Because writers must be brave and stealthy, he had said, most importantly true to truth at the cost of all – that's THE KEY. He had made her fearless, evidenced by all the journalistic awards she had received for ducking bullets and taking shrapnel which had given her a permanent limp as a badge of honour. She wanted to talk of those old times but, when she turned to blabber, his face discouraged her with its semi-sadness, his head bowed, staring at his toes peering out of rubber sandals.

Instead she said: 'Do you still write sonnets?'

At this his face kindled and he rose with stretched lips. She knew he may have stopped writing creatively – officially – but he would never abandon his sonnets. A lot of things might change, even his allegiances, but never that. She was as certain of it as she was that his spirit mated with hers.

'Yes, I have written 142.'

'Eleven short of Shakespeare's mark!'

'Yes, I am that close.' He raised his right hand and extended a small space between his thumb and forefinger.

'So you will be publishing soon?' The prospect excited her: maybe the old galon was hiding behind his vulture plumage, to dazzle bright upon his return to the literary coliseum.

'No.' The word hit her right between the eyes like a well-placed slug, instantly contorting her brow.

'Why not?'

'The style is Eurocentric.'

'But it's the English Sonnet, and you are writing in English.'

'Language is only a medium of expression, form is the shape

of the mind. Publishing them would be very unpatriotic.' He took his hand off the wall and stood legs akimbo. She was beginning to see flickers of the boy she knew in the ash. She half-turned and smiled, a glitter of enchantment revving in her narrowed eyes. It used to be like this; he would spill his philosophies into her and they would argue until they were babbling with laughter and no-one would win the argument.

As the familiar pleasures past crept in, she decided to bait her prey. 'Then why do you write them?'

In a fragment of a second he had winced and straightened his face, cocking it to match his tone when he said: 'If you know yourself and know your enemy, you will never be in peril in a thousand battles.' His head rocked lightly; yes, there it was rippling to the surface, that arrogance. 'Sun Tzu Ping Fa,' he crowned the quote.

In the old days he would have smiled or laughed because then he used the tone and posture to mock those who played the character earnestly. This time his face was stern as a guerrilla's; he didn't stop for her to respond, he was lecturing now. 'You see, the mind is the last frontier; these people have taken everything from us and cloned us: language, identity, we even think in English now. We took our political independence by the gun. They would not give up the means of production, so we took it by force and they fought back; they crippled our economy with sanctions, now we are claiming our minds. We will have our full sovereignty one day. That will be true independence.'

There was a joke that had done the rounds in her circles when The Simian was saying Fat Cheeks asked for sanctions from the West. It said The Simian is the one who had told Blair to keep his England, which technically was a request for sanctions. Of course she wouldn't say that to him.

'We are at war on all fronts; the West is trying to undermine the sovereignty of Zimbabwe. They have tried everything from name-calling, sanctions, to puppets like Tsvangirai to undermine us at every turn. Now they have their agents of neocolonialism trying to destroy our culture with gay nonsense. We do not need them and their filthy ideas.'

She wanted to retort that no organism or country can survive in isolation, wanted to ask if he sincerely thought the murder of the agricultural sector had no impact on an agrarian-based economy, but at that moment a retarded boy who was known to roam the neighbourhood ran into the green outcrop of grass, dropped his pants, stuck a bisected black moon at them and coiled a brown rope onto the grass. She looked away. The man hadn't seen it. She wanted to say something but he was terrifyingly absorbed in his utterance, with more emotion in his voice than a heartbroken Pavarotti.

'We must safeguard our independence that was paid for dearly with life and limb. They envy us, the soaring majesty of our lands, the glorious sun that kisses like an adulterous god. They want to be like us, so how must we be like them? We must enjoy what we fought for; what we fought for is beautiful.'

She looked away. She couldn't look at the green because that kid might still be there, expelling ropes in the open, so she looked at the road in raw disbelief, with a sliver of disappointment. Her eyes were in time to capture a cyclist making a narrow escape by veering into the road to avoid a neat silver Audi with Mpumalanga numberplates evading a pothole the size of an average moon crater. The bike was Lamborghini-yellow and its trendily angled arm read Diablo. The colour seemed an odd coincidence of time, considering that, as it slid out of view, a man rolled past pushing a yellow Scania pushcart. It reminded her of a John Eppel poem, *Aluta Continua*. Although the exact wording evaded recital, she recalled the irony the poet presented, of an ex-combatant who spoke proudly of a time in the Seventies – during the war – when his landmine took out a Rhodesian Army Scania while pushing his Scania along Robert Mugabe Way. This pusher may have been lean with the toil of his occupation and the choking of suffering, but his hair, ash-of-decades drizzled to look like guinea-fowl plumage, suggested he was old enough to have fought in the war.

From my authorial vantage-point I can tell you that he trained in Moscow with The Black Russian: Dumiso Dabengwa and the infamous Black Swine, who once stepped onto a podium loaded with explosives as Dabengwa's doppelgänger and ended up hanging from a tree by his intestines. He survived with horrid belly scars that made for spine-tightening drinking-stories until his death in 2012 at Mpilo Hospital. Mpilo, that's life, had failed to give him life lying there in his own bedding, next to other patients sleeping on the floor because the hospital had run out of beds. Dabengwa is still alive though, running a government-affiliated Non-Governmental Organization that has for decades been said to be bringing water from the Zambezi to drought-prone Matabeleland.

When the Scania had rolled away, it revealed a woman she hadn't noticed before, squatting at the roadside with a fire, roasting mealies. She would not have noticed her, had it not been for the customer screaming at her in Shona for giving her change in South African rands. He was wearing a Ruling Party t-shirt, once green now lime. It was only a guess because she couldn't see most of the inscription on the back but she wagered that only a Ruling Party shirt would be printed with something that definitely ended with the word 'sovereignty'. *Sovereignty with no currency* she thought to herself. It was odd to her that anyone would be wearing a Ruling Party shirt in Bulawayo, considering that, even though it had secured a three-quarters majority in the last elections, it had failed to secure a single seat in Bulawayo. Once, discussing it with her editor, she had remarked that the city had not voted for Fat Cheeks, rather against The Simian for no-one could take Fat Cheeks seriously, especially after winning an election and settling for an imaginary position for five years. What was the popular phrase? Rather a donkey than a geriatric Simian. Despite the rude customer's loudness, she couldn't hear a word because when she had left the country Shona wasn't a language one heard every day in that part of the country. She could only make out the details by the woman's responses made in Ndebele, which were chorused by the rhetorical 'what should I do then?'

Saddened by what she saw, she turned fully away from the window. 'Can I see the sonnets?'

'Sure,' he said, and went to get them. They were concealed beneath his mounted suitcases. He was glad she had asked: he loved showing her his work but most of all it untangled the awkwardness. He handed her the counter-book filled with his scrawl. She could read it legibly; she could always read his handwriting, at times better than her own. She leafed through and at random stopped on this one:

I lay my head on my pillow and ignite a dream,
The night illuminates with phantasms of you,
Of me, of us in cryptic dance, moonlight beam
Like a limelight. The world's a theatre it's true,
And we the players on the grand proscenium;
Galleries watch our art. A god and a queen,
Pan and Elizabeth, can spawn to the coliseum
A race of Thoth avatars, silence the muezzin,
Religious defecation and deification refigured,
A dynasty of forever, daughters of immortals!
Was Spenser's Elizabeth so fiercely courted,
Or was he unworthy in deficiency of laurels?
My queen, Magdalene, a god bows a request,
Follow me and we put eternity to the test!

When she finished reading it she turned to him. 'Is this a love letter to NoViolet?'

'No, hell no!'

She's a sellout, he wanted to add, she guessed. The time spent in his presence had revealed how bitter and uncharitable he had become. When he continued, she smiled, sadly.

'She sold out her country: that's why they wanted to give her the Man Booker. They only offer it to people like her and Rushdie.'

She didn't agree with him: as an expatriate, she related to NoViolet's work. And she wanted to point out the similarity between Rushdie's Civic Beautification Programme from *Midnight's Children* and Mugabe's 2005 Operation Murambatsvina when 'illegal structures', including people's homes, were razed to the ground on a promise of resettlement in lands yet to be cleared for construction. It uncannily coincided with an amendment of the electoral law that required people to vote only in the constituencies they had registered in. Deprived of a home in the icy grip of June; disenfranchised too.

If she had pointed out the similarity, it wouldn't have ended there. She would have dragged Orwell into the scene – *Animal Farm* – for she figured the aptitude of the prophecy in this regard: in 1980 after running out Mr Jones or Smith in the local context, all animals were equal but before that very year was done, a genocide had reared its serpentine head. By 1983 the North Korean-trained Fifth Brigade had wiped out more civilians in Matabeleland than the 'terrorists' it claimed to be hunting down. She didn't say anything.

He had taught her most of this history, which was never found in her school syllabi. She had studied history for six years, only to be convinced that nothing significant had occurred between Lancaster House and the Unity Accord. It was he who had encouraged her to look with a more perceptive eye. To question why the terms of the Accord dubiously sounded like a peace settlement without the mention of a war in her books. A Vienna without Napoleon, a Versailles without the Great War. He seemed to have forgotten his own lessons. They had stolen her love away.

She turned the page again, hoping for something different. It seemed even a simple love poem could get political with him. And then she found it. And she knew like the *mantengwane* knows it will rain, that it was about her, for her – though she might never have seen it but for that visit. She knew because purple had always been her colour.

Pout your lips like pistils discharging sweet poison,
Honeyed dew on purpled precipices of ecstasy.
Flower of eternity; let me climb your stalk to the sun
Like Jacob scaling his ladder in a bout of lunacy
And knock back vast vats of the heady wine
Of your mouth. That mouth, let me hear it spew
Incantations with its pours of the forbidden divine.
Let me climb and burn in your lips' bloom like dew,
O let me climb from this heath to the hearth
Bones of death-somnambulist kings would renew!
Kiss me long, kiss forever and swallow my breath,
In beautiful dying let my whole be shed into you!
Time always stills when I am in your watch,
In the taste of your lip eternity would crouch.

He looked down and crossed his legs. Recently he had come to think it unmanly to show such emotion. And her reading of that poem had made him feel like she had decoded the cipher of his soul. That wasn't the only reason he didn't slake his thirst for her kiss; he was also scared. She had changed so much and he had taken a turn in the opposite direction. He felt... unworthy.

When she read the sonnet, her heart was elated because now she knew, not just in her heart and spirit but also by evidence, that she was not alone in her feeling. He wanted her too; to share his breath into her mouth and rekindle the ambers of a golden time. South Africa had made her more liberal; before, even with him, she would have hidden her desires, because that is how she had been raised, to be modest like an unfeeling, metallic being – subject to the whims of a man. She had been taught to put up with all hardships in relationships and, in marriage especially, to let the man lead – to follow like Ruth, no matter how much she had to take, and hopefully survive and live, unlike her poor aunt who had been knocked into a daze with a burning log by her husband and denied medical attention until, five days later, her spirit gave out. But she was a different person now, and she would get what she wanted.

'I live my life to the full at every moment, I don't like to have regrets. I think it's better to regret something you have done rather than what you have not.' Her voice was low and slow, her eyes dazed.

He knew what she meant but didn't know what to do. The angle made it more awkward: if she had been standing, he would have worn bravado until it turned to bravery, but, the way they sat, his oft-praised imagination was frozen. He tried but to his horror found that he couldn't move. His bottom was stuck to his seat like a dictator to his throne. His tongue grew heavier, his eyes wide with fright. A legion and a cavalry marched in his chest. In the silence, threatened by his booming heart, he heard the radio from the next room, it was the four o'clock news and it began like almost every news bulletin: 'The head-of-state and government, commander-in-chief of the Zimbabwe Defence Forces and First Secretary of ZANU(PF), his Excellency comrade Robert...'

He shot up like porcupine quills arming. 'I need to use the bathroom,' he announced and made his exit, leaving her wide-mouthed. As he walked into the corridor to the communal facility, Hummond walked in. Hummond knelt before her, told her how beautiful she looked and how his soul had thirsted to see her, how grateful he was to her and Providence for her visit – even if it was for a short while. Hummond was also a sonneteer. She began to speak but he raised a finger to hush her. Then he spoke:

'If it is love, say it with closed lips;
I'll hear only the voice in your chest.
Mine is poised for what yours speaks,

Tell it about the pleas in your breast.
Say not one word, just shut your eyes;
Have you not heard love has no sight?
I taste your breath, swallow your sighs,
Drop your gown, unclothe your heart,
Crush the wick and kill the candle:
Let's make our love as blind as Cupid.
Say nothing, I will read you in Braille...
...Your blood is ink, lucid and livid.
How your body speaks to my feel,
Two deep chasms each other fill.'

With that he clasped his mouth to hers and eclipsed the day.

All the while, our friend in the bathroom was gaining tightrope-walking efficiency on the bathtub edge. He wobbled and almost crashed his skull open on the mist-cooked wall. Despite his restlessness, he decided to be still for a few moments, stood at the far end with the taps between his feet and looked out of the window, at the township which had only deteriorated since Independence. On the roofs among other junk were rusting bicycle frames and Springmaster beds.

To Hummond, the bicycles would have symbolized aborted journeys, a long wait for beds, lying while politicians lie. Two spare-limbed police officers ambled down, the female staggering under the cumbersome load of an FN assault rifle. Hummond would have made a sarcastic remark about gender equality. Hummond, being the cynic he is, would have remarked that their frames suggested honesty on their part, or junior rank – probably recent recruits. The FN, which proved inefficient in the hands of Rhodesian forces matched against guerrilla Kalashnikovs, in the hands of the police was a dark symbol of retrogression. But Hummond was more concerned with fulfilling fantasies.

The man watching didn't see things with Hummond's eyes. In fact, he saw but didn't notice the police; he was figuring out what he would say to her, how he would initiate the kiss they both wanted so badly but he couldn't get himself to angle for. Softly, as a lover's morning whisper, the words came to him:

> It is not enough that we think our love,
> Love's gluttony demands I swallow your air
> To weave my heart's fingers like a glove
> Around it and watch the poetry flare.
> Apollo's sun will wilt, witlessly struck by
> The ray of your brazen flair leaping from
> Twenty-six characters poised to fly:
> The ugly-duckling grown into a swan's form,
> Verbal origami, still animation,
> Thoth thought-vexed tumbles to the ground,
> Pleads his submission. Poetry in motion
> Heavenward spiralling, twirling every cloud
> Into its vortex until all the gods are dethroned,
> You are their queen, and I your king crowned.

There it was again, the godly inference. He smiled: he would have been a god with her kiss. He had been once but circumstance had dethroned him. There was not enough justice in the world. Once he had felt free, but now the yoke of purpose burdened him. Most of all he tried not to resent her for being a more successful journalist. Served him right: he had once called it an artless profession but it became a solution when the question of paying the rent arose. It was bad enough that he was good at a job he didn't like; worse still that she was better, that his protégée had beat him outside the classroom.

While he sulked to the open opaque window, in the other room she was laughing and peering at Hummond with dilated pupils, her blink rate increased. He touched her and she relaxed in his touch, he was going to kiss her again and the situation would escalate. She anticipated his slow methods which would boil her blood to a level that only their combined sweat could cool.

The man, spreading his gaze over the symmetrical township rows out the window, willed himself into going back in there but his courage failed to rise to the call. So he stood there, while she giggled with Hummond, the hazy eyes of the love-drunk somnambulist dancing on the surface of his face like a spirit-medium in a frenzy of possession, closing in on the kiss ages thirsted for.

With a heave such as Kirsty Coventry would take before plunging into the blue after an Olympic medal, he alighted from his cowardly perch and strode, with the steps of a man intent on executing a coup d'état on the other side. He opened it and she felt a gust of air flee his figure at the door while he stood like Napoleon, sick of Elba, returned to all his glory.

She swallowed Hummond.

They locked eyes like sparring buffalo bosses, the atmosphere thickening, each breath threatening to burst the time-tested walls. He was heaving deep, her mouth parted in silence, he took a step and she stiffened, anticipating him, eager for him in an unholy way, though the purest of love rippled in her chest like some mythical monster, the Nyaminyami perhaps, stirring beneath Kariba waters. That creature, humongous water serpent stirring the meniscus of her eye, sought to swallow him whole. He took another step, two more towards a heaven religion could not offer – he took the first in her direction, but, to the dismay of both, then veered towards the window, where he hung on the burglar bars with his back to her. He wished he could turn round, but there was so much he had to overcome. The shame of not rising to the occasion was even more emasculating than erectile dysfunction.

Couldn't he see, how she thirsted for him like the desert for the rain? Couldn't he see how she yearned to make art with him, or let him make an artwork of her, paste her as a mural on the wall, write dancing hieroglyphs of forbidden pleasure on the caves of her soul in his breath, spread it into her like the Holy Ghost yeasting Maria's belly? Couldn't he see how she wanted him to conjure ghosts of Hummond's form in the hollows of her inner being? And she would give out her soul in heaving, sweet delirium, gasping to the sky like an uninhibited Alleluia, as the tension built within, ecstasy expanding her chest high, high, higher, tilting her head back in the quenching of half-a-decade's thirst, until finally relinquishing itself in a spray of aural graffiti that would shake the sky and tumble heaven into her gaping mouth. Couldn't he see the wanting she had for him? The silence pleaded, it was written on her face, her eyes spoke it – why, why couldn't he do it?

She stood up. They were facing away from each other, he out the window staring at teen boys sharing a quarter-jack of a popular dollar-whiskey smuggled from Mozambique, and she staring at the wall. If her eyes could see what they were facing they might have seen smudges that someone had once suggested looked like a cracked map of Zimbabwe.

'I was wondering,' he began in a cracked voice, before he paused right there to correct it. He hated the way he sounded, but he had failed for too long and the aching within would not relent. He continued: 'What your lipstick tastes like.'

She had tilted her head to the side at his first words. In this position, hung low, her mouth released: 'It tastes purple.'

He turned. 'That has always been my favourite flavour.' He walked towards her.

She was looking the other way, which helped his bravado such that every step felt lighter. By the time he reached her, he was walking on cushions of air, like a stairway to heaven. He clasped his arms around her shoulders, her hair was in his face but he didn't mind; the scent was intoxicating and he was an addict of that aroma so long denied. Instead of being weaned off it, want had only grown as fat as the time between. His head fitted perfectly in the angle between her neck and shoulder where he had dreamt contentment and freedom seemingly eons ago. The only movement she made was to drop her shoulders in relaxation. Sweet, old, familiar, the misty ghost of history condensing into a present: a gift of time. They rocked sideways, in a silent rhythm for a while, until she turned and drowned in his eyes. Their torsos did not touch but their hearts could hear each other pounding a mutual song. They had synchronized in desperate beating, breaking tempo only when his courage was dry, but now the time had been corrected and they beat to the same staves. In fact, when they stood facing each other, immobile, their hearts shifted to align one to the other, so that when they clasped bodies their hearts would also be touching but for the flesh and ribs caging them from their most sincere desire. They watched each other, front to front forming a palindrome, Shakespeare's beast with two backs. His head was slow in its arching to the right, hers too turning in a mirror image, mouths anticipating ambrosia. Right before noses brushed, eyes shut like a moment of peaceful dying when breaths of heaven whisper to the pious. They could feel each other's breaths, ghosts of fire, but before their oyster mouths clasped over the pearl, her phone vibrated in her pocket with such violence that she jumped and he would have fallen flat had he not staggered two steps back. She could have ignored it but the moment was already broken.

She looked at the screen and her brow crumpled, realizing who was calling. She gasped at the time passed. It was already 4.30pm. She answered it while he stood, intent on completing his mission, but his courage soon wilted and he drooped into a chair like his withered heart when she turned from him and told the caller she was on her way.

When she hung up she watched him for a while. He did not hide his disappointment; she didn't enjoy wounding him because it hurt her too. Let me refrain from resurrecting a scar of history and unravelling gory details. Let me say she left soon after that to meet her fiancé who was parked not far from there.

They walked out into dazzling sun. The despot in the sky seemed more oppressive than ever. When they reached the car, she introduced the two men, one of whom felt he should have been the other, wearing a stiff deep red polo-shirt, smiling unconvincingly and shaking hands reluctantly.

She slid into the front seat – equally reluctant. She wanted to hug the man, but not in view of the driver who had heard a lot about the disappointing figure. She smiled at him sadly.

'It was good to see you,' he said in farewell, hoping she would at least tell him when she would come see him, since she now knew where he would be found the entire time she was in the country. Maybe then courage would not conspire against him. The engine leapt to life, roared like a beast asserting territorial dominance.

'*Soixante-neuf*; the pleasure is mutual,' she said, craning her head back as the car rolled away towards Christmas dinner with the driver's folks, slow as a baiting coquette.
Soixante-neuf, a neat turn of Gallicism, he thought, considering that, in French, a culture famous for kissing with tongues, anything could be a sexual innuendo, even a number – especially if that number happened to be sixty-nine. He watched the car roll away.

Hummond was sitting on the driver's lap, pretend-grasping the steering wheel, watching her more than the road, his hand slung over her shoulders.

Back in the room the man watched the stains on the ceiling, but he couldn't watch for long. He felt like his whole inner being had evaporated only to be splayed above in the abstract of the Sistine Chapel. How close he had been to touching the hand of God.

Do not kiss me goodbye ray of December,
I cannot bear to separate myself willingly
From your fragrant bosom's bower;
Do not tempt my mouth to speak sinfully.
Just go, but when you are there write,
That our fragile moments may strengthen
And lend their solemnity to my art.

When all the world sleeps may it awaken,
Armed to sculpt emotion from a rock face,
Burn it to ink, paint with words an aureole
As bold as an aurora of rage into place
Above your head while tears shed like fall,
Significant of winter coming after you go.
Au revoir, when do we meet to part no more?

There was a mirror behind his stiff shirts. He brought them down and viewed himself. The image clawed at the wound the meeting had inflicted in his spirit. Clawed such that his innards spilt onto the floor and he watched them with appalled scrutiny, rearranged in the lingering spirit of the meeting hovering about the room. *What have I become?*

He looked into the mirror. Hummond wasn't in it. Hummond should have been in his mirror, but Hummond wouldn't have been living there, his story would be entirely different. Hummond would have been a successful novelist and, if he could help it, he would never have let her out of his sight. He wouldn't be peering at mirrors because Hummond would have spent every spare moment having and holding her as his wife.

The man blinked and saw to his horror that Hummond was standing in the mirror, hollow eye-sockets accusing in silence. Hummond's throat was slit and black blood gushed, washing down his naked body, bloodying his feet like a crucifixion. It pooled on the floor and rose to drown him. He turned away from the mirror, but ghastly Hummond was everywhere around the room in various poses of desolation and persecution. The man fell to the floor and clutched his head as though to snap it off the twig-neck. Jesus, he wept.

He looked up again and Hummond was standing over him. He shook and fell back.

'Stay away from me; you are not real!'

'Yet here we are.' Hummond's voice was metallic and scraped in his ear like a nail of judgement.

'What do you want from me?'

Hummond's bloodied finger shook as he spoke. 'I am the vision you dreamt and poured into her figure as a messiah. I am the bloom your bud threatened but you have crushed the beauty of the promise. I am the heart of truth you have concealed behind tinted eyes and a hollowed tongue. I am the fulfilment of you. Give me life.' Then Hummond walked towards him. The man froze, shook like an epileptic, as the fierce doppelgänger stepped into him. As Hummond entered his body, the man opened his mouth and, with a frightening scream, released his broken form to the sky. He looked down, found a pen and began to write.

THE LAST SONNETS

Patria Mori
My country's offspring are scattered like ashes
In the wind across the orb fertilizing other
Lands. What remains are skeletal sketches,
Marrow of the portrait vanished into despair.
Our eternal culture of bacterial resilience
Survives a hope once hinged on the anti-air,
Winged there by a spear thrust in the defiance
Of spirit mediums who said *kill the flesh*
but you cannot harm the breaths of revolt
Clamouring for freedom. So what is a nation,
When all we know is toil-sweat and its salt?
Is it still my country when I fight it to stay alive
Or is my country, my home, yet to arrive?

Legacy
There on that acre of heroes and heroines
Shall they partition a gulf in the belly of the
Earth like they dug for Mama Mafuyane
When she bowed, to swallow thee
When fallen Caesar. The spray of madrigals,
Of madmen twirling with virgin girls,

The beardless boys and blazing veldts,
Friends, foes and cynics' scenic tales,
The fish in Kariba humming harmony with
The basalt and granite of Masvingo (the true
Zimbabwe) shall perfume the air with myth.
What song, dirge or mirth? Grins or blues?
What colour shall be your name
After the red has clotted in your vein?

Pro Patria Mori
Patria mori is a mirage so near yet ever far,
A distant mass-dream of promises ever looming,
A child trapped in gestation, fathered by a martyr
Too long gone to ask when shall be the blooming.
My nation's most apt symbol is the flame-lily:
She is a lily to some and a flame to the rest.
She is that most majestic and wild filly,
We would go far on her back well harnessed.
O flame-lily watered in the tears of a man-child,
Where is the nectar for which he wept?
Ophir, land of milk and honey of legend,
Not so fair, keeper scored by the bees he kept.
The land of birth should be the land of abode,
But mine is choking me with my umbilical cord.

Children of Death
Behold the chaff your rain could not wash!
We are the foetuses that shrank from the stabbing
Of the bayonets but crawled out with the gush
Of mother's intestines. Our first sight was her dying.
We are the stalks that survived the Whirlwind,
Though leaning our crowns almost to the ground
Rose again, watered in blood to stand like kings.
We have returned to salt and pepper your wounds,
We, sons of the Lots that survived your holocausts
O ancient demi-god of abominable pleasures,

We, sprinkles of those who spat at death in revolt!
Herod, see the Christs you sought in the manger?
We do not seek vengeance or to feed you your bile,
Our vengeance is our existence, revile our smiles!

The House of Hunger
In the house of hunger teacups are missiles,
Especially the Kango ones that can be reused.
I crouch over my pad composing missives
Of bleeding whores, turning menstrual fluid
Into image of cuntree bleeding but won't die.
Mother cursed me Marechera, hunger arming
The teacup again. She tossed it, let out a sigh
As the feeble throw refused any hurrying
At my mane, withdrawn in time to let it pass,
Crash into the wall behind where flies perished
In wait of manna from starving gods' mouths.
Civility has perished, polished façades buried
Behind loud epitaph of form alongside dignity.
And now strides the animal side of humanity.

Benevolent Leader
Statesman, pith pouring pitch and molasses,
What hellish night clouded your heart so?
Burning at bearing cruel countless crosses?
Is that the colour of reluctant scars of war?
Son of Nkrumah spared your father's fate,
Did you not ever think it, that Fate withheld
A hand so you'd undo the ill your father did?
Your longevity into a curse you have turned,
I pity your sons with so long to live after you,
One of them wears your fouled names both.
As for your daughter what fate do you ensure,
For your spouse, Macbeth's harpy in loathe?
Will Wisdom be vindicated by her children?
Far too long from light have they lain hidden.

Dulce Et

If you were to walk down Joshua Nkomo Street
And ask those girls why the statue faces North,
They will not say, they only know how to greet
You with a smile, tell you the price not the worth
Of great Mqabuko's life as recorded in a book
Much thinner than the one the man actually wrote.
They will speak about his arm, a shepherd's crook
All embracing, but not the gallant words he spoke
In his historic address from the Mahomva shops.
They will not tell you about his Pelandaba home;
Bullet-riddled as he escaped by the hair of his nuts,
Nor will they tell how the Unity Accord was born.
They will simply say he was a great man and one,
As though they were placed there to dim his sun.

Waiting for Godot

On a familiar strip of earth I watch walk
Dante and Virgil. The latter acting guide,
Points forward at a silver-black snake
And beyond to words too far to be read.
A boatman called answers to 'Charon'
And rows over the serpent I call Limpopo
But Virgil to Dante names River Acheron.
Then the fire-branded words start to show:
ABANDON HOPE ALL YE WHO ENTER HERE.
A muzzled crowd marches under a cockerel
Banner around, around. Dante with a tear
In his throat, a cry on his face turns to Virgil:
'What invisible cord is it that binds them
That they keep looping about this hem?'

Waiting For Godot II

'What holds them fast to this self-imposed slavery
Of perpetual indifference that they trudge every day,
Loyal as the rising day, seemingly not growing weary

Until their souls bleed through their soles to the clay?'
Virgil raises his brow and follows its height with voice:
'This where we stand is quite a peculiar kind of hell,
These we watch here, saunter through life indecisive
And thus are eternally condemned to this vestibule,
To follow the cockerel's banner through all eternity.
They live a life unworthy of praise and unworthy of
Blame, theirs is simply existence. They are the Ignavi.
See how they are stung yet don't wave the wasps off?
They keep waiting for one who his own coming forgot,
They keep waiting for their messiah, waiting for Godot.'

Philani Amadéus Nyoni was born in Bulawayo, Zimbabwe in 1989. He is the author of two poetry anthologies: *Once A Lover Always A Fool*, which received a National Arts Merit Award in 2013, and *Hewn From Rock* (with John Eppel). His work also appears in *Splinters of A Mirage Dawn, Migrant Poetry from South Africa*.

Eko Hotel

Chinelo Okparanta

Agbomma and Ikem were on Victoria Island, on Bar Beach, alongside Ahmadu Bello Way. They were walking at the far end where the rocks rose high, grey rocks glowing silver in the sun. Along the perimeter, broken shards of beer and stout and mineral bottles: Star, Gulder and Guinness; Coke, Fanta and Sprite. Umbrellas stood in a neat line: blue, orange and purple-striped, yellow and green, red. Now they stopped at the edge of the beach where the ocean turned to foam on the sand. They stood together, holding hands.

'We could lose ourselves in all that water,' she said. 'Very beautiful.'

He had been contemplating her hair – the smooth, silky look of it. It was long hair, and even with the curls it flowed down past the small of her back.

But now he allowed his mind to consider the ocean. He nodded. 'It's a beautiful view indeed,' he said.

She thought she heard something teasing in his voice, the way he said the word 'beautiful'. She felt suddenly self-conscious, ran her fingers through her hair.

He watched her, his mind once more back where it had been. Standing there by her side, in his short-sleeved shirt, he was grateful that she was just the height that allowed him to feel the softness of the hair on his arm. He wanted to touch it directly with his hands, wanted to run his own fingers through the locks, but he reasoned that it was still too early for that.

***

She saw the horse rider approaching from the corner of her eye and turned to steal a look. Today the horse rider was wearing a green and yellow rastacap. His sunglasses hung in the space where the hat met his forehead. On his shirt, strewn across his chest, was the yellow banner that proclaimed his trade: HORSE RIDERS. She knew that he was leading the mare in search of customers who were willing to pay and ride. She knew also that for a lesser sum of 600 naira, one could be photographed on its back. She turned back to the ocean, intent on evading him.

Ikem saw the horse rider now. How romantic it would be for he and Agbomma to ride together. It might be a thing she might like. A thing she might never have had the money to do. And how wonderful to be the one to provide her with the opportunity to do it.

'*I choro igba inyinya?*' he turned to ask her.

She looked at Ikem. From the start, he had been nothing but kind to her. But there was the matter of his age; he was older than her. Early forties at the least, she speculated. Still, she felt a security in his age, in being under the protection of an older man. His forehead was wide and furrowed, and there was that gap in the middle of his upper teeth which she did not think quite suited him. Nevertheless he had a neat appearance, which was attractive in its own right. The presentation of a proper businessman, as he had put it that first meeting of theirs, now about a month ago. And his eyes were kind.

He looked up at the sky. It was early evening, perfect time for a horse ride, if there were ever a perfect time for such a thing.

The sun hung droopily above, that lazy brightness before it began to set. He took in a relaxed and languid breath. The air smelled of palm fronds, salty and sweet at once. '*I choro igba inyinya?*' he asked again.

The last thing she wanted was to ride the horse. Could he not tell? But, of course, how could he possibly tell? She thanked him for the offer all the same. '*Da'lu,*' she said. And then she tugged at his arm and steered him away from the horse rider.

***

Not far from them a hawker was carrying a tray of knock-off wristwatches, chanting, 'Rolex and Seiko, Fossil and Swatch! The best of the best!' At a distance from the hawker, a white-garment spiritualist knelt, praying; she was not wearing any shoes. Another white-garment spiritualist was bathing a young woman with a small bowl of water near the tip of the ocean. The young woman was completely unclothed, and her breasts were perfectly round on her chest. Her sides dipped into a small waist from which her hips swelled again: a set of flawless curves. This second spiritualist was a man, and he appeared to be reciting a prayer as he poured the water on the young woman. The water streamed down from the bowl and, as it did, the spiritualist ran his free hand up and down the young woman's body – up and down her head, her back, her chest.

'*O dikwa egwu,*' Ikem said, sighing, thinking what a shame that the beaches were more and more littered with these sorts of religious spectacles – ritual cleansings and baptisms, all in plain sight.

'It's ridiculous indeed,' Agbomma said in response. 'How can they really believe that the water will wash away their troubles?' She sighed too, out of a frustrated acceptance of the way things were. A sort of resignation.

They carried on in the direction of Kuramo Beach. He continued holding her hand. She noticed the warmth and firmness of his hand on hers. She always noticed the warmth and firmness of the men she picked up at this beach.

He noticed the way the fences around the buildings were topped with shards of clear glass. He always noticed the glass when he walked with ladies along this path.

***

They were now inside Eko Hotel. All around them, Lagos élites – businessmen in pin-striped suits carrying leather briefcases – strolled in and out of the hotel's glass doors.

It was he who had reserved the room for them. It was a deluxe room, which called for top money. He had been hesitant at first, but now he was feeling happy with the idea. Anyway, he had booked the room at a discounted rate of 55,000 naira for the night, and for just this final night, the culmination of their time together, it was okay. It would be like a celebration. And afterwards, he would recoup the money with the sale.

There had not been any question about whether they would stay at Eko on her part. This was her territory, after all. Any man who was worth her time would either pay for a stay at the hotel or forego his time with her. This was the way that she was weeding out 'lesser' clients these days. Lagos élites only, nowadays. Those were the only ones who could afford to be with her.

He pushed the button, but the lift was taking too long to arrive, so did she mind taking the staircase up to their room? She did not mind.

They walked up the steps, separately. He no longer held her hand.

****

Agbomma walked toward the windows at the far end of the room. The windows were large, and the purple drapes were drawn open. The sun had set by now, so it was dark enough outside that the glass of the windows was now reflecting images, like a mirror. Her hair was still in place. Lips still perfectly coloured. All was well. She settled into watching Ikem's reflection now through the glass. What a man he was: every passing minute more intriguing than the minute before. Was he even real?

He was sitting on the bed – a king size, with a white poof comforter. He was unbuttoning his shirt now, and peering at her. What a woman she was – a little shy, gentle, soft spoken. Unexpected. He had actually grown fond of her. He had spent quite a bit of time with her already, and here he was now, spending even more time with her.

She ran her fingers through her hair, her usual tick. And suddenly she was no longer looking at him, and no longer thinking of him. Now she was thinking only of her hair: of the wonderful softness of it, of the way she felt so beautiful owing to it. Of how long it had taken her to save up for the purchase. It was no small amount of money, 320,000 naira, but the hair was human hair, and imported, and very much worth it. It was her most prized possession, no contest. She reached into her handbag and took out a wide-toothed comb. She combed gently, like a caress.

Now he was in his undershirt – a white, ribbed singlet that was tucked into his trousers. He had pretended to make himself busy by removing his shirt. But really, all the while he had been sneaking glances at her. How she ran her fingers through her hair! He was now feeling that earlier longing to run his fingers through it. How he wished that he could substitute his fingers for her own. How he longed for a feel. But all that fussing! Surely so much touching was bound to ruin the hair!

She was back to watching him through the glass. Earlier in the day she had noted how perfectly tailored his trousers were, expensive-looking. Now she found herself noting how even his undershirt looked redolent of money, the kind made of rich cotton, a bright sort of whiteness that appeared incapable of getting stained. He was loosening his belt now, and untucking the singlet from the trousers. There was a magazine on the bedside table. He picked it up after untucking the singlet, began flipping the pages.

It occurred to him that he was flipping through the magazine a bit too quickly. He needed to pace himself. He would not, after all, want her to know the effect she was having on him. He would not want her to see his nerves at the thought of making love to her. Because, of course, this was somehow different from all his other hair encounters. For one thing, he had never taken any one of those other girls to bed. And for another, if he ever had felt inclined to take any of them to bed, he doubted he would ever have waited nearly a month do so.

She realized now that he was watching her. Maybe he had been watching her all along but somehow his eyes on her at this particular moment felt like a surprise. She pulled the drapes closed, walked towards the bed, set her handbag on the nightstand. She unzipped her skirt, allowed it to slide down to the floor. She unbuttoned the back of her blouse, lifted it carefully above her head. Her undergarments were pale pink and lace. She knew that the cups of her bra were tight enough so that her flesh appeared on the verge of spilling, the dark brown of her nipples peeking out at the cups' hem.

She moved closer to the bed, sat on the edge of it, and hunched her shoulders forward out of a strange, unexpected shame.

'Don't stay so far away,' he said, pulling her closer, making room for her by his side. And now he thought that she was looking even more demure than he'd seen her looking in the past month. There was a shadow on the wall, just above where her head formed its own shadow, and he thought that there was something sacrosanct about the image, the way the shadow appeared like a halo around her head.

'You should know that I really like you,' he said to her now. It came out suddenly, unexpectedly.

She looked at him, a little stupefied. This was not the way it ever went.

'Don't look so shocked,' he said, firmly, but a little jokingly too. But, as the words came out, he acknowledged to himself that these were words merely uttered in an attempt to compose himself.

She attempted to compose herself, by sitting up straighter and staring idly in the direction of the windows.

'What?' he asked.

'What do you mean, "what"?'

'I mean, what's the matter?'

'Nothing. Just sitting,' she said.

'Why so straight?'

'To hear better,' she said.

'Then I should sit up too,' he said, straightening himself up on the bed. After a moment he asked, 'Do you hear them?'

She listened to the silence. What again was she even listening for? She asked him: 'Hear what?'

'The lizards and grasshoppers. Sometimes you hear them scurrying across the walls and thumping on the glass panes of the windows.'

They were on the sixth floor. 'I didn't think they got up this high,' she said.

'You never know,' he replied.

'I suppose they have just as much right to climb as high as they want.' Immediately she thought that there was something shameful about the statement. It seemed to her now a little like a defence.

He shrugged. 'I don't know.' A pause, and then, 'Please come closer to me. I want nothing more than to be close to you right now.' He nearly bit his tongue after the words came out. Because he had of course used those same lines before on other girls. And it didn't seem right that he should now use them on her. Because there was certainly something different about her. With her, the words were actually true. The truthfulness of them, he realized, was what was making him feel self-conscious. He repeated them anyway: 'I want to be close to you,' he said.
'Do you mean that?' she asked.

He nodded. 'Of course I do.'

She believed him and felt a little less ashamed now, a little more like her other self: more confident in her skin. She scooted closer to him, hooked her fingers into the belt loops of his trousers, tugging gently. She took in the scent of his faded cologne. Beneath the scent of the cologne was his musty male scent. She breathed it in. Musty, like the beach.

***

'I fly out of Lagos tomorrow,' he announced, a half an hour later, out of the blue. 'To Port Harcourt for business. *I chori bia*?'

She smiled. 'Maybe. But if I go with you, you will make it worth my while?' She felt a sudden sickness in her stomach at the sound of the question. Again, the shame. Because the thing was that she did want to go with him. In one very major way he was unlike any of the other men that she'd ever picked up, on Bar Beach or anywhere else: he had stayed with her all this month, just getting to know her, not demanding anything of her, not even now. It was she who had insisted that they come to Eko.

'Make it worth your while?' he asked quietly, like an echo. He laughed softly when he was finished uttering the words.

The thing, for him, was that he really did want her to come along with him. In the last month, she had really grown on him, this intermittent shyness of hers, this strange guardedness. Now he could honestly say that it was too bad that he had met her under these circumstances.

He sighed. There was a thumping in his heart, a salient distress: he was feeling more strongly than ever the obligation to cancel the deal. But his partners in Port Harcourt were counting on him. Already he had wasted so much time.

He should hold off on inviting her until he knew for sure which way he would go: cancel the deal or carry on with it?

'You don't have to decide now if you'd like to come with me or not,' he said, finally. 'Let's just play it by ear.'

She remained silent, flipped her hair behind her shoulders. She nodded, continued to sit by his side.

He reached out and stroked the hair. Finally, he thought. Finally. There was a sense of elation in him. The hair was just what he thought it would be. As soft to the touch as to the eyes. A silky feel that was at par with the silky look. Quality hair, exactly the kind good deals were made of.

***

Later, she told him about the child. 'You, a mother?' he asked.

She nodded. 'An eight-year-old girl,' she said.

He was astonished. She was hardly old enough to be the mother of anyone, he reasoned, let alone an eight-year-old. He thought now of his sister, Nkechi, whom he adored and had practically raised himself, due to family hardships, circumstances he no longer cared to revisit. Agbomma looked to be only a little older than Nkechi, which was not very old at all, because Nkechi was only now finishing up her youth service. How young, then, Agbomma must have been when she had the child! He wondered at the story behind the pregnancy. Perhaps a job-related accident. But he did not dare to ask. Instead he said, 'You kept it from me all this time.'

'It didn't come up,' she replied. 'Besides, this isn't the ideal situation to bring up the topic of a child.'

He nodded. He certainly could not argue with that.

For a moment neither one spoke.

She broke the silence. 'Izuchukwu is her name, but she likes to go by Yellow. You see, her favourite colour is yellow.'

She paused, hating to rattle off this way, but then she could not help herself. She continued: 'She cooks for me. Mostly she boils things. For breakfasts, for instance, she boils eggs and serves them with thick slices of agege bread, slathered with margarine. By the side of each plate, two cups of Lipton tea. Continental Breakfast, she calls it. Don't ask me where she learned that one. Probably television.'

'Probably television,' he agreed.

'And it's not just breakfasts that she serves. There are lunches and dinners too. For lunch, she sometimes cuts up plantains and boils them along with a couple of eggs. Then she peels the plantains and shells the eggs and divides them evenly for us on two plates. Sometimes she coats the plantains with margarine, as if they were slices of bread. Sometimes she even cuts up tomatoes on the side. And sometimes she sings as she serves the meal, and the sound of her voice is more than a little like the brightness of yellow.'

She really did sound like a miracle of a child. To match this wonderful miracle of a woman who was sitting before him. 'What a delightful child,' he replied.

Agbomma nodded. 'Who would have thought that I would actually enjoy being a mother?'

'The way life surprises us,' Ikem said.

They sat silently again.

'So where is she now?' he asked. 'What do you do with her while you're at work? Daytime, I imagine she's at school. But evenings and night-time?'

'She has a grandmother,' Agbomma replied, and just as she said it she took note of the harshness of her voice. She should have controlled herself better, she reasoned silently to herself. But it was too late now. The response – the sourness of its tone – was already out, and certainly he had heard.

He took note of her sour tone. He noticed, too, the worried crease that had formed now on her brow. He imagined soothing it away.

'Her grandmother comes to my flat and watches her when I'm gone,' Agbomma said.

'Her grandmother? Your mother?'

'Yes,' Agbomma replied. 'My mother. Very demanding woman. If you asked her, she'd tell you I was working the overnight shift as a nurse. She believes it. If she only knew. But the truth is, even nursing is a compromise. If she had her way I would be a doctor. Clearly, I'll never live up.'

Ikem remained silent. He was unsure how to respond.

'Anyway, point is, I'm not like all the other girls. I'm a mother. This is just business, so that I can provide for my child.'

It was silent again in the room. But now the sound of the air conditioner seemed amplified to him, a persistent hum. He listened to it as he mulled over all the things that she had said.

'I still really like you,' he said after some time. 'And from the sound of things, I'd like your little girl too.'

Agbomma laughed, one quick, quiet burst of ha!

He shook his head thoughtfully. 'I really do,' he said. 'I really, really do like you.' He paused. 'I could prove it to you.'

'Prove it to me?' Now it was she who was thoughtful. After a moment she replied: 'OK. Sure. Why not?' She acknowledged to herself that it was a dare, because of course she did not see how he could possibly prove anything to her. He was different, yes, but perhaps he was also the same: the type of Lagos man who made grand, elaborate declarations – lies – and then insisted on proving them. More to feed his own ego than for her benefit. 'Go ahead,' she said defiantly. 'Why not? Go ahead. Prove it to me.'

'I will,' he said. And just like that he proposed: 'Marry me,' he said.

And, of course, she agreed.

***

It would be a small, private ceremony. After all, why announce to the world that he was marrying a lady of the night? Not to mention that he was not in favour of large, elaborate weddings. He felt that too much ceremony had a way of diluting the essential.

As for the site of the ceremony, they could hold it on the beach, in a recessed corner, far from the spiritualists and hawkers and horse riders. He didn't imagine a small wedding like theirs would draw anybody's interest on the beach. The same way that the nude bather had not managed to draw any interest.

It would take place whenever he was able to get some time off from his business travels. He wouldn't need too many days off, because there would only be one wedding – the white wedding, no traditional wedding. It would be better that way, even necessary.

Of course, her family members could come. He would like to meet them. He'd like to see if she held any resemblance to her mother. If they shared that same look of concern, if not the demandingness. If she had any sisters, they would of course be invited too. He'd like to meet them also. And her father, and any brothers. Finally, he'd love to meet Izuchukwu – quite an impressive little girl, from the sound of things. Perhaps she would arrive dressed in yellow, a single daffodil in an expanse of white and grey sand.

It was March now, the end of the dry season, and so perhaps they would wait till August or September to be married. There was the brief return of the dry period during that time of the year – there always was – and so they could expect not to be disturbed by rain if they held the wedding then.

He would wear a plain linen *buba* and *sokoto*, and she would wear a simple ivory-coloured gown. They would not bother with shoes, so that they would be able to feel the warmth of the sand beneath their feet. She would pick up a bouquet of flowers from the florist shop in Ikoyi. Or, better yet, as there were hedges all around Lagos from which flowers grew, perhaps she would collect from them some white or yellow or red flowers, and she would use these as her bouquet.

The minister in his robe would say a brief benediction, conduct a brief ceremony. The only music would be the cawing of birds. There would be the chemical scent of her make-up, of their perfume, and maybe the slight scent of the bergamot in her hair.

He imagined it this way.

***

After he had stripped her of her pink lace and found his way into her, they lay side by side on the bed, on their backs, looking at the square tiles on the ceiling.

'Was it as you like?' she asked.

'Yes. Even better,' he replied.

She thought of the horse rider now. The memory came back to her. She had picked him up in one of the bars in Lekki. He had not been so gracious when she asked him if it had been as he wanted. Later, he had refused to pay.

She felt a sudden apprehension, an unease. 'I think I'll go home now,' she said to Ikem.

'What's the rush?' he asked.

'Nothing. Just tired. Besides, *m mechanam*,' she said.

It was true, she told herself. She had finished. She had earned her keep. She had spent more time with him than with any of her other clients. So much time just hanging out, and finally, one night of this. Now, she could collect her money and go. It was too bad, though, when she reasoned it, that it had turned out this way, the same way it always turned out: her lying in bed after having been used this way. After *allowing* herself to be used this way. He had not even demanded it of her. He had offered the money whether she slept with him or not. All he had wanted was that she spent some days with him. And then the days had tumbled into weeks, and finally into a month. Now he was going away on business.

Well, perhaps she should have just accepted the money. 25,000 naira was nothing to sneeze at, especially when he had not demanded much from her. But had she accepted, she would have felt as if she had somehow cheated, as if she had not really earned it. She wanted to *earn* the money. If not, she would have felt like an even more corrupt version of herself.

He was not yet ready for her to leave. '*Kedu mgbe ugbo gi na'bia?*' he asked. What time was she planning on catching the bus? And was she sure she wanted to go home?

Yes, she said, she was sure about wanting to go home, home to her little girl, and to relieve her mother of watch duty. But she was not sure when the next bus would arrive.

He had forgotten for the moment about the girl. 'That's right,' he said. 'Makes sense. A mother should go home to her child.'

She nodded. 'This mother would like nothing more than to go home to her child.' And now she found herself talking once more about the child. She could see it now, she told Ikem: crawling into Izuchukwu's bed to kiss the girl goodnight. She always did, because the girl demanded it of her. And always, as she lay there, the girl would turn around so that they were facing each other, and she'd gape at her, her little eyes squinting to see in the dark. And she'd ask, 'Are you alright?' 'Of course,' Agbomma would reply, nodding. Yes, she was alright. Even if that was not exactly the truth. How the girl worried over her! An angel of a child. She could not bear to make her worry more than she already did.

But it was already late into the night now, Ikem said. In an hour or so it would be midnight. The buses might no longer even be running. So maybe she should catch a taxi instead, he said.

She nodded.

After a moment he said; 'Stay with me just a little while longer, won't you? Later you can leave. A taxi has no schedule. And I'll even pay for it.'

There was a pause, another moment of reflection during which she cleared her throat. When she was done clearing her throat, she asked, 'Then afterwards, what?'

'Afterwards, what?' he repeated. It came out a little like mimicry, but he was thinking seriously about the question.

Some time went by.

'No answer?' she asked.

'There's a lot to think about yet,' he said.

'Typical man,' she replied.

He laughed softly, assured her that he still planned to marry her, assured her that that had not changed. Soon he was pulling her to him, holding her tight. They stayed that way. When he finally let go of her, they returned to their former positions, once more facing the ceiling, their backs on the bed.

He thought of all his previous transactions now. All of those other women had been momentary encounters, touch-and-gos, which was of course necessary in order to preserve the longevity as well as the integrity of his business: in a line-up, there was no way they would be able to recognize him.

Well, she was certainly no touch-and-go. But perhaps it was best that he simply carried on with business.

He knew what he should have done next. 'Let's take a stroll,' he should have said. 'A night stroll under the stars and moon.' Then they would make their way back down the narrow staircase, back to the lobby, and out the glass doors. Perhaps there, on the beach, they would make love again. The palm leaves would be thrashing in the breeze, and they would tumble in the sand. Darkness would surround them like a veil, and her screams would attempt to pierce the veil, but he would wrestle with her so long and recklessly that he would render her breathless, and tired, and confused. Too breathless and tired and confused to go chasing after him.

Those still on the beach would conclude that this was, after all, what lovers did. They would pay them no mind.

He would do it then. Having exhausted her, he would pick up a shard of glass and slash the threads carefully. He would pull the hair off her head. He would rise then and walk quickly away, the loot in hand.

She shifted on the bed.

There was the soft creaking of springs, and only now did he notice that she had curled up on her side in a posture a little less taut than the foetal position. Only now did he notice that she had fallen into sleep. He found himself watching her, just watching, the way her breaths caused her nostrils to widen and contract in a barely perceptible way. The way her lips twitched every once in a while. Her creased forehead, that look of concern that seemed to be permanently pasted on her face. And that hair: the way it dispersed itself across the satin sheets. Good thing that these were satin sheets. Better satin for the sake of the hair.

He continued to observe her. She appeared to be sleeping as peacefully as a child, though she was not quite a child. But she was young – 25 at the most. How tragic the things that young women were doing these days for money. He thought of his sister. '*Tufiaka*,' he whispered, crossing himself at the chest. God forbid.

The air conditioner was still humming. All along the temperature had suited him fine, but now he felt as if it were blowing frigid gusts of air. Shivers raced down his spine, jolting him into a state of greater wakefulness.

He got up momentarily to dim the lights. There was a series of soft knocks on the door just then. He looked around for his trousers, found them, put them on, walked over to the door to answer.

The server was dressed in a yellow-and-black uniform, a beret on his head, holding a tray with champagne and two glasses.

'Compliments of Eko Hotel, Sir.'

The glasses were not filled, but the server was offering to fill them.

'No, thank you,' Ikem said. 'The lady is already asleep. Maybe another time.'

'Sir, I should take the champagne back?'

'Yes, please,' Ikem said.

The server continued to stand there, smiling impishly.

'Something else?'

The server's face turned supplicatory. 'Sir, abeg, I dey hungry o. Find me something, Sir, abeg o.'

Ikem dug into his pocket, pulled out a hundred naira note. It was not much, but he knew it would do. He handed the note over.

'Thank, Sir,' the server said, bowing his head. He repeated it, bowing his head twice more. 'Thank, Sir.' Now he was off on his way.

Ikem closed the door softly, walked in the direction of the windows. He pulled the drapes open just a bit. Above, a bright moon. Below, the stretch of sand. In the distance, the ocean surged.

His eyes lingered on the water. He watched as the waves rose high and then crashed onto the shore. Over the years the beach had become more and more eroded by these surges. He was aware of the erosion; most people on Victoria Island were. Lagos authorities routinely made efforts to keep the waves in check, but there were still frequent floods that washed debris ashore and onto the roads and brought traffic to a standstill on Ahmadu Bello Way. It seemed the ocean would continue to surge. The shoreline would continue to recede. The government would continue its containment efforts.

His thoughts returned to Agbomma. He had gone after her instinctively, out of his habitual pursuit of money. It was justifiable. After all, one did not make a living by sitting around, pursuing nothing at all. He had been innovative with this business endeavour and had built a small empire out of it. He was as good as any other successful entrepreneur. He held this as a fact, and he thought that he would still hold it as a fact even if he were outside of himself, even if he were an objective observer of himself.

He drew the drapes back closed now. He walked over to the bed, took off his trousers, got into bed. Beside him, she lay, still naked, and still fast asleep. He stared at her.

She was beautiful and, though he had never considered having a wife for himself, perhaps she was what he wanted his wife to be like. She was broken, damaged goods, but so was he. They were perhaps the perfect match. Perhaps in their union, they could become different people, begin to live different lives, normal lives. He would no longer be a thief and she would no longer be a lady of the night. What would they do instead? If money were not a factor, then the possibilities were endless.

But money was a factor. Money was always a factor, and so perhaps it was easier simply to carry on with the way of life that he had already worked so hard to create for himself.

So what now? Well, perhaps two or so days before their wedding he would ask her to the beach, once more to Eko Hotel, and they would find the restaurant there. It would not yet be evening, not yet dinnertime, but still they would share a meal – a late lunch or an early dinner, some rice and stew, or some *ofe oha* and pounded yam.

He would have just finished his meal, and perhaps he'd be looking into her face when he'd suddenly announce his change of heart.

He'd simply look at her and say, 'I can't do it.' There was, after all, the eight-year-old child to think of. Great as Agbomma made her out to be, was he ready to be a father? No. Not yet at least. Not even to a perfect eight-year-old kid.

And so he'd smile at her, weakly squeeze her arm, tell her how sorry he was. He'd try to convince her of what a mistake it would have been.

'I just can't do it,' he'd say. No real explanation, only that he'd been mistaken, only that he'd suddenly realized that things would not work out between the two of them.

For her it might be like getting the breath knocked out of her. Or, like being given life only for that life to be just as soon snatched away.

But for him it would be like having a death sentence revoked.

He continued to look at her. The air was no longer frigid in the room, but there was an intermittent cold. He felt it now, but he did not think of himself. It occurred to him, instead, that she might be cold.

I'm sorry, he thought, as he turned to her, lifted up the comforter from where it lay at her feet and pulled it up to her waist. *I'm so sorry.* Of course, he did not say any of this aloud – first, because he was not yet ready to announce his change of heart, and second, because he was being cautious not to rouse her from her sleep.

But all along she had not quite been asleep. Silently she acknowledged to herself that she was a little like a bullfrog: not that she never slept, but that she had grown accustomed to needing very little sleep. She acknowledged, too, that, as calmly as she lay, and for all this time, there was no way for him to know that she had all along been awake.

She felt his touch on her. The fool, she thought. Falling for the bit about the child. They always did. Not that she used the bit about the child often at all. She only used it for the special men, the ones in whom she saw a sort of promise. So far, if she were to count, she must have used it for no more than a handful of men. And, always, they swallowed up the lie as easily as a gulp of water. He had done so too. To believe her a mother, let alone of an eight-year-old! He was not unlike the other men in that way. But where the other men had simply paid her more money on account of their empathizing, only he had gone so far as to propose marriage.

Well, a marriage would come out of it, and thank heavens for that. She could see her future now: wife to a wealthy businessman, enough money to buy all the things her heart desired. How would she explain the absence of the child? Well, never mind that for now. She trusted herself to come up with something.

She moved around on the bed, repositioned herself, still feigning sleep.

Rules

The prize is awarded annually to a short story by an African writer published in English, whether in Africa or elsewhere. (The indicative length is between 3,000 and 10,000 words.)

'An African writer' is taken to mean someone who was born in Africa, or who is a national of an African country, or who has a parent who is African by birth or nationality.

There is a cash prize of £10,000 for the winning author and a travel award for each of the shortlisted candidates (up to five in all).

For practical reasons, unpublished work and work in other languages is not eligible. Works translated into English from other languages are not excluded, provided they have been published in translation and, should such a work win, a proportion of the prize would be awarded to the translator.

The award is made in July each year, the deadline for submissions being 31 January. The shortlist is selected from work published in the five years preceding the submissions deadline and not previously considered for a Caine Prize. Submissions, including those from online journals, should be made by publishers and will need to be accompanied by six original published copies of the work for consideration, sent to the address below. There is no application form.

Every effort is made to publicize the work of the shortlisted authors through the broadcast as well as the printed media.

Winning and shortlisted authors will be invited to participate in writers' workshops in Africa and elsewhere as resources permit.

The above rules were designed essentially to launch the Caine Prize and may be modified in the light of experience. Their objective is to establish the Caine Prize as a benchmark for excellence in African writing.

The Caine Prize
The Menier Gallery
Menier Chocolate Factory
51 Southwark Street
London, SE1 1RU, UK
Telephone: +44 (0)20 7378 6234
Email: info@caineprize.com
Website: www.caineprize.com

He was looking at her. He observed the gentle way she moved as she repositioned herself and continued to sleep. He carried on looking at her for some time before finally giving in to the temptation of stroking her hair. He allowed his fingers to caress the hair. He was deeply regretful. *I'm sorry*, he thought again. *I'm very sorry.*

There was that burst of cold once more. Once more, he thought of her. He pulled the comforter all the way now, upward from her waist and over her chest, adjusting it just so, until it seemed to her that she could not possibly any longer be cold.

Chinelo Okparanta is the author of *Happiness, Like Water.* A recipient of a 2014 O'Henry Award, she is a finalist for the 2014 New York Public Young Lions Fiction Award as well as for the 2014 Lambda Literary Award for Fiction. Her stories have appeared in *The New Yorker, Granta* and *Tin House,* among other journals.

Music from a Farther Room

Bryony Rheam

The afternoon hangs suspended in the drowsy heat of late October. The house is quiet with the softness of sleepers. It breathes in and out, gently; the sleepers are drunk with heat and tiredness soon overcame them. The tin roof creaks and a thick triangle of yellow sunlight cuts across the red veranda floor. A lizard tiptoes up the wall, lifts his head and ponders the view from his great height. Somewhere in the distance, a woodpecker sounds twice; a grey lourie plunges noisily into the top branches of a syringa and the lizard scuttles under the eaves of the veranda roof.

It is an old house: it has felt many things: heat and storms and the cold bite of winter. It remains solid, immovable, as it spreads its tentacles of flower beds, palms, pots, a long green lawn, vegetables and herbs; a wheelbarrow, even. At night, it lies open to the dark and winks at the owls, the stars, the night wind, all who come to look for the original brown bush it was built on. And it laughs.

There is a movement from inside the house. There is a slow creak of the wooden floor and two figures appear at the doorway. One is a nurse. She is large and efficient-looking. Her wide, open face is smooth and wrinkle-free. There is the slightest gleam of sweat at her temples, her uniform stretches a little too tightly over her expansive bosom and her wide stockinged feet look uncomfortable in narrow black shoes.

Her ankles are slightly swollen; her breath as she helps the old lady, stick thin as she is, into a chair, comes a little fast, a little shallow, but otherwise she exudes a warm, capable endurance.

The old lady watches her now, as she does often. There is something in her demeanour, perhaps it is her broad chest, which seems to speak of years of care, of love. She imagines new-born babies laid against her shoulder and children bathed by those soft brown hands. She wonders if they, too, will get old, will one day lose their plump firmness, wither and weaken. Will she, too, one day begin the process of forgetting her self, her selves, leaving them behind, faded watercolours in a dusty album?

She turns her attention to the garden. A heart beats through the afternoon. Despite the heat, she can't sleep. She enjoys this time, the time she catches while others sleep. The garden lies bathed in sunlight. Bees hum in half-hearted drones at flowers that nod sagely like monks at prayer. The intermittent coo of a dove sounds, but the air itself is still.

There is a sudden noise from the doorway, the brisk sharpness of shoes tapping down the veranda steps. It is Amelia with the boy. The grass is soft and springy, but she hardly notices for it is the sun which occupies her attention. It beams down directly, a great hot light, and even insects, lizards and birds move restlessly away from it. It is not yet the time for the sprays to be switched on, for the cool tic-tic-tic to remind her that the day is nearing its close. She sighs. She is aware of the time she holds resentfully in her hands. She wants to spill it, to throw it away, but hold it she must and the burden is heavy.

Her son runs at her heels. His small, unstable legs take him rolling across the grass. He cries and she stoops to pick him up. She sighs again and somewhere inside of her, the sigh resounds. She wants to run, to put him down and run, run away. Instead, she feels his skin soft against hers. He is sticky with sweat and his breath is sweet with the sleep he has just woken from. He wriggles and she puts him down, watching him run and fall, run and fall over oceans of grass. She wonders, as she has wondered before, how she would feel if he kept going, through the flowerbed, thick with Julia's daisies and fuchsias, geraniums and petunias; if he crawled through the bougainvillea hedge and carried on into the next garden, and the next, and the next. If he never stopped to look back, if he kept on going and going, his little white legs stumbling, falling, but going ahead, through gardens and flower beds until... then what?

A very slight breeze lifts from somewhere. She shifts her feet and lets the thought detach itself. She hopes it will flutter away, but it drops again, lying heavily next to her. A rustle in the dry leaves makes her start suddenly, but nothing appears.

The old woman and the nurse share a look, a half-smile. There is not a lot of need for them to talk. The nurse is well-versed in the needs of the old. She knows how they squirm under a barrage of talk, she understands how life has become a process of watching and waiting, noticing the little details in life, appreciating quiet. People say how the elderly become like children, but that isn't right. They have a fascination for things in the same way that a child has when seeing something for the first time, but they don't need to touch or examine. They notice what they hadn't seen all their lives long, while other things, like people and words and places fall away into some empty space behind them.

The old lady, Julia is her name, looks at the garden again. She remembers other days, days pressed firmly like petals in a book. The feeling of grass between toes, the taste of salt on skin, that wonderful exuberance of youth that will never fade, never run out, when life stretches on in an unrolling succession of days without names, without numbers.

She remembers, too, the romance of the young woman

cutting white iceberg roses, snipping off withered heads: confident, meticulous, in control, feeling the power of life at her disposal; arranging flowers for a vase, fingers tweaking, lips pursed. She remembers a polished wooden floor, the slant of soft light through a corner window, a child sleeping in a pram, the years that stretched on, ordered and neat. Christmas card lists, holidays to the sea, mending sheets, storing seeds for next year's beds, seasons that folded softly into each other.

There were occasions when she had groaned a little under the weight of time. Times when she wondered just how long it would go on, this making of Christmas puddings and darning of holes. As a child, she loved to climb trees and watch the world from the top of branches. She loved the height and the disguise of leaves and how no-one could find her, although she saw them, the flashes of blue and green of her mother's dress and the white of the cook boy's apron, way beneath her, darting here and there like frightened birds. Sometimes she would imagine she were up there again and she could hide in the thick canopy of green forever.

But the tree was cut down, a long time ago, chopped up for firewood and, besides, her tree-climbing days were over. And so she had continued to mend socks and wipe children's tears. It was worth it, wasn't it? Those little arms around your neck, the soft kisses, the smiles even while they slept and dreamed it was them climbing trees, climbing and climbing, further and further away into the clouds and beyond.

Forty, Amelia thinks. They had said, hadn't they, that it was too late? You'll be tired. Exhausted. You're not used to children. Having responsibility. The time you need to give up. Your time is not yours. She closes her eyes as she feels time turn elastic. Minutes, hours, all stretched away and away, beyond the garden, beyond all the gardens. Away and away from her, until she is just a small speck, a tiny dot of nothingness. She isn't Amelia, she isn't a mother, she isn't a wife. She is just this tiny spot on a piece of continent, waiting to be whispered away.

Out of the corner of her eye, she sees Julia on the veranda. She knows the old woman's sharp blue eyes are on her. She wonders what she is thinking, of what one can think when one's life is a succession of moves from one room to another, when life has become a routine of waiting, not doing, waiting for an end which must come soon. Life now must surely be whittled down to its basic functions, and even those are not easy.

The nurse gives a little wave and Amelia looks away. She is irritated. Why? The nurse's smile is warm, her face is open. There was an incident. This morning. The boy was crying, his face twisted into ugly red ribbons of childish anger. The breakfast bowl fell from the table and cereal exploded in warm mush on the floor. Amelia picked him up by one arm and took him into the bedroom. He screamed and thumped and lay on the bed, kicking his fat little legs into the air. She turned and closed the door and ignored the pleas to let him out.

She went out onto the veranda, picked up a magazine and flicked through it, seeing nothing but a blur of pictures and tears. Then there was a quiet, a sudden quiet and she realized she couldn't hear the sobs and the sound of the door being repeatedly knocked. She felt a sudden alarm, a tightening of the chest and throat, and dashed along the corridor to his room. The door was open and at once she thought of the goldfish pond and the thick lush green of the water.

Then she heard a voice speaking quietly and the soft shudder of a child's sobs calming into nothing. She saw the nurse carrying him through the garden, talking gently, pointing out flowers and bees and lizards in exaggerated tones of surprise and joy. She saw his little hand grip the nurse's shoulder, his little head nod as she pointed out this and that. His voice still came in hiccups of tears, but he smiled tentatively and the nurse wiped his face.

Julia thinks back down the years, years that flicker and glimmer like a spool of film unravelling. The house had expanded with the laughter of children and dinner parties, friends and visiting family. Her memory jumps from one picture to another: her son receiving a certificate on speech day, her daughters pirouetting through performance after performance and the youngest, another boy, with his Scouts badge. The initial quiet when the children left home was a welcome one. The house sighed with space, but it was never lonely, never empty. She was still the centre, the pivot round which they all swung and to which they all returned. The kisses were less frequent, except when soothing broken hearts, but telephone calls and letters were more insistent.

When she thought they were old enough and she wanted to do something else, something that didn't involve cooking or cleaning or mending, they looked at her as though she had left, as though she stood at the door with her suitcase in hand and kissed them all goodbye. She saw fear in them, the fear of an empty house, as though they couldn't imagine such a life, such emptiness. She stretched out her hands to reassure them it wasn't true, but they didn't believe her, so she folded her dreams away like one of her embroidered cloths, and placed them right in the back of the drawer.

Amelia does not want to be here. It isn't her home or her country, but her husband insisted and hung on to his dream of returning home. So clearly had he painted it with the colours of nostalgia that even he was disappointed with the picture he then discovered. He is away all the time; he is getting them a house, he says. Things would be so much better then. If she could just wait, if she could just see what he has tried to tell her all the years they have been together; but even he knows, she thinks. Even he knows, and there is nothing quite so angry, so vicious, as a disappointed soul.

The old lady despises her, she knows that much. She disapproves of the way Amelia dresses and the way she smokes and the way she answers calls on her cellphone, standing outside the house and trying not to let her voice be heard. Be kind, he said, she's very old. She's lonely. Speak to her, please. But Amelia doesn't think Julia is lonely; she is too old to be lonely. Julia mutters to herself and drinks her tea alone and is in bed by eight. There is the nurse who is there all day, humming in the kitchen or singing a few bars of a song or directing the maid where to clean and the gardener where to prune and Amelia can't stand it. She hates the woman's usefulness, her ability to plan and arrange. The nurse made her a cup of tea one day and put it in front of her with a biscuit in the saucer, but Amelia pushed it back ungraciously. I don't drink tea, she said.

At some point, the house had swelled again with grandchildren who fell and tumbled on the soft blanket of lawn or ripped the heads off flowers and plucked the petals out in jest, for such are the actions of the young, who hold life, glimmering and over-brimming, in their hands and then let it spill on the earth at their feet.

Then, gradually, they had started to go. First it was her husband, then friends. People stopped coming to see her; family grew up and moved away. The house contracted. She closed rooms, emptied cupboards, stopped driving. She felt the cold, which seemed to settle in her bones, take up residence with a genial animosity. Her teeth were a problem. Then her leg. And now, the nurse.

Suddenly they were back; her grandson from Australia and his wife and the little one. They clattered and banged doors and left cellphones and car keys on her polished dining table. There were muttered conversations that didn't include her and, from her bedroom, she heard them talking late at night. Sometimes there were the soft sobs of a woman and the sound of doors closing. At times, she wanted to say something, but the woman was hard and unmoving. She wore t-shirts and jeans too tight for her and her mouth was a thin, straight line that smoked cigarettes one after the other. She was always looking somewhere else, out of the window, but not into the garden. Far away, somewhere else, perhaps.

She wonders what will become of the house when she is gone. Her children are scattered throughout the world, not one on African soil. They've all asked her to live with them; they used to plead for her to sell the house and move in with them, but she always shook her head and gave a little laugh. Gradually, they stopped asking. They used to write, letters and postcards. Then just postcards, just Christmas cards. There are occasional phone calls, but sometimes she shakes her head and the nurse tells them she is asleep.

Now, there is her grandson and his awkward little family. She glances at Amelia who watches her little boy collecting leaves with a look of bored abstraction. She wants to tell her she will be all right. Would it help if she put her arm around her? She fears the girl will revolt against her sagging skin and her bony shoulders and her swollen arthritic hands. Everything passes, she wants to say, everything, but Amelia's phone has rung and she picks up the little boy and takes him off to the other side of the garden. The nurse sighs and gives a little shake of her head. She suggests tea and moves off into the house to put the kettle on.

Julia looks up, high into the branches of the syringa. The sun is still bright, still hot, but she feels a shade fall on the house. She leans back in the chair and closes her eyes. She imagines she is a child again and she is climbing, climbing, climbing. High, high up she goes, right to the top of the great tree. Looking down, she thinks she could perhaps fly if she jumped. She would fly around the house and above the flowers and the top of the hedge. She would fly down the road and then back again. This time, however, she is not interested in flying low. The branches have ended, but she carries on climbing. It becomes colder and lighter and a fine mist comes down and now she is in the clouds. Somewhere, very far away, she hears a tea cup placed next to her, the tiny tinkle of a teaspoon placed in the saucer. She hears those hard feet tap up the steps and go inside, but she doesn't mind. She lets go and falls and then swoops and dives.

The garden is hot and silent. The branches of the syringa stretch motionlessly in the sun. Inside the house, it is quiet and dark. The stone floor of the kitchen is cool on bare feet. The little boy wanders from room to room, toddling here and there, looking for the cat that has darted away from his outstretched hands. He disappears into the garden and the house is quiet again. A curtain lifts slightly in a rare breeze and tiny motes of dust dance in a slant of sudden sunlight. The house sighs once more, deeply and slowly, and then it lets her go and she flies.

Bryony Rheam was born in Zimbabwe in 1974. She completed her further education in the UK, graduating with an MA in Literature from the University of Kent at Canterbury. After teaching for a year in Singapore, she returned to Zimbabwe in 2001 where she worked as an English teacher. In 2008, she moved to Zambia where she still lives with her partner and their two children. In 2009, her debut novel *This September Sun* was published by amaBooks (and in 2012 by Parthian in the UK). She has also had numerous short stories published in various anthologies.